AT TH
LAST MOMENT

The Jewish Struggle for Emigration
from Poland before the Holocaust

IRITH CHERNIAVSKY

Producer & International Distributor
eBookPro Publishing
www.ebook-pro.com

At the Last Moment
Irith Cherniavsky

Translation from the Hebrew by Yehuda Oppenheimer
Cover photo: Warsaw 1933, Departure From Jews who are Leaving To Palestine
Photo credit: Narodowe Archiwum Cyfrowe

Contact: cheririt@gmail.com
ISBN 9798667582656

I dedicate the book to my children: Yony, Dandy, Yael.

AT THE LAST MOMENT

The Jewish Struggle for Emigration
from Poland before the Holocaust

IRITH CHERNIAVSKY

Contents

Acknowledgments 9

Introduction 11

Foreword 26

1 Poland and Polish Jewry During the 1930s 40

2 How Polish Jewry Imagined Eretz Israel 58

3 Polish Jewish Migration in the 1930s 99

4 The Workings of Aliyah 119

5 The Fight over Immigration Licenses 146

6 Conditions of Aliyah and the Characteristics
   of Immigrants 178

7 Epilogue 274

Statistical Appendix 285

Bibliography 305

Acknowledgments

The basis of this book is a doctoral dissertation written at the Hebrew University of Jerusalem that dealt with the *Aliyah* and emigration of Polish Jews in the 1930s. My deepest thanks are due to my supervisors in this work: Professor Hagit Lavski and Professor Yaakov Metzer, who accompanied and continue to accompany me with good will and patience from the initial idea stage through the research to the present.

While processing the doctoral dissertation for the book, the work was rewritten and shortened, and an effort was made to produce an accessible, readable, and interesting composition not only for the research community but also for the general public. I hope this goal has been achieved, if only partially. The doctoral thesis won several awards and scholarships: Scholarship from the Scholarship Fund of the Institute of Contemporary Jewry at the Hebrew University in Jerusalem, an award from the Dinur Center, and an award from the Dr. Ernst M. Adler Foundation.

The historical sources were collected mainly from the Central Zionist Archive (CZA) in Jerusalem, from the Netanya archives, from Kibbutz Ramat Hakovesh, from Kibbutz Yagur, from the Central Archive for New Documentation (Archiwum Akt Nowych - AAN) in Warsaw, and from the Polish Central Bureau of Statistics

(GUS) in Warsaw; from the YIVO archive in New York, and from the periodical collection in the National Library in Jerusalem. I thank all the staff at these institutions.

Thank you to all my family and friends who supported me and encouraged me throughout my long years of dealing with immigration from Poland.

Introduction

THE ATTEMPTED ALIYAH OF
THE MEZERITCH BRUSH MAKERS[1]

In the Podlasie Province of eastern Poland, about 90 kilometers east of Lublin, there is a town known as Mezeritch (Miedzyrzec). Before World War II, there were about 20,000 inhabitants, about 12,000 of whom were Jews. One industry unique to the town, in which Jews operated most of the businesses, was the manufacture of handmade hog hairbrushes.

The raw material was brought to Mezeritch from Russia, Ukraine, and Siberia, and processed in the many workshops of the city. The finished products were exported throughout Europe and even overseas. This industry, in addition to the local wool, fur and leather industries, entailed extensive import and export and thus furnished the inhabitants – especially the Jews – with extensive European connections and thus earned the town the nickname "Little America." Hog processing was done in small and medium-sized workshops, each employing a few dozen workers, about 2,000 in all. The work was done under harsh conditions and entailed standing for long hours alongside hot containers in which the bristles boiled in toxic acid.

---

1   CZA (Central Zionist Archives) S6/2740.

The financial situation of the Jews of Mezeritch was apparently good relative to other places in Poland. The town's Jews would spend long summer holidays in the surrounding villages and frequently traveled to fairs. The vibrant community established many Jewish institutions: a hospital, fire department, orchestra, sports clubs, gymnasium, "Tarbut" school, many synagogues, and a *Beis Midrash*. Until the outbreak of World War II, no less than three Jewish journals were published in Mezeritch.

In 1937, a brush-making cooperative was organized in Mezeritch to help its members emigrate to Palestine (Israel). Correspondence concerning the rise of this group began in mid-November 1937 and continued until July 1939. Most of the correspondence was between an activist in the Jewish trade unions in Poland, Pinchas Steinwachs, and various officials in Palestine - members of the *Aliyah* department and the Trade and Industry Department of the Jewish Agency, various elements in the *Histadrut* (The General Organization of Workers in Palestine), the Center for Cooperation in Palestine and more. The Central Zionist Palestine Office in Warsaw also became involved. For much of this period, Pinchas Steinwachs stayed in Palestine to promote the *Aliyah* of the members of the cooperative. However, despite considerable efforts and constant pressure from the cooperative's representatives, the brush makers were unable to achieve their goal of *Aliyah*, and thus most of them perished in the Holocaust.

The correspondence began in November 1937, when a memo on behalf of the brush makers' cooperative was transmitted from the "Haoved" (Worker) department of the *HeHalutz* organization in Poland to the Jewish Agency's *Aliyah* Department in Jerusalem. The memorandum dated November 15, 1937, signed by the organizing committee of the "Berschter Cooperative in Mezeritch," described the brush industry, the organization of the cooperative and its plan to emigrate to Palestine. A representative of the Haoved department of *HeHalutz*, who was sent to Mezeritch to investigate, and "concluded that the matter was practical and could be realized." He also noted that "this is a very uncommon industry, for there are only a few places in the world where this industry is being developed. In Poland, it is the only such city, [...] and the members of the cooperative are experts in this work." The representative asked for a serious discussion regarding this issue. On November 19, 1937, a similar letter was sent by W. Romanowski from the Center for Jewish Professional Trade Unions in Poland to A. Dobkin, the head of the *Aliyah* Department in Jerusalem. Dobkin responded to the "Haoved" on December 20, 1937, stating that the material was being transferred to the Trade and Industry Department of the Jewish Agency for their opinion. On December 24, Tishbi from the Department of Trade and Industry sent a detailed reply to the cooperative's request from Mezeritch. Tishbi examined the prices of raw material (hog hair) and produce (brushes) on the international market, the conditions of the credit, the required investment, and labor wages, and concluded that the venture should continue to be developed. He recommended changing the organization from a cooperative to a Limited Company (Ltd.), adding: "With the appropriate organization of the plant, the business will succeed. It will be able to hire many employees, secure high wages, and provide acceptable conditions for the shareholders."

On December 27, 1937, Dr. P. Rottenstreich, head of the Trade and Industry Department of the Jewish Agency, wrote to the Center for Professional Trade Unions in Warsaw, affirming that the Agency is willing to endeavor to make immigration certificates available to the members of the cooperative, but cannot provide them with working capital credit. However, when the experts would arrive in the country, it would be possible to help them obtain credit for export.

On January 11, 1938, A. Dobkin conveyed this letter of intent to the Cooperative Center in Tel Aviv and to the Center for Professional Trade Unions in Warsaw. On February 18, 1938, a reply was received from P. Steinwachs, the representative of the organizing committee of the Berschter Cooperative, to questions that had been raised by Tishbi regarding the venture. In response, on March 3, 1938, H. Barlas, the then director of the Immigration Department, communicated to the Center for Professional Trade Unions in Poland: "We are coming to terms with the Department of Industry at the Jewish Agency regarding this matter." On March 16, 1938, V. Romanowski of the Trade Unions Center informed the *Aliyah* Department that they were sending a representative to the country to expedite the cooperative's affairs. That representative was Mr. Pinchas Steinwachs, Secretary of the Professional Trade Unions establishment by the Poalei Zion party and Polish *HeHalutz* organization. Confirmation of receipt of the letter by A. Dobkin was sent to Poland on April 11, 1938. Earlier, on April 8, 1938, Steinwachs had transmitted an economic assessment of the hog hair processing plant in Poland and Palestine to the *Aliyah* Department. The memorandum contained a detailed breakdown of production, marketing, and gross and net revenue. For example, the 30 families that will immigrate will bring with them 3,000 Palestine pound (PP), in addition to travel expenses. Of that, 700 PP will be used to purchase raw material, 1,300 PP as credit for removing the merchandise from the warehouses; the remaining 1,000 PP will be used for rent, initial arrangement and salaries in the first months of living in Eretz Yisrael. According to the calculations, the expenses are expected to be slightly higher, and therefore, a credit of 400-500 PP will be required.

Pinchas Steinwachs' activities to raise the cooperative continued vigorously. Besides contacting the relevant departments in the Jewish Agency, he contacted the Histadrut, the credit cooperatives, the settlement bodies, and other entities. On April 27, 1938, a letter was sent to the *Aliyah* Department from the Tel Aviv Cooperatives Center, explaining that the center had decided to support the brush industry. The writer noted that the thirty candidates for the cooperative are experts in the profession and are willing to invest 100 PP each in working capital. The immigrants will finance their travel expenses themselves and will bring 20-25 PP for initial arrangements. This 3,000-PP total will be enough to purchase raw material in Romania and the Balkans; finished goods will be shipped to England. The cooperative will be located in a settlement or *moshav* near Tel Aviv or Haifa. The group required 30 certificates. At the same time, a letter was sent to the *Aliyah* Department from the Committee of Settlements and Organizations connected to the Jewish Agricultural Workers Association in Israel. The Committee recommended that Steinwachs, the representative of the brush factory, settle in the Hefer Valley, on the assumption that this industry would employ hundreds of families, at a time when the economic and political situation in the country required the addition of people. A letter of support for the brush-making cooperative was sent on April 29, 1938, by the Executive Committee of the Histadrut. The *Aliyah* department was asked to make a special effort to ensure the *Aliyah* of the brush makers.

On May 2, 1938, Pinchas Steinwachs sent three letters: to A. Kaplan, to H Barlas, and to A. Dobkin of the Jewish Agency, detailing his activities in the country to promote the *Aliyah* of the brush makers. He set up meetings with: D. Horowitz and Professor Rottenstreich from the Institute of Economic Research; Dr. Oplatkin, director of the health department of the Tel Aviv municipality; Zvi Yehuda from the secretariat of the workers; Zelig Lubianik from *Shikun*, and with Ben-Zvi from *Kfar Vitkin*, all of whom supported the plan. A few days later, Ben-Zvi sent an enthusiastic request to the Jewish Agency from the *Emek Hefer* Regional Committee, which was very keen on establishing the factory in their area. At the same time, Steinwachs noted in his inquiries that the people of Mezeritch had contacted importers in England who were interested in the goods to be produced. Furthermore, the project is ready for implementation and now depends only on the allocation of 30 certificates. This will enable Israel to become a transfer country for the global hog hair market. Besides, Steinwachs noted that with the success of the project, many Polish Jews would be brought into the Zionist movement. On May 8, 1938, Kaplan, of the Commerce and Industry Department of the Jewish Agency, responded that the application had been relayed to Dobkin. However, he was aware of the difficulty in securing certificates from the current schedule (quota). Nevertheless, he wanted to get more detailed calculations.

Two days later, Steinwachs again contacted Dobkin and Barlas reported on his inquiries to England and the United States, which were well received. The party's secretary in England helped contact importers and received a serious response. Mezeritch residents in the United States also expressed their willingness to help with finances and with organizing the import of the brushes.

"My dear Steinwachs," Barlas wrote on May 11, 1938, "you know [...] the conditions of immigration during this period, and you will surely understand that we cannot easily decide anything." In reply, Steinwachs wrote, "I am sure that you will continue as you have until now to do everything in your power to get positive results." On the same day, another letter of support for the transfer of the factory from Poland to Israel was sent, this time from the *Aliyah* Center of the Histadrut, seeking a list of names of the skilled workers in order to allocate licenses to them.

On May 20, 1938, Dobkin replied to Steinwachs that the reduction of the (certificate) quota forced him to postpone the discussion about the Mezeritch cooperative to the possible allocation from the next quota, which was due to be released in October 1938. However, 10 certificates from the current quota (at the expense of industrial workers) would be provided, subject to an agreement being reached with the Department of Commerce and Industry. Dobkin sent a copy of this letter to C. Rosenstein of the Histadrut, to Yitzchak Gruenbaum, a member of the Jewish Agency's governing body, and to A. Kaplan of the Agency's economic department. That same day, likely even before he received Dobkin's letter, Steinwachs sent four desperate inquiries: to Dobkin, Barlas Shapira, and Silberberg, all from the Agency's *Aliyah* department. Steinwachs sought assistance and intervention to arrange for the certificates.

I have already spent six weeks in Palestine, and I have only a few days left to stay. The first few weeks were devoted to discussing and proving to our economic and organizational institutions the practical reality and importance of this project; I succeeded in receiving a positive response from all those institutions. The only delay is the question of immigration, and unfortunately, this point is the most important and most resistant to being solved. I am well aware of how small the number of immigration licenses granted in this schedule is, and

I know of the high demand for the certificates — I know how many are knocking on your doors every morning and evening. Nevertheless — and specifically because — the schedule is small and cannot even slightly satisfy the need for a large and broad Aliyah; precisely because the number of certificates to be issued is so small — we must utilize them for the establishment of a new industrial plant in the country. The plant will be a source of great blessing to the country, providing a significant source of needed employment. All this — apart from mentioning the good...that this will cause for the entire Zionist movement in Poland.

It will be very difficult for me to return to Poland without finalizing the matter. I will not be able to explain to my friends and to the movement that the matter was utterly destroyed simply due to an inability to provide the certificates (to Dobkin) [...] it would be an unjustifiable sin if everything we have built up to now will be demolished solely because Immigration certificates were not granted (to Barlas) [...] I find it imperative and vital that you try as hard as possible to positively resolve our request and to see to it that certificates are granted for establishing the Cooperation Center for the Hog Hair industry with immigrants from Mezeritch (to Shapira) [...] Forgive me for troubling you so much, it is also unpleasant for me, but I feel that you will not have any resentment toward me [...] My request of you [...] is that you look after the matter and help us to conclude this matter positively (to Silberberg).

On the same day, another letter of support was sent to the *Aliyah* Department, this time from the *Mapai* (Palestine Workers Party): Steinwachs complained about his difficulties in obtaining certificates for the people of Mezeritch, and the party members asked the *Aliyah* department to look favorably upon his request. On May 22, 1938, Steinwachs again wrote to Dobkin, complaining of the recanting of previous promises and of conditioning the granting of the licenses on a waiver by the Department of Commerce and Industry of the licenses that had been granted to them, which would not be forthcoming. Steinwachs asked for a decision in principle regarding the 30 certificates: ten to be granted in the current schedule, and first priority for the other experts in the next schedule, as well as nullifying the veto by the Commerce and Industry Department. The next day, the *Aliyah* Department received a letter in a similar vein from the Histadrut executive committee: "Although the problem of the limited certificates is great and it is not easy to implement a program that requires the inviting of 30 immigrant workers, it is difficult for us to understand why you have made the 10 certificates conditional on the agreement of the Commerce and Industry Department."

At this point, the potential immigrants from Mezeritch intervened. On May 27, 1938, a telegram was sent to Dobkin from Mezeritch with three words: "Don't interfere. H E L P!" On May 31, 1938, Steinwachs sent two letters: one to the board of the Brush makers' Cooperative in Mezeritch, where he reprimanded the management for the telegram and praised Dobkin's activities, and the other — an apology letter to Dobkin in which he wrote, among other things:

I am very sorry for the fuss made by our friends from Mezeritch, Poland [...] I attach the letter I sent today to friends in Mezeritch [...]. I can't understand how my friends allowed themselves to send a telegram like that, and on what basis? [...] We must not neglect this sacred matter. We will work with all our effort and strength to make this happen. We must not consider the nonsense committed by some irresponsible members; it is necessary to conclude the matter in a positive way. I assure you that our legal authorities in Poland will certainly not be silent regarding what happened.

On June 7, 1938, a letter from the *Aliyah* Department in reply to Steinwachs' May 20 request was sent: "We have been informed that the chances of fulfilling your requirement [...] are even less than a few weeks ago, because the number of licenses we have received this season will probably be reduced greatly." The following day, Steinwachs received another reply, from M. Shapira of the *Aliyah* Department stating: "We have decided to recommend to the Department of Trade and Industry to set aside 10 licenses for the Cooperative from those that were reserved for experts invited by Industrialists in Palestine [...] This decision cannot satisfy you. Please understand, however, that in the special situation that the current schedule presents, we could not decide otherwise." On June 14, 1938, Dobkin wrote to the cooperative in Mezeritch: "I demand that you explain to me the meaning of the words [in the telegram] 'Don't interfere' — who do you suppose I am? Where did you receive such information?" A second letter was addressed to Steinwachs explaining the impossibility of assigning 30 licenses and the promise to respond regarding the 10 licenses within two weeks.

On June 15, 1938, Steinwachs again wrote to Dobkin and Zilberberg asking them for help in arranging for the *Aliyah* licenses. In reply, Dobkin replied that he could not expedite the processes. In the meantime, an apology telegram was sent from Mezeritch to Dobkin: "We appreciate your actions; please forgive us. We ask for your help — the Cooperative." In addition, an apology letter was issued to "our dear and very respectable friend Dobkin" by the Cooperative's management. The Mezeritch writers made two major arguments for the sense of despair that led them to send the telegram: One — the huge contribution to the Palestine economy if it succeeds in moving the hog hair industry from Poland, an industry that will provide many jobs and in addition will contribute to the development of the country's international trade; and the second — the great contribution that will be made through the success of the venture toward the transfer of Polish Jews from the Bund movement to the Zionist movement. Thus, they chose to end their letter:

Dear Friend! We know you well and greatly appreciate your actions in the field on behalf of the Zionist movement in general and the *HeHalutz* in particular, since the time you lived among us as a leader of the movement in Poland. It did not occur to any of us to suspect you of interfering with such an important enterprise as ours [...]. We are sure, dear friend, that you will erase the insulting phrase from your memory and just focus on our cry of "Save us!" Please do whatever you can to ensure that the efforts of our friend Steinwachs will not go unnoticed and that our great pioneering enterprise will be carried out.

Dobkin's response to this letter was laconic: "I received your letter from the 21st of this month regarding immigration licenses for members of the Cooperative of hog hair processors in Mezeritch. Details of the situation in this regard will be given to you by P. Steinwachs who is returning to Poland."

At this point, the political factor - the struggle between the Zionist movement and leftist movements on the Jewish streets in Poland - was mobilized for the Cooperative's desperate efforts. It was claimed that when the initiative for the *Aliyah* of the group of brush makers became known in Mezeritch, there was a move away from affiliation with the Bund and Communist movements and toward the Zionist movements; however, with the lessening of the chances that this *Aliyah* will happen, there is a consequently a concern about the strengthening of the left-wing movements in Mezeritch and the collapse of the Zionist movements in the city. The Bund members also spread rumors that the entire project of the *Aliyah* of the Brush makers' Cooperative was a ruse designed to recruit supporters for the Zionist movement. Inquiries highlighting the danger to the Zionist movement in Poland with the failure of the venture were sent to the immigration department by the Zionist organizers in Mezeritch – from the Executive Committee of the Histadrut and from the "Ichud" in Israel – and there was extensive correspondence between these bodies and the immigration department.

In a letter dated July 22, 1938, Dobkin explained to the Histadrut's executive committee why he could not grant licenses to the people of Mezeritch: From the remaining 100 licenses that had been designated by the government for those who were in Palestine illegally, 80 of them were reassigned and sent to Vienna and Berlin for prisoners in Dachau. The remaining 20 licenses have been designated by the government for special cases in Austria." The correspondence between Dobkin and Steinwachs resumed upon the latter's return to Poland, with Dobkin explaining that the licenses had been assigned to Austrian Jews and expressing his hope of helping the cooperative in the next schedule. Although they were unable to advance the venture, the Cooperative members of Mezeritch continued to prepare for their *Aliyah*. Meetings and conferences of immigrant candidates were held, a list of 36 candidates was formulated, and inquiries were sent to the Zionist Office in Warsaw and to the Immigration Department in Jerusalem. On August 15, 1938, they asked that the Zionist Office in Warsaw send a representative to Mezeritch to examine the candidates. The Zionist Office, however, chose not to send a representative due to concerns about raising false hopes for the city's Jews.

At this stage it became clear that licenses should not be expected even under the new schedule. On September 1, 1938, Dobkin wrote to Steinwachs that he could not guarantee anything. Nevertheless, Dobkin instructed the Warsaw office to send a representative to Mezeritch for examining the candidates, while stressing that the examination should not be regarded as a commitment. On October 2, 1938, the director of the Zionist Office in Warsaw, J. Kashtan, visited Mezeritch to examine the candidates for immigration. Thirty-six applicants were tested. Seven were disqualified for reasons of health, personal mismatch, age, and family size, and another candidate was disqualified for political reasons ("extreme circles" and disloyalty to Zionism). Twenty-nine candidates were approved, 12 of whom were former "Bund" or "extremist" members (formerly a Communist code name) who had recently joined the Poalei Zion. At the beginning of November 1938, the number of permits requested for the cooperative dropped to only 15-20.

On November 16, 1938, Steinwachs wrote to Dobkin in London, reminding him of the cooperative's interest. Another letter was sent to Dobkin on December 27, 1938, after the latter returned to Palestine. On January 10, 1939, Dobkin replied: "To my great sorrow, I cannot fulfill your request [...] in light of the terrible tragedy that has befallen the Jews of Germany and Austria we are powerless to help." Between January 13 and 16, 1939, Steinwachs wrote four letters to members of the Immigration Department, all desperately asking for help in obtaining at least 10 certificates.

On January 20, 1939, Silberberg replied to Steinwachs: "The 40 immigration licenses allocated to experts commissioned by industrial enterprises [...] through the Association of Manufacturers were distributed to important experts from Austria and Germany, aside from 3-4 to experts from other countries." On January 25, 1939, Shapira replied to Steinwachs: "At the height of the situation of the Jews of Germany and Austria, we could not even think of the possibility of setting aside any number of licenses for this purpose in the current season." On January 29, 1939, Silberberg replied: "It is impossible to assign even a single license to the people of Mezeritch."

Barlas's reply of March 3, 1939 was: "it is hopeless. As you have already been informed, the matter is being registered for a special hearing on obtaining licenses for the period beginning in April."

On May 16, 1939, Dobkin wrote: "Despite the hopes, we have not yet received the approval for the new schedule. Even if approved, there is no hope that the number of licenses will be high and the chances of arranging the matter are very low." On July 10, 1939, J. Bachar, Secretary of the *Aliyah* Department, wrote to the people of Mezeritch: "We announce that we were not, unfortunately, able to approve special immigration licenses for your members. H. Dobkin is now abroad, and we expect that he will visit Poland as well." On

July 17, 1939, about a month and a half before the outbreak of the war, the last letter on this subject was written. Bachar wrote, this time to the Central Committee of the Trade Unions in Warsaw, that Dobkin was abroad and there was nothing to do be done with the brush makers from Mezeritch.

Group of workers in a stubble factory in Mezeritch
Source: The "Mezeritchim Laborers and Revolutionaries," a photo album by the Mezeritch Olim Association in Israel, 2010

Foreword

In the Thirties of the previous century, a thousand years of Polish Jewish history raced to a tragic end. The Jews tried to leave Poland in every which way, but their attempts were unsuccessful, and only a handful of them succeeded. America closed its doors to immigrants, and Israel became virtually the only possible destination for anyone trying to escape a country that offered only poverty, anti-Semitic harassment, and exclusion. Unfortunately, the gates of Palestine were also not open.

Jewish immigration from Poland was part of a broad immigration movement: Between 1931 and 1938, about 515,000 immigrants emigrated from Poland; some 119,000 of them were Jews. The quantity of Jews among the immigrants was 23 percent – more than twice their proportion of the population. Close to 60 percent of Jews who left Poland in the 1930s immigrated to Israel. Other important immigration destinations were the United States and Argentina. Two key factors affected immigration in the period between the World Wars: Restriction of immigration to the United States (Quota laws 1921, 1924) followed by the restriction of immigration to other countries, and the economic crisis that began in 1929. These two factors resulted in diverting the center of gravity of Jewish immigration from the United States to Israel.

After World War I, the extent of international immigration narrowed. Among Jews, the volume of immigration dropped from 60,000 to 50,000 immigrants for the year before the First World War and averaged 26,000 after that. However, in the interwar period, more Jews emigrated from Poland than from any other country and Palestine was the leading destination of this migration. In the 1930s, some 256,000 immigrants arrived in Israel, more than a third of them from Poland. When the state was founded, those born in Poland constituted 35 percent of all foreign-born persons in the country, and 22 percent of the total population. These immigrants had a considerable influence on the character of the State and its way of life in its early years, an influence so significant that it can be felt until today.

Jewish immigrants from Poland were the last to succeed in escaping the horrors of the Holocaust even before the outbreak of World War II, and they can be seen as an important group of survivors, in addition to other groups of survivors: 100,000 survivors who survived War World War II on Polish land, and about 200,000 survivors who fled to the Soviet Union when the war broke out.

Despite its importance, this *Aliyah* of Polish Jewry has not been studied so far as an independent issue. The literature dealing with the impact of the various waves of immigration on the Jewish population in Israel regards immigrants from Poland as a key element only in the Fourth *Aliyah* (known as the Grabski *Aliyah*), in which the immigrants from Poland accounted for about 50 percent. However, the immigrants from Poland also accounted for the majority of the Fifth *Aliyah* (1930-1939), in which immigrants from Central Europe (Germany, Austria and the Czech Republic) accounted for only 15 percent. Still, the Fifth *Aliyah* is regarded as the "German immigration." In the research dealing with this period there is a great deal of material dedicated to the immigrants of Germany but the information about the immigrants from Poland is sparse, and includes mainly numerical data based on the classification of permits that were issued for entry into the country. This book is focused on the Polish immigrants of the Fifth *Aliyah*: It discusses their demographic, occupational, social and economic characteristics, and especially the background of their immigration and their journeys to Palestine.

The political and institutional side of immigration has been studied in-depth in Aviva Halamish's book *B'Merutz Kaful Neged ha-Zman*[2]. In this book, this policy is examined as it played out "on the ground" – in the activities of the Israeli Land Office in Poland, in the relationship between the main office in Israel and the office in Warsaw, and in the practical implications of the policies outlined in Jerusalem. Most of the extant research on this topic was done from a Palestinian-centric perspective, focusing on the effect waves of immigration had on the *yishuv*, the Jewish community in Palestine. In this work, the center of gravity of the discussion moves from Palestine to Poland.

According to the basic pattern accepted in immigration research, the migration process consists of three types of factors: 1) factors related to the place of origin; 2) factors related to the destination; 3) factors related to the process of transition. The present work focuses on the first and third types. We discuss the factors that pushed people toward emigration and that were related to the place of origin, i.e., the condition of Polish Jews on the one hand; and factors related to the transition process on the other hand. It turns out

---

2   Halamish, *B'Merutz Kaful Neged ha-Zman* [A Dual Race against Time: Zionist Immigration Policy in the 1930s, Hebrew], Jerusalem: 2006, p. 539.

that the transitional factors, which are generally seen as marginal in the immigration process and thus given scant attention in research, were central – even critical – to the immigration process, especially to the emigration attempts from Poland in the 1930s. This was a result of the immigration restrictions and the procedures required, in addition to the high economic and psychological toll that immigration exacted – all these together prevented the majority of Polish Jews from taking advantage of the opportunity to begin a new life on foreign soil.

This book seeks to shed light on the emigration from Poland, in a way that has not been done so far; namely, to examine this process against the background of the situation of Polish Jews at that time and the possibilities they faced regarding immigration and *Aliyah* to Palestine. At the center of this analysis is the individual, the conditions he had to face, the difficulties with which he had to cope and the immigration options he faced. Also, the economic and social situation of Polish Jews in the 1930s and the motives for the emigration that resulted from it; the atmosphere and mood of Polish Jews in relation to Palestine and *Aliyah* and the image of the country as depicted in the Jewish press; the emigration of Polish Jews against the background of all emigration from Poland at that time; examining the immigration options that were open to Polish Jews; the characterization of those few Jews who had the opportunity to emigrate compared to the "others" who constituted the majority of the Jewish people in Poland, and for whom there was no room to even consider this possibility; exposing the "behind the scenes" of the emigration and *Aliyah* efforts from Poland – all these are the main subjects of this book.

***The Balfour Declaration and the conquest of Palestine by Britain opened a new era. The government that came into power recognized the right of the Jewish people to a national home in Israel, and the Zionist Organization received the status of representing the Jewish people with regard to the establishment and development of its national home. There was a sense that the gates of the land were opening wide to masses of immigrants. Upon the establishment of civil government in July 1920, the Zionist Organization was granted permission to bring immigrants into Israel, subject to an agreement with the government, provided that the Zionist Organization could secure employment and living expenses for their first year in Israel. This principle of economic absorption capacity of the country was the guiding principle in establishing the quota of immigrants allowed in the succeeding years. Later, it was joined by the principle of maintaining the demographic balance between Jews and Arabs. In 1922, the principle of economic absorption was officially approved in Churchill's White Paper. The events of August 1929 led to a re-examination of immigration, and this time the national issue and the relations between Jews and Arabs in the country were at its center. Following the events, an inquiry committee was appointed – the Shaw Committee. In October 1930, the White Paper was published, which stated that regarding the subject of immigration, the political situation and the concern of Arabs about the scale of Jewish immigration should also be considered. After the outbreak of the Arab revolt in April 1936, a royal commission of inquiry – the Peel Commission – was sent to Palestine. The committee's conclusions were published in July 1937 and included the recommendation for the termination of the British mandate and the partition of the country. The recommendation was partially adopted by the Zionist Organization and rejected by the Arabs. About two months later, the Arab revolt resumed. The Partition Plan was dropped from the agenda, and on May 17,

1939, the MacDonald White Paper was published, which stated that within ten years a Palestinian state with an Arab majority would be established in Israel, that for the period of 1940-1945 only 10,000 immigrants would be allowed annually into the country, and that, in addition, the onetime entry of 25,000 refugees would be allowed immediately. Jews were also restricted from buying land.

The principle of absorbing immigrants according to existing capacity divided immigrants into three types: immigrants who were economically self-sufficient, immigrants who depended on the residents of the country for their livelihoods, and immigrants who would be able to integrate into the labor market (the "working *Aliyah*"), on condition that it was proven that there was a labor shortage in the country and that the immigrants were fit for employment.

Immigration policy and negotiation with the Mandate authorities on the number of certificates and their subdivisions were the responsibility of the Jewish Agency's administration and its political department. The Agency's immigration department dealt mainly with the practical aspects of immigration. The department operated two bureaus in Palestine – in Jaffa and Haifa – and had overseas branches that were called the "Palestine Ministry." Every six months, the Agency's management applied to the government for the quota – the "schedule" – which was based on the absorption capacity of the country. Initially, full authority was given to the Jewish Agency to distribute licenses to the "working *Aliyah*" among the Diaspora countries. With the rise of the Nazis to power in Germany, these powers were reduced. Until 1937, the distribution of the certificates was made according to considerations of the country's needs and absorption options, but political considerations and pressure by family members in the country also influenced the decision-makers quite a bit. A significant factor in the decision to distribute the "working *Aliyah*" licenses was the financial situation of the Agency that was required to support the absorption of pioneers and was exempt from this obligation for relatives and professionals. As the Agency's economic resources for the absorption of immigrants diminished, preference was given to relatives and the "middle class" (craftsmen) at the pioneers' expense.

The head of the *Aliyah* Department from 1930 to 1933 and from 1935 to 1937 was Dr. Werner Senator, an immigrant from Germany who represented the non-Zionists in the Jewish Agency. From 1933 to 1935 the department was headed by Yitzhak Gruenbaum, a major leader of Polish Jewry who immigrated to Israel. Beginning in 1935, two deputies were added to the department's administration: Eliahu Dobkin, one of the leaders of Mapai and an immigrant from Poland, and Moshe Shapiro, the "Mizrahi" representative; they also ran the department after Senator's resignation in 1937. Chaim Barlas, another immigrant from Poland, also played a major role in the *Aliyah* department, and served in various positions, including secretary of the department.[3]

The *Aliyah* Department had a great deal of power: close supervision of the Zionist Offices, who were required to obtain the

---

3   The Consul of Poland in Jerusalem feared that the appointment of Senator would hurt Jewish immigration from Poland: "Senator, until recently a German citizen, [is] not a man of wide horizons, he thinks in a typical German way, characterized by a love for order and a lack of understanding of wider problems ... He never had contact with the masses of the people as his predecessor, Gruenbaum, did; he did not grow up in that kind of environment...and there is a fear that he would give preference to German Jews..." AAN-MSZ (*Archiwum Akt Nowych, Ministerstwo Spraw Zagranicznych*) t.6288 s.5-6.

department's approval for their activities, as well as control of the salaries of the department heads and their employees and all their financial affairs. The Zionist Offices served as an address for all those interested in immigration and represented the Jewish Agency in their countries. Their job was to provide information on immigration conditions and conditions in Israel, conduct medical examinations, handle certificates and documents, and organize transports. These offices were operated by two arms: the administrative arm staffed by officials selected in coordination with the *Aliyah* Department in Jerusalem, and the community arm – community representatives who served on the "Palestine committees" of the ministry offices. From 1933, members of the Palestine Committee were selected according to party affiliation and the results of the elections to the Zionist Congresses.

With the rise of the Nazis to power in Germany, when constitutional and structured persecution of German Jews began, the British government began to determine the number of licenses to be given to German immigrants, without increasing the number of licenses delivered to the Zionist Organization. Thus, a situation was created in which the certificates handed down to German immigrants came at the expense of the Jews of the other European countries, particularly Poland. German Jews were favorably treated in other ways: National foundations and worldwide Jewish organizations allocated special funds to aid the *Aliyah* and absorption of German immigrants in Palestine, funds that could not be used for other purposes. Another privilege granted to German immigrants was flexibility in fulfilling the criteria required for obtaining the licenses. The heads of the Jewish community in Palestine and Poland were aware of the injustice caused to Polish immigrants as a result of the government's preference for German Jews. Ben-Gurion, Katznelson, Gruenbaum,

Dobkin, Farbstein, Rottenstreich, and others raised the issue of the deprivation of Polish Jews compared to German Jews, even at a time where the former's condition was seen by many, at least until Kristallnacht, as more difficult than the situation of German Jews. After the first wave of harassment against the Jews of Germany, when their situation stabilized a bit, the relative number of licenses granted to them diminished; however, after the Nuremberg Laws in 1935, the share of the total number of certificates granted to German Jews again increased. This was so even though the situation of Polish Jews worsened after the death of Polish leader Jozef Pilsudski that very same year. The rate of certificates handed over to German immigrants increased steadily in 1935-1937 and reached more than 50 percent by 1938.[4]

In 1924, with the end of the economic recession in Palestine, a relatively large number of immigrants began to arrive. This wave of immigration, which lasted until 1926 and included about 60,000 immigrants, is known as the "Fourth *Aliyah*." In 1926 another economic crisis hit the country. During these years, immigration was almost completely halted, a large wave of people left the country, and even a negative migration balance was recorded. Beginning in 1929, immigration resumed, peaking in 1935. After this record-breaker, the number of immigrants dropped sharply in 1936-1937, and rose slightly in the last two years before the war.

---

4   Halamish (2006): pp. 312-338.

Table 1 - Number of immigrants to Palestine 1930-1939

Year	Number of Immigrants
1930	4,944
1931	4,075
1932	12,553
1933	37,337
1934	45,267
1935	66,472
1936	29,595
1937	10,629
1938	14,675
1939	31,195
Total 1930-1939	256,742

Source: Sicron, Haalyia L'Israel (1957), Statistical Appendix, Table A1

Nearly 257,000 immigrants officially arrived in Palestine in the 1930s, more than 40 percent of them from Poland. Another major country of origin during these years was Germany. Other immigrants came in small numbers from other countries. As a result of this wave of immigration and with, in addition, natural growth, the Jewish population in the country increased from approximately 165,000 persons in 1930 to approximately 432,000 persons in 1939, and its proportion of the general population increased from about 17 percent in 1931 to about 30 percent in 1939. The Jewish population in the country was relatively young, with a notably high proportion of working-age people. The immigrants of the 1930s, like their predecessors, settled mainly in cities. As early as 1936, about three-quarters of the Jewish population were concentrated in Tel Aviv, Jerusalem, and Haifa. The trend of concentrating the Jewish population in cities continued until the end of the decade.

Compared to previous immigration waves, the abovementioned *Aliyah*, known as the "Fifth *Aliyah*," was more "family oriented": 57 percent of immigrants came in a family setting, compared with only 30 percent and 44 percent in the third and fourth immigrations. Approximately half of the immigrants in the Fifth *Aliyah* came as part of the working *Aliyah* movement, about a quarter of them as economically self-sufficient, and slightly less than a quarter as dependent on the residents of the country; six percent of the immigrants were students.

During the 1930s, as in the previous period, alongside the officially recognized *Aliyah*, illegal immigrants arrived in Palestine through three avenues: tourists who became illegal aliens, land-based border thieves who arrived through Egypt, Lebanon, and Syria, and immigrants who arrived by sea. In 1932, thousands of tourists arrived in the country as part of the first Maccabiah and the Eastern Fair, and many of them stayed there. *Aliyah* under the guise of tourism continued in the years to come; however, with restrictive measures adopted by the government, this stream of *Aliyah* considerably narrowed. In 1934, the "*halutz* [pioneer]" operation succeeded in landing 350 illegal immigrants who had arrived on the ship *Wallace* on the shores of the Land, but another similar operation failed. These clandestine operations ceased until they were renewed under the leadership of the Revisionists starting in 1937; such efforts were carried out by the Labor movement as well.

The absorption policy that developed in the 1920s included caring for the immigrant until he was settled in a job, and this consisted of securing a short-term residence (in camps and immigration housing), medical assistance and a loan for immediate needs. This policy was the result of a worldview in which the immigrants who arrived were ideologically motivated and, accordingly, were trained in agricultural work or labor. The limited assistance was provided on the assumption that the immigrants would be able to settle in the country within a few days, and it was specifically tailored for immigrants who joined the movement to settle the Land, or the workers' union in the cities.

Jewish society in the country was organized in a series of voluntary institutions and organizations that were referred to as the "organized community." The "unorganized" part of the settlement mainly consisted of the ultra-Orthodox, Communists, and Revisionists[5]. During the period of the Mandate, two national systems operated simultaneously in the country: Worldwide institutions, as in the Zionist Organization (later called the Jewish Agency), and the local institutions, as in the Knesset of Israel, the Assembly of Representatives and the National Committee. The former were dominant during the Mandate period because the local institutions had no fixed financial sources; only part of the Jewish population in the country took part in the local institutions, and, in addition, the status of the Zionist leadership was enshrined in the Mandate, while the local institutions were only partially official. The Zionist leadership was the senior body that negotiated with the British government and regulated most of the matters that affected life in the *yishuv*, the Jewish community. The two main camps in the political-social system were the Labor Movement and the Revisionists. The strengthening of these movements occurred simultaneously in Palestine and within the global Zionist movement. Until the late

---

5   Horowitz and Lissak. (1977) pp. 307-309.

1920s, the political center's delegates constituted the majority of the Zionist movement. At the 16th Congress in 1929, the power of the Center's delegates for the first time declined. In the following years, the main ideological movements – the Labor Movement and the Revisionists – were strengthened. The Revisionist movement that was established in Israel in 1923, and which was strengthened in the years to come, was in many respects an opposition to the Zionist leadership led by Chaim Weizmann. In the 1930s, these two movements fought for hegemony in the Zionist movement.

In the elections to the Third Assembly in January 1931, Mapai won more than 42 percent of the vote. The Revisionists received 22 percent. Thus, Mapai became the dominant factor under the leadership of the National Committee, and Yitzhak Ben-Zvi was appointed Chairman. At the Seventeenth Zionist Congress in 1931, the Labor faction rose to 29 percent, while the Revisionists gained 21 percent. The new administration included representatives of the Labor movement, and the political department was headed by Haim Arlozorov. In the years 1931-1933, the Labor movement and the Revisionists fought fiercely. On June 16, 1933, Haim Arlozorov was murdered, and the struggle between the two movements intensified fiercely. Before the Eighteenth Congress in 1933, Ben-Gurion went to Poland, the stronghold of the Revisionists, to convince voters of the justice of the Labor movement. Jabotinsky also made a similar journey. Ben-Gurion ultimately had the upper hand, and his list – the League for a Working Israel – won 42 percent of the vote in Poland, twice the number of votes given to Jabotinsky. Thus, the Labor movement came to control the Zionist movement, which now stood under the leadership of David Ben-Gurion, Moshe

Shertok, and Eliezer Kaplan.[6]

In 1935, the Revisionists announced the departure of the Zionist Congress and the establishment of the New Zionist Organization (the "Tzach"). Mapai became the dominant factor in the Zionist movement. Ben-Gurion was appointed head of the Zionist administration, Shertok was appointed head of the political department, and Kaplan – head of the finance department.[7]

Until the outbreak of World War II, Polish Jewry was the largest and most vibrant of the Jewish centers in Europe. The political parties and movements in Palestine attributed great importance to it, both as a source of *Aliyah* and as a pool of supporters. This book is devoted to the study of Polish Jewry and the opportunities that existed for its *Aliyah*.

6   *Ibid*, pp. 336-339.

7   Naor, Giladi. (1991) pp. 218-229.

1

POLAND AND POLISH JEWRY
DURING THE 1930S

The fate of sad young Jews [...] We have nothing to do, we live aimlessly. Where to go? What to do? [...] This stagnation paralyzes our youth and is a spiritual death. [...] The Polish environment is hostile to me, Poland is deporting me as a Jew, treating me as a foreigner. I look around and see that Poland is not mine; here I am not free. The parks, the avenues, public buildings - are not mine. Even as a guest, I am not wanted [...] all the roads here are closed to me. [...] I began to take an interest in Zionism [...] My dream of Aliyah is like a beautiful and unattainable fantasy. [...] I see myself behind a plow with a rifle on my shoulder. [...] But I doubt this distant dream.[8]

At the end of the First World War, the Second Polish Republic was established, which lasted until the outbreak of World War II. Before the establishment of the Republic, Poland had been subservient

---

8   Szandler (2002) pp. 377-378. (Translations of documents from here infra are mine – I.C.)

to and divided between Russia, Prussia, and Austria. When borders were set, independent Poland became a multinational state. Only about 65 percent of its population were Poles; a third were Ukrainians, Belarusians, Jews, and others. The three areas under the pre-war powers – eastern and central Poland under Russia, areas of western Poland under Prussia, and southern Poland (Galicia) under Austria –differed economically, socially, and culturally. The Russian domain consists of two regions with unique characteristics: central Poland (Congressional Poland), and the eastern provinces (the Kresy).

With the establishment of independent Poland, 16 districts were designated: in the central region – Warsaw, Lodz, Kielce, and Lublin; in the southern region – Krakow, Lvov, Tarnopol, and Stanislav; in the eastern region – Vilnius, Bialystok, Novgorod, Polesie, Volhynia; and in the western region – Szlask, Poznan, and Pomoze. The Ukrainians and Belarusians were concentrated in the eastern provinces; the Germans – in the west, while the Jews were scattered throughout all the Polish provinces.

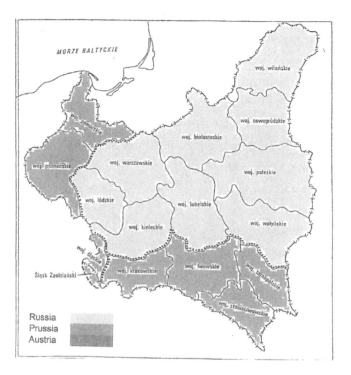

Division of Poland from before 1914

Poland between the wars was mainly agricultural land. At the beginning of the period, the rural population accounted for 75 percent of the total population. With the urbanization processes that took place between the wars, its rate dropped to 70 percent. The urbanization process mainly led to the growth of the big cities and had very little effect on the population of the towns. Poland was a poor country compared to the countries of central and western Europe, which was expressed in part by the volume of consumption of basic commodities in Poland compared to other countries. For example, the annual per-capita consumption of sugar in Poland in the 1930s was only nine kg compared to 50 kg in Denmark and England, 45 kg in the United States, 24 kg in France, and 19 kg in Germany. Data on infant mortality rates and the level of the communication systems in the country also indicate how underdeveloped Poland's economy was during those years.

The Polish village was characterized by great backwardness, outdated methods of soil cultivation, and poor agrarian structure: vast estates that were in private hands and which were only partially developed, and a sharp reduction in agricultural land per-capita in villages. In the years between the two world wars, Poland suffered two economic crises: the first in the mid-1920s, from which the Polish economy recovered at the end of the decade; the second, which was part of the global economic crisis, began in Poland in 1930 and peaked in the mid-1930s; recovery began in 1936. Parts of the rural population that could not make a living from agriculture were called "redundant people," and their number was estimated at 2.4 million in 1935.[9]

Some estimate that the number of unemployed in cities at that time reached a million or more.

Only half of the 500,000 young people who entered the job market each year were able to find employment, resulting in a situation where a significant proportion of those aged 25 and under were unemployed. Eighty-three percent of the unemployed lived in one room apartments; the density reached seven and sometimes even 10-15 people per room. Only nine percent of the unemployed had a bed for themselves. Many of them suffered from starvation. Their diet was mainly based on potatoes, and the glycemic index dropped almost a third compared to the time that they were employed.

Not only the unemployed suffered from poor living conditions:

9   Mahler (1968) p. 13.

the condition of the partially employed and those of the lower working classes – artisans and peddlers – was not much better. Following the liquidation of large and medium-sized businesses, a great many small trading businesses and workshops were opened, many of them in residential apartments. From 1928 to 1932 the number of workshops in Poland declined by 35 percent or more. Particularly affected were small operations such as shoemakers, tailors and small shops, who eked out an income of only 30-60 zlotys a month. The standard of living of these business owners was extremely low. A monthly income of 30 zlotys dictates a life of starvation.

Polish Jews

Polish Mother, with your last pennies you are educating your child, but what source of livelihood will you be able to give him after those are gone? What will happen to him? After all, there are no jobs, the village is too crowded, and overseas countries are closed to immigration. Thousands of energetic youth who should be the pride of the people instead increase the army of the unemployed, those without the means of existence, people of despair. Consider that your beloved child, as well, may yet be bread-less in his be-loved homeland. To avoid this, we must begin today to prepare a source of livelihood. And so, Polish Mother, you must help us in our economic war against the Jews. For the place of every Jew expelled from Poland will be opened for Christian businesspeople, artisans, and craftsmen -- perhaps the opened position will be for your child. Therefore, do not patronize Jewish businesses; buying from the Jew is not less expensive. If he is selling it to you more cheaply, he is cheating you. ("Self-Defense" publication, Poznan)

The above text accompanied the caricature below, which was typical of Poland in the 1930s.

Przez kupowanie u żydów, szukajcsz straszną przyszłość
swoim dzieciom — oraz nimi będą!

Matko-Polko!

Za ostatnie grosze kształcisz swe dziecko, lecz jakie dasz mu później źródło do życia?
Czem ma być? Wszak posad zabrakło, na roli za ciasno, a zagranicę nie wpuszczają.
Tysiące młodzieży pełnej zapału i sił do pracy, która powinna być chlubą i dumą narodu, powiększa kadry bezrobotnych, a więc ludzi bez środków do życia, ludzi rozpaczy.
Pomyśl, że i Twe ukochane dziecko może w przyszłości w swym rodzinnym kraju nie mieć kawałka chleba.
Żeby tak nie było, żeby nie czuło się ono parjasem na ziemi swych ojców, musimy już dziś przygotować dla nich źródło do życia i dlatego

MATKO-POLKO

powinnaś nam dopomóc w walce gospodarczej z żydami, gdyż
na miejsce każdego usuniętego z POLSKI żyda do handlu, rzemiosła, urzędów i wolnych zawodów wejdą chrześcijanie,
a może i Twoje dzieck . A więc

NIE KUPUJ U ŻYDA!

Typical Anti-Semitic Caricature

Half of the Polish Jews lived in the center of the state in the districts of Warsaw, Lodz, Kielce, and Lublin; a quarter in the southern region that belonged to the Austrian division; slightly fewer Jews lived in the eastern region that was under Russian influence; and only one percent in the western region. One-third of Polish Jewry lived in "second" Poland in the underdeveloped areas.

The Jews of central Poland and the south were subject to three primary sources of influence: Hasidism, Zionism, and Polish education and culture. In these areas, various groups held activities and the Hasidic movement was thriving. The large Hasidic movements were Belz and Sanz Hasidim in Galicia and Gur Hasidim in central Poland, and dozens more, perhaps even hundreds of smaller groups. The most important yeshiva of this period was in Lublin: the "Chachmei Lublin" yeshiva, under the leadership of Rabbi Meir Shapira. In addition to the influence of Hasidism, Central Poland also showed influences of Polish culture and language, which led to acculturation and assimilation. Polish influence was especially evident in Jewish intellectual and artistic circles as well as among the wealthier bourgeoisie, but over time it spread to the general Jewish public as well. Signs of the increasing influence of Polish culture could be seen, among other things, in the rapid increase in the use of the Polish language in the schools educating its youth, and in the development of Jewish journalism written in Polish, in addition to the existing Yiddish press.

In the eastern regions of Poland, the situation was different. Poles in these areas constituted a minority among the Ukrainian, Belarusian or Lithuanian majority. Although, in the 1930s, the influence of Polish culture and language increased in this area as well, Jews were less affected by this. The impact of Hasidism in northeastern Poland was relatively minor as compared to central Poland and the south, and the region was mainly under the influence of "Mitnagdim" (opponents of the Hasidic movement) on the one hand, and the Zionist movement on the other hand. Vilna was the capital of Jewish-Yiddish and Jewish-Hebrew education and culture. The cultural-religious differences between Lithuania and other parts of Poland were so significant that the "Lithuanians" ("Litvaks") who immigrated to central Poland were perceived as threatening to religion and Jewish tradition. In the West, the former Prussian occupation area, there was a small number of Jews that were heavily influenced by German culture. Many of them immigrated to Germany even before 1918.[10]

Despite the differences in cultural-geographical background, the influence of Polish language and Polish culture in the 1930s increased among all Polish Jews. This effect stemmed from the fact that the vast majority of Jewish students received Polish education in general schools in which Polish was the language of instruction and daily speech. This resulted, during the interwar period, in a steady increase in the number of Jews whose primary language was Polish.[11]

Half of Poland's Jews lived in small towns and cities, about a quarter in the five big cities: Warsaw, Lodz, Vilnius, Krakow and Lvov, and another quarter in the rural villages. The high proportion of Jewish residents of cities (75 percent) was in contrast to the low percentage of non-Jews, of whom only 22 percent lived in cities and towns. (This changed somewhat over the decade, as the economic crisis affecting the Polish village intensified the migration of a rural population to towns and cities.) Thus, the proportion of Jews among the inhabitants of cities in Poland was almost three times their proportion in the general population. In some major

---

10   Tomaszewski (1993) pp. 176-178; Mendelson (1987) pp. 18-24.

11   Shamruk (1997) pp.9-18; See also Freilich (1999).

cities the proportion of Jews was especially high: in Warsaw, about 30 percent of the population was Jewish; in Lodz – 33 percent; in Lublin – 35 percent; in Zamosc – 42 percent, in Chelm – 47 percent. Jews accounted for the majority in many smaller towns as well.

Polish economic policy since the crisis of the 1920s took a greater toll on the Jewish population than on the general population. The nationalization of some sectors of the economy and deliberate policies resulted in the removal of Jews from the nationalized industries both as businesses and as business owners. For example, the nationalization of tobacco, oil, and railways led to the dismissal of thousands of Jews.[12]

Grabski's tax policy, which was based primarily on raising property taxes, seriously damaged Jewish businesses. In addition, Jews were harmed by anti-Semitic discrimination that included an economic boycott and business harassment. The decline of the village pushed the wealthier and resourceful of the peasants into cities and towns, where they tried to find a living in trade and crafts, thus squeezing out many of the Jews who traditionally engaged in these industries. Some of the non-Jews who lost their government jobs during the Depression also moved to trade and crafts, further increasing competition with the Jews in the cities and towns.

The occupation structure of Polish Jews was typical of the inhabitants of cities and towns, and consisted mainly of crafts and commerce, industries in which nearly 80 percent of Polish Jews were employed. Sixty-four percent of Jewish workers were self-employed. The vast majority of them worked by themselves, sometimes with the help of their families, and did not generally hire employees. About a quarter of the employed were laborers, and only

---

12   Garncarska-Kadary (2001) p. 67.

eight percent were classified as workers not engaged in physical labor.

As a result, in the early 1930s, 80 percent of Polish Jews were either salaried or craftsmen or small independent merchants, most of them in businesses that provided only a very small income. During the 1930s, the economic situation of Polish Jews deteriorated, and by the end of the decade the percentage of those employed in low-paying industries increased significantly.[13]

At the same time, the economic competition between Jews and non-Jews, together with political and social influences from Germany, strengthened anti-Semitic movements and increased their activity in Poland. Thus, vandalism against Jewish property increased steadily, as well as did the boycott of trade with Jews, poisonous anti-Semitic propaganda, physical injuries, and even pogroms. Gruenbaum described the desperate situation of Polish Jews in his speech at the end of February 1930:

> This process [of pushing Jews out of livelihoods] oppresses a large community of people ... who find no place for themselves, are superfluous, especially when it comes to traders and small brokers. ... But, ladies and gentlemen, this process concerns hundreds of thousands of people. What should happen to them? What are they supposed to do? Where are they to turn and how are they to act?[14]

The Jews of the eastern provinces were more affected than the

---

13   Mahler (1968) p. 50.

14   Landau and Tomaszewski (1982a) p. 341.

Jews in the other provinces. As there was no industrial development in these areas, the inhabitants of the cities and towns found
a livelihood only in commerce and crafts, both of which had been
adversely affected by the impoverishment of the Polish village and
the increased competition in cities and towns. The rate of Jewish
"passives" (unemployed of working age) reached 50 percent, so
that every "financially" active person was forced to support several
people, including adult children, while he sat in his store most of
the day hoping for customers. Not only the unemployed or partially
unemployed suffered from poverty and hunger, but also some of the
fully employed. According to estimates of the time, 20 percent of
employed persons lived below the poverty line. Thirty percent lived
on the brink of poverty.[15]

Child labor was widely accepted in Poland in general, and among
Polish Jews in particular. An average workday lasted nine to 10
hours. The weekly income ranged from four zlotys for children
aged 12-14, to 15 zlotys for those aged 17-20. According to surveys
conducted of Jewish street vendors, a common Jewish occupation,
profits ranged from 9 to 12 zlotys per week. About 40 percent of
all Jewish craftsmen, traders and workers were earning less than 10
zlotys a week, with a family of four requiring 35 zlotys a week for
basic needs. Surveys conducted of Jewish workers in 1926 and 1930
show that only five percent of workers lived in relatively uncrowded
quarters defines as one person or less to a room. Nearly half of the
interviewees lived in crowded quarters of six people or more to a
room, with about 50 percent sleeping two or more to a bed. Another
survey conducted in Lodz found that 73 percent of Jews' living

---

15   Garncarska-Kadary (2001) p. 143.

quarters were one-room apartments. A significant portion of them were basement apartments or attics; some doubled as workshops.[16] The agreement regarding minorities in the Treaty of Versailles required Poland to grant equal rights to all minorities in its jurisdiction. In its official policy, the Polish government adopted an equitable policy toward all minorities, including Jews, and in March 1931 all discriminatory regulations against Jews were formally abolished. The reality on the ground, however, was far from equal: the right-wing parties and their circles embarked on an organized anti-Semitic campaign throughout Poland; anti-Semitic organizations were set up in central Poland, Krakow, Poznan and elsewhere. The anti-Semitic activities included circulating leaflets, publishing hateful articles in the press, boycotting Jewish shops and businesses, destroying Jewish booths in the markets, and attacking Jewish students at universities. During the 1930s, "waves" of anti-Semitic incidents erupted, some of which led to Jewish and non-Jewish injuries and fatalities. In the second half of the 1930s, the influence of nationalist radicalism in Poland increased. After Pilsudski's death in 1935, the anti-Jewish faction in the government became stronger. Their approach was illustrated by Prime Minister Felicjan Skladkowski's famous statement on June 4, 1936: "My government believes that in Poland it is forbidden to harm anyone, just as a decent homeowner would not allow anyone to be harmed in his home. Economic struggle – certainly, but no physical harm."[17]

This statement legitimized the boycott campaign against Jewish businesses as well as the intensification of government policy against the Jews, although veiled in secrecy. Thus, for example, the central

---

16   Bronsztejn (1963) p. 79. Mahler (1968) p. 192.

17   Meltzer (1982) p. 55.

policy toward the Jews was formulated in a secret memo of the Consular Department of the Polish Foreign Office in April 1938:[18]

> The Jews' struggle against Poland bears the character of a struggle against the character of the state (System) and not against its very existence. Jews want to live in a country where there is no absolute majority for the indigenous nationality. Jews flourished only during periods that Poland was weak. A weakened Poland is necessary for the Jews; in order to achieve this goal, it is essential, according to the Jews, to fight against the nationalization of the Polish economy and its politics – Poland must be weakened internally or become multinational.

In light of the above, the following conclusions must be reached:

1. There is a conflict of interest between Judaism and Poland.
2. With the strengthening of the Polish Nation, these conflicts of interest will be further exacerbated.
3. In light of this, the objectives of Poland's policy are:
    (a) Reducing the Jewish population and emigrating "excess" Jews from Poland.
    (b) Nationalization of economic life in Poland.19
    (c) Finding another immigration territory for Jews, besides Palestine.

---

18   Tomaszewski (1996) p. 125.

19   Transfer of businesses to Polish hands; not under direct government control.

4. A uniform policy of all government institutions toward Jews must be created:

   (a) Prevention of the growth of political strength of Polish Jews, which would result in a unified Jewish bloc. This can be accomplished by strengthening the New Zionist Organization of Jabotinsky (by the Polish government), At the same time, this movement should also be prevented from reaching a monopoly.

   (b) Encouraging loyalists to Poland found in Palestine who were fighting against the Arabs and the British (the New Zionist Organization)

   (c) The liberation of the economy and government from Jews, both in domestic and foreign trade.

5. The Foreign Ministry's policy should aim for:

   - Paralysis of anti-Polish moves that Jews are implementing in the world through appropriate Foreign Ministry activities in the United States, England, France, the Netherlands, and Belgium.
   - Coordination with other Polish entities to replace Jewish activity in international trade.
   - Prevention of the opportunity to return to Poland for Jews of Polish origin who are living abroad.
   - Independent organization by the Polish government of immigration of Jews to countries outside of Palestine.
   - Search for new territories for Jewish settlement.

6. Directing all public energy to constructive anti-Jewish activity, which would create strong pressure from Polish Jews on Jewish organizations around the world, leading those organizations to give priority to the immigration of Polish Jews over the immigration of German and Austrian Jews.

From 1936 to 1939, anti-Semitic incidents intensified, and the boycott against Jewish businesses grew stronger. Competition between Jewish and Polish businesses also intensified, a trend that was aided by the establishment of government-sponsored cooperatives of Christian manufacturers, marketers, and consumers.[20]

The peak of violence against Jews came in 1936-1937. In 1938, while there was a decrease in anti-Semitic violence, the economic boycott at the same time became more institutionalized. Hostile demonstrations in front of Jewish shops became a daily occurrence. "Ghetto stalls" were established in the markets.[21]

Another place where discrimination stood out was at the institutions of higher education. The *Numerus Claus* proposal was supposed to have already ended in the 1920s. Although the proposal was rejected, 27 educational institutions supported the enactment of the *Numerus Claus*, with only nine opposed.[22]

During the 1930s, "ghetto benches" were enforced in many universities – establishing separate seating areas for Jewish students with the excuse of preventing harm to them. In those years, fewer and fewer Jewish students were accepted into higher education.

---

20   Garncarska-Kadary (2001) p. 91.

21   Meltzer (1982) pp. 216-229; Leschinsky (1952); Zyndul (1994); Rudnicki (1985).

22   Tomaszewski (1993) pp. 186.

The quest to isolate Jews in all spheres of life spread to all the right-wing circles: the move toward segregation in the universities extended to high schools and even elementary schools in the late 1930s. Campaigns for segregation in the markets and for removal of Jews from various organizations such as the Association of Lawyers, of Physicians, and of Merchants intensified. Right-wing circles in Poland approved of the Nuremberg Laws and tried to emulate them. This extreme anti-Semitic campaign slowed in early 1939 with the deterioration of Polish-German relations. Anti-Semitic activity in general, and agitation for the enactment of the Nuremberg Laws in particular, did not extend to the entire Polish population. Voices against these trends were also raised, especially by left-wing circles. The Polish Socialist Party (PPS) and the illegal Communist Party (KPP) acted against the anti-Semitic incitement.[23]

A central question that arises around the issue of the immigration of Polish Jews is whether the primary cause was the economic situation or whether it was a result of anti-Semitism. There is disagreement among the researchers.[24]

The question of what the main catalyst of Polish Jews' desire was to immigrate is difficult to determine, as both factors – a very challenging economic situation, and anti-Jewish activity – were simultaneously present and were intertwined. A review of autobiographies by young Jews in Poland in the 1930s, written as part of a life story competition conducted by YIVO, does not shed light on this issue. Their stories raised both issues in parallel: on the one hand, the hopelessness of their economic situation; and on the other, the writers' sense of being seen as foreign and rejected by the

---

23   Meltzer (1982) pp. 62-63, 191-192, 341.

24   Alroi (2008) pp. 49-50.

Polish public, a feeling that prevented them from seeing Poland as their homeland. The depth of despair among the Jews of Poland, especially the young ones, is evident in letters and diaries of the period. For example, a young man from Zamosc wrote:

> Only 15% of Zamosc youths have regular work, 50% work occasionally, while 25% do not work at all. The rest are supposedly helping their parents in trade. The girls serve as workers...many of us love our girlfriends, but marriage is a rare phenomenon.[25]

A young woman from Kolomyia who called herself "Gina" wrote:

> We are facing a tough situation ... In 1933 we suffered a sharp blow with the fall in prices ... I saw that the struggle for existence would be in vain, and thus wanted to go to Palestine, where you can only get to through Zionist *Hachshara* ... In Poland, we have no existence... If we would work so hard anywhere else in the world, we could eat our bread quietly ... I want to go to Palestine, but I cannot go to *Hachshara* because my father needs me in the shop ... my cousin goes to *Hachshara* ... and when he gets the certificate he will take me along, and once I am in Palestine, I will work to bring my parents there. Can I plan anything else? Will my plans come true?[26]

---

25   Garncarska-Kadary (2001) p. 92.

26   Cala (2003) p. 392. Gina's plans never came true. She was murdered by the Nazis in Kolomyia.

A young man by the name of "Sturman" wrote in his autobiography: "My future is as black as a moonless night. [...] Without work without bread, without family help, I go out naked into the world."[27]

Polish Jews, especially the younger ones, did not see the possibility of a future life in Poland, and many of them aspired to immigrate. However, the gates of most traditional destination countries were closed: first, those of the United States and then the gates of other countries. From 1933 to 1935, the influx of immigrants to Palestine increased, but from 1936 severe restrictions were clamped on this destination as well. Three developments occurred simultaneously that exacerbated the situation in which it became impossible to leave Poland: severe economic depletion, the rise of anti-Semitism, and a growing sense of foreignness. On the eve of World War II, all these factors led to feelings of despair and hopelessness among Polish Jews.

---

27   Shandler (2002) p. 262.

2

HOW POLISH JEWRY
IMAGINED ERETZ ISRAEL

Polish Jews received information about Palestine from various sources: from the letters of their relatives, from immigrants and tourists who returned and told about their experiences, and from articles in the press in Poland. The picture of Palestine as depicted in the newspapers, by 1936, was optimistic and enthusiastic, painted in bright colors. Writers marveled at its views, its vegetation and climate, the "New Man" who lived there, the city and the countryside, the atmosphere of pulsating activity, the vibrant nightlife of Tel Aviv, the high cultural level of the city and the village, the efforts of the pioneers and workers, and the beautiful homes in the cities. Only rarely did a tone of criticism or disappointment creep into the descriptions of what was happening in Palestine. One example was Janusz Korczak, who returned to Poland after a visit to Palestine in December 1934, and poured "cold water" on the flowery descriptions published in the pages of the Jewish daily *Nasz Przeglad* (*N.P.*)

> Do you marvel at the fact that Jews work hard? On Nalewki Street I saw old Jews carrying heavy loads as well [...] Are you enthusiastic about Jewish farmers?

> There are also some in Poland. The enthusiasm for
> physical work of Jews is a diasporic phenomenon, [...]
> Indeed, why should a person coming from Europe who
> is unaccustomed to the harsh climate of Palestine com-
> pete for the hard physical work for which the old inhab-
> itants of the Land are used to? [...] Even the legends
> about oranges found in Palestine throughout the year
> are all exaggerated. I spent several weeks there and did
> not encounter a single orange.[28]

A critical note was woven as well through the reports of Benny
Weinstock, a reporter for the *N.P.* who was sent to Eretz Israel,
depicting the darker side of life in Palestine in a picturesque and
humorous way. Also, in *BaDerech*, a Hebrew weekly published in
Poland, a series of articles appeared entitled "Lights and Shadows in
Eretz Israel." Apart from these, however, most of the articles reflected an enthusiastic attitude toward Palestine, which was acceptable
to both Zionist and proto-Zionist circles in Poland.

The Jewish press in Poland painted a broad picture that reflected
the different aspects of life in Palestine. It reported on the economic
development, cultural flourishing, the development of the big cities
– Tel Aviv, Jerusalem, and Haifa – and the rural settlements, the
nature of the land and its landscape, the "new person" a Jew could
be, and the growth of its youth. One could also learn a little about
what was needed to "get along" in Palestine and also about the
"others": immigrants from Germany, immigrants from the Oriental

---

28   *N.P.* (Nasz Przeglad), 19.12.1934. Reported from a press conference
      with Korczak after his return from Palestine.

countries, indigenous Arabs and Bedouins. Although most things were written from an enthusiastic Zionist point of view, it was still possible to get a rather detailed (though incomplete) picture of what an immigrant to Palestine was likely to face.

Dizengoff Square, Tel Aviv, 1935
Source: Library of Congress, Washington

"Blue sky, clear and springy weather even in the midst of winter, bright sun, green fields, wildflowers, citrus blossom scents, plenty of fruits: grapes, plums, peaches, apples, pears" — thus, Eretz Israel was portrayed. The reader also became acquainted with her unique landscapes: the Waterfall in Metulla, the Degania cemetery, the Kinneret, Mt. Hermon, Meron, Safed, Tiberias, the Galilee colonies, the Valley, the Sharon colonies, the Dead Sea, Haifa, Jerusalem.

There is no actual end of seasons, no complete wilting ...
The end lies in a new beginning, in constant renewal, as
in the Song of Songs that is read on Passover, eternally
reflecting spring ... Flowering, growth, and ripening are
in Palestine almost the entire year. I arrived in Palestine
in Adar, right out of the frost and snow, just when the
almond trees were blooming. A month later, the orange
trees bloom, and the scent of their perfume spreads
throughout the area. After the oranges, the strawberry
ripens and in the Galil, wheat is harvested, melons and
watermelons are gathered. On Shavuot, the crops ripen
and then – the grapes. In the summer [sic] the oranges
and lemons are picked, and then the olives also ripen
and fall from the trees. Nature never falls asleep.[29]

The howling of the jackals is quite impressive. While the newcomers panic and become depressed, the old-timers are used to these
voices, reminiscent of a baby cry. Other voices of the night are
braying donkeys: "a wailing filled with passion capable of melting
rock and the female's heart, and the ringing of bells of the camel
caravans." All these instead of the nightingale voice of Polish nights.
Rarely mentioned are the *hamsins*, the harsh heat, which necessitate
a daily shower and installation of shower rooms in all of the apartments. From the letters of young readers to the newspaper, one can
clearly see how they saw the land of their dreams:

In the future I want to work in Palestine, and I imagine
what my homeland looks like: wheat fields, vineyards,

29   *N.P.*, August 18, 1930.

large oranges... I see myself working in agriculture. Even if I will have a lot of money, I will give it to an important cause so that I, like the others, can work hard. I will share my fate with the fate of my people. My life will be based on the love of the homeland and the love of others.

Allenby St. Tel Aviv, 1934
Source: Eric Matson Collection, Library of Congress, Washington, 3135

And in another letter:

I keep thinking about how most quickly to travel to Palestine. I will finish elementary school and go to the 'Eretz'. I will study in an agricultural school. I imagine: everyone gets up in the morning, goes out to the field, and works all day. There is no difference between adults and children. The children live a free life, in the day they study, dance, and sing, in the evening the adults come to them, and they play together.[30]

Oranges held a special place in the descriptions of Palestine, and over time they became a symbol. The tourists marveled at the quantity and low price of this fruit, and so wrote an immigrant child: 'You, there in Warsaw, stand outside a shop window looking at oranges. Only if you are very ill will your aunt visit you and bring what you so dreamed of – an orange. Here in the 'Eretz,' there are so many oranges that even the camels feed on

Harvest in an Orchard
Source: PikiWiki_Israel_1198_Agriculture_in_Israel

---

30   *N.P.*, December 12, 1930.

Another feeling that comes from the writing is the feeling of home. The writers were excited that they were among their people, that all those around them were Jews. They marveled at the Jewish policemen, the Jewish street cleaners, the postal officials and the Jewish builders, and of course, the Jews working in the fields and orchards. Tel Aviv, the "100 percent Jewish city," gave them a feeling of home and freedom. Walking around the streets of Tel Aviv, one of the writers felt that, despite being a tourist, he was on his own land and under his own roof. Thus, a resident of Tel Aviv is quoted as saying: "Although each house is not mine, the entire city of Tel Aviv is ours. It belongs to me; it belongs to you; it belongs to all Jews."[31]

A tourist who came to Palestine for the first time wrote:

> The first impression upon your arrival in Tel Aviv is that there was not even an ounce of exaggeration in everything they told about the first Hebrew city. When you enter the city, you walk like a visionary and dreamer and can hardly believe it yourself: do we already have all this? Hebrew policemen, Jewish street sweepers, Hebrew chimney cleaners, Hebrew theaters. When you see all this with your own eyes, you will be overcome with emotion.[32]

The economic and cultural development of Palestine had a strong connection to Tel Aviv, so the reporting was mainly about Tel Aviv. Indeed, most of the articles and reports dealt with this city.

---

31   *BaDerech*, March 16, 1933.

32   *BaDerech*, September 28, 1934.

The city is lively; nothing is missing here. Everything is beautifully organized, the children are well looked after, there are even street carts where books are sold, and everything can be found in them – from a rare French book to a Latin dictionary. The new neighborhoods are garden cities with houses that look like they were moved here from the most beautiful resorts in Europe; there is a lot of greenery; there is a wonderfully high level of security in this city.[33]

Tel Aviv Beach, 1930s
Source: Library of Congress, Washington

---

33   *N.P.*, November 17, 1930.

Again, and again, comparisons were drawn between Tel Aviv and Paris, Vienna, and the resorts of the European Riviera. In 1931, it was noted that there are already 30 bookstores in the city selling 100,000 books a year while the municipal library housed over 30,000 books. Those reporting marveled at the rhythm of the city, at the streets flowing with traffic like the major metropolitan areas of Europe, at the shops with brightly lit windows, at the colorful advertising signs, at the crowds of young people on the streets, at the private houses dubbed "small palaces" surrounded by greenery and flowers, at the cleanliness of the streets. Tel Aviv was the "Great Cosmopolitan City," a city of glory, wealth, and well-being.

> The Jewish tourist walks around the streets of Tel Aviv like a drunkard [...] The fashion shows at the luxurious San Remo Hotel, beautiful models showcase the latest and most luxurious fashions from Paris and London. The cafes are just as good as those of Berlin, Paris, and Vienna. Nightlife, cafe musicians, abound in streets full of noisy life. New luxurious neighborhoods, the latest architecture. Through the well-lit windows, you can see rich furniture and equipment. This house cost £10,000, another house - £15,000, another - £5,000, £8,000. Parked in front of the houses are shiny new cars. Here live rich industrialists, landlords from America, from the Netherlands and Germany, consuls, and bank executives. In the reception parties of these circles, Hebrew mixes with English, which is considered "bon ton"

among those with fortunes exceeding £10,000.[34] The women are heavily made-up, and the men are smoking cigars. All the above notwithstanding, the street still belongs to the pioneers: they dance and sing until very late at night. Alongside the fancy houses there are gray tents and barracks where the pioneers live.[35]

As the economic situation in Palestine improved, Tel Aviv was increasingly described as a city of the rich and of "the good life": "On Allenby Street limousines, private cars, and carriages line the streets... everything spells 'Prosperity.'"[36] In another article from February 1935:

Thousands of smaller and larger three-story houses. All the houses are bright, enveloped with the greenery of eucalyptus trees [...] Sunlight reaches all the streets [...] In the evening the streets are lit by flashlights and neon lights, the music of phonographs and orchestras emanates from the cafes, the people dress elegantly, many in white. Newcomers, tourists, speculators, dreamers, idealists – everyone is looking for a new life.[37]

Alongside the dozens of articles praising Tel Aviv, there were also, as mentioned above, voices of criticism. A Jewish-Polish architect

34   When German immigrants arrived, it was reported that in their high society parties, only German and English were spoken.

35   *N.P.,* November 6, 1932.

36   *Ibid,* February 6, 1935.

37   *Ibid,* February 6, 1935.

criticized the city's planning: there was no public transportation plan suitable for a modern city, the streets were narrow and ignored the proper orientation toward the sea, the streets were too long and lacking plots for public buildings. The architecture of the buildings is a patchwork of many styles: everyone has brought his hometown and pasted it on to Tel Aviv.[38]

An article published in "*BaDerech*" discussed the economic and social gaps in the city, as exemplified by the "*Kerem HaTaimanim* [Yemenite Vineyard]" neighborhood:

> During the day Tel Aviv is noisy and very busy; at night it is all lit up [...] Night after night, hundreds of cheerful and laughing men and women gather around the cinema [...]the street is bathed in light and pulsating with life. But I also saw a different Tel Aviv, right next to this Tel Aviv. In that Tel Aviv, there are no bright electric lights, no cinema, and no paved roads. In that Tel Aviv, streams of wastewater flow through the streets while flies buzz by, and dozens of sick, dirty, and hungry children roam around. The poverty, hunger and disease found there make their mark on everything, even on the glowing Tel Aviv beside it.[39]

Another criticism stemmed from the ideological struggle against city life and hedonism. The worldview of the early Zionist movement centered on an ideology valuing productivity, satisfaction with a minimum of material needs, and modesty. In line with this

---

38   *Ibid*, November 4, 1934.

39   *BaDerech*, October 15, 1937.

ideology, the hedonistic lifestyle of the city and its inhabitants was viewed negatively. Palestine, it was felt, needs pioneers and workers, not commerce, cafes, and restaurants: "In Palestine at this time, luxuries are premature. Immigrants from the west [Germany] who fled here because of the economic crisis brought along with them a craving for luxury and snobbishness. The rich get richer on the backs of those who labor hard on a daily basis."[40]

Similarly, in 1934 it was written: "Immigrants and tourists come to rest and spend time in the luxurious hotels of Tel Aviv - *Sapir* and *Tarshish* - but we need people who are working to build a healthy economic structure."

Additional criticism was directed at the "foreign spirit" that infiltrated Tel Aviv in the form of the New Year's "Sylvester" parties celebrated mainly among the German immigrants.[41]

Much space was devoted, as well, to the problem of land and houses. In November 1932, real estate prices were reported to have risen by 15 percent over two weeks. In January 1934, the main problem in Tel Aviv was a shortage of apartments and a run up in prices. A company was formed to provide cheap housing to German immigrants; at the same time, construction of hundreds of shanty houses was approved by the government for new immigrants. Between 1931 and 1933, rents in Tel Aviv doubled and reached £3 per room per month. Land prices "jumped" three-fold, and the price of half a dunam reached £1,500. The inflation of real estate prices, according to a newspaper essay, caused damage on two levels: It enriched

---

40   *N.P.,* November 16, 1932.

41   An *N.P.* article of February 21, 1935 described a group of Arabs in the bank after they had sold their land to Jews. They sat on the floor and split the money between them.

the Arabs who sold the land to the Jews, and it raised the cost of housing. This particularly burdened the immigrants and the lower socioeconomic class in the cities.[42]

Raising of the rents also hurt trade because of the high cost of renting a store on the main thoroughfares. Concerning the status of the real estate market, Benny Weinstock humorously commented:

> A middle-class tourist from Poland comes to Palestine to invest in something here and have security for his old age. If he doesn't want to spend time consulting with knowledgeable acquaintances, he'd better go straight to Herzl Street and enter one of the cafes. There he will learn all he needs to know: why houses "fall" and why construction sites "rise." Here sit the "actors" on whom the fate of Palestine truly depends; not – as erroneously thought – on the High Commissioner of Palestine. This is where significant capital is created, and where it is also lost. The tourist wants to buy a house, and the agent happily goes out with him. It becomes apparent that all of Tel Aviv is for sale: new homes, old homes, big houses and small houses; existing houses, and future homes. It is hot and humid in Palestine; it is hard to think and plan; the tourist is sweating. Time passes, and he cannot decide: to buy or not buy? Will it go up or down? Should he buy a house or a lot? A lot or maybe an orchard? Toward Jaffa or maybe better toward the sea? After two days, *Polonia* sails back before he could visit anywhere

---

42 An *N.P.* article of February 21,1935 described a group of Arabs in the bank after they had sold their land to Jews. They sat on the floor and split the money between them.

or see anything; he did not visit the holy places, nor did he have a single quiet night. He travels to Jerusalem to the Western Wall, leans his head against its cool stones, and bursts into tears. He thinks: Maybe he should buy the Western Wall? The tourist goes back to Poland and the whole journey seems like a nightmare. This returnee to Poland urgently needs a vacation.[43]

Compared to the plethora of descriptions and reports about Tel Aviv, relatively little was written about Haifa and even less about Jerusalem. In many cases, it was the difference between Jerusalem and Tel Aviv that was emphasized: "In Jerusalem the air is too clear, the people are too serious, the city is too heavy. It is only 70 km from Tel Aviv, but it is a different world. Jerusalem has all the beauty in the world, it is great and holy, but it is not pleasant. There are many disparate communities and they are all enclosed within themselves."[44]

Thus detailed a writer in April 1932:

The first impression is a disappointment. The Holy City broadcasts misery. Poor and dirty shops, including Arab and Jewish merchants, also dirty. Small and lowly houses are crumbling. Jews from all over the world - Persia, Bukhara, Yemen - dressed in strange clothes, red hats, blue belts on their belly, yellow tunics, white socks. The Jews of Jerusalem comprise 65 percent of the Jewish population but do not participate in the building of

---

43   N.P., December 30, 1934.

44   Ibid, May 24, 1931.

Palestine. This is a group that is large in quantity and small in quality. The children speak Yiddish in ugly jargon. The only advantage of *"Chaluka Jews"* is the large number of children that they rear – 8 to 12 children per family [...] on the way to the Western Wall are stifling narrow alleyways and bad smells. At the Wall - 48 meters in length, 18 meters in height, Jews pray in ecstasy. Even a non-religious person is moved there to tears.[45]

However, even in monolithic and oppressive Jerusalem, a new way of life is emerging. New Jewish neighborhoods are rising. Despite the ban on dance halls and theaters, there are dances in the "Vienna" and "Grand" cafes, although the participants are few; the city's residents are serious and inhibited. At ten o'clock, the streets are empty; only on Saturday night if one goes to Jaffa Street will he get to observe somewhat of a parade of city residents.[46]

The future of Jerusalem is depicted as bleak:

Tel Aviv is the city of the future. Jerusalem, dedicated to the three religions, will remain as a museum, a labyrinth of stone alleys where the past slumbers. Politically, the city will never be a Jewish city. It will remain a city of education and religion, a center of officials, and clerics. It will be a holy city, not belonging to anyone. Nevertheless, the city is developing and changing: new neighborhoods are being built overnight, big and modern shops are opening, the Jews have also set up cinemas, and

45   *Ibid*, April 20.1932.

46   *N.P.,* April 22, 1932.

there is also "Cafe Vienna." The English high society gathers in the evenings at the King David Hotel, which is a modern monument, the most magnificent hotel in the Middle East, and one of the world's most beautiful. After dinner, they dance on the marble floor to the sound of the jazz band, elegant men smoking, and ladies in evening dresses. Here is the meeting place of the English and Jewish "high society."[47]

The writers displayed a more positive attitude toward Haifa. They highlighted the beauty of Mount Carmel and the city developing on its slopes. In November 1933, a festive opening of the harbor was held. A journalist who reviewed the ceremony wrote: "Haifa is a wonderfully picturesque city. At the top of the Carmel, nestled among pine groves, are vacation villas and health spas. The neighborhood of *Hadar HaCarmel* is a miniature Tel Aviv, with shops, coffee houses and a lively movement of city buses."[48]

Allocation of building land in Haifa was done according to classes and sectors: *Kiryat Haim* was defined as a working-class neighborhood, with 450 dunams allocated to the middle class, 300 to "*Hapoel HaMizrachi*" and another large area for German immigrants.[49] On April 5, 1935, it was reported that there was a housing shortage in Haifa. The rent for a room in *Hadar HaCarmel* came to £3.50 a month. The reporter continued to gush about the beauty of Haifa: "Carmel is a beautiful mountain with fig trees, carobs, palm trees and pines. These are interspersed with beautiful

---

47   *Ibid*, November 9, 1932; November 12, 1932.

48   *Ibid*, November 15, 1933.

49   *Ibid*, February 26, 1934.

Neapolitan-style villas. On Herzl Street, there are beautiful show-case windows, large white houses with balconies and gazebos."[50]

The reporters toured the country and visited the colonies and kibbutzim. *BaDerech* reported in detail on communities such as *Ein Harod, Givat Brenner, Bat Shlomo, Mesha, Menahemia, Gedera, Rishon Lezion, Gan Yavne, Beer Tuvia, Rehovot, Nes Ziona, Karkur, Pardes Hanna, Givat HaShlosha* and the *Emek Hefer* settlements.[51]

In their reports, rural settlements were painted in rosy colors and described with great enthusiasm. This is how *Magdiel* was described, a colony where immigrants from Poland accounted for about half the population: "*Magdiel* is a sun-drenched garden, made up of white houses with balconies. The smallest apartment has a bathroom, electricity, radio, and a phonograph.

Aliyat HaNoar students
Source PHRS/1404980 – National Govt. Archive

---

50   *Ibid*, April 12, 1935.

51   *BaDerech*, October 11, 1933; July 3, 1936

The faces of the residents radiate joy and contentment. Everyone speaks Hebrew. Cultural life is also well-developed: people are reading books, attending theater and opera."[52]

Degania was seen as an estate: "Beautiful houses, similar to villas; rows of palm trees, cactus beds, lots of flowers; the orchards are filled with grapes, grapefruits, bananas; there is even a cowshed."[53] Members of the kibbutzim and moshavim were portrayed as "beautiful people." The ideal man is one whose main occupation is manual labor, but who also excels at a high cultural level: Beethoven's music, books, chorus. Every kibbutz has several engineers, doctors, economists, and philosophers. In the cities of Palestine and in the village, the "new Jewish man" is rising. A rejection of the Exile was prominent; there was a highlighting of the gap between this "new person" and the Jews of the Diaspora. As soon as the Jew steps on the soil of his homeland and begins productive work, his personality is revolutionized – it is then that the Jewish soul is resurrected:

"The younger generation is quite different from that of Poland. The youth of Palestine live with nature; there is not the same pessimism that characterizes Polish Jews." The fashioning of the "New Man" already begins on the ship bound for Eretz Israel. The familiar type of Polish Jew was transformed on the deck of the *Polonia* into something new: standing upright instead of in frightened subordination, this "New Man" is in control; he bears the new look of a man proud to be master of his own fate on his own land.[54] In an article entitled "The New Jew in Palestine" a tourist's impressions are given:

---

52   *N.P.,* July 24, 1932

53   *Ibid,* Jul 17, 1932

54   *Ibid,* March 1, 1931; May 10, 1932; March 12, 1934.

> I was in Eretz Israel and saw the new Jew…the self-respect-
> ing posture, the countenance and the general appearance
> of the Jews of Eretz Israel are of a people utilizing the ma-
> terial blessings of a land which is natural for them.[55]

The change is often attributed to village life, proximity to nature and especially to physical work:

> Life in Palestine is full of enthusiasm and optimism.
> There has been a change here in the image of the typical
> Jew; life in the village and agricultural work have creat-
> ed a new type of person, both physically and spiritually.
> With the aspiration to breathe the air of Eretz Israel,
> to immerse our hands in the soil of its land – we are
> already transformed into new people.[56]

The descriptions of the "New Man" give special mention to the children: They are described as blond, healthy, beautiful, dressed in clean clothes; work for them is the supreme ideal; they grow up as sturdy and healthy villagers intimately connected with nature.[57] Thus, a reporter for *N.P.* described the "Sabra" Ruth that he met on a ship on her way back to Palestine after visiting her mother's parents in Poland:

> Laughing eyes, happy face, a carefree smile, Ruth sings
> the songs of Eretz Israel. It doesn't even occur to her to

55   *BaDerech*, October 25, 1935.

56   *N.P.*, July 24, 1932.

57   *Ibid*, April 3, 1932; April 12, 1932; July 24, 1932; October 2, 1932.

be embarrassed. The most amazing phenomenon is the children and youth, the likes of whom are not found in any city in the world. They are full of joy, health, and magic. It is a new generation with a new mentality – they grow up in the air, in the sun, by the sea; they do not know fear, or humiliation; they grow up free, simple, happy. The Jewish children here look like a different, new breed.[58]

An important feature of the "New Man" is health and sportsmanship: the youngsters in Palestine ride horses; the girls from the *moshavim* excel in riding and children are already riding well from an early age; groups of laughing girls can be seen on the streets of Tel Aviv on their way to work. At the opening of the Maccabiah march:

"Adloyada" (Purim) in Tel Aviv
Source: Zoltin-Kluger, Government Press Bureau, D 826-123

---

58   *Ibid*, 3.4.1932; 23.11.1934.

> Tall, erect, athletic girls in light blue shirts and white skirts wipe away with their white tennis shoes the sad and depressed characteristics of Diaspora Jewry. Jews typified in paintings by Chagall and Mana Katz – pale, bent, and frightened – fade into the air, replaced by a marvelous new generation.[59]

The above is a fair sampling of the spirit with which the "New Man" in the country was depicted in the writings of the time. Criticism, however, did occasionally creep in, especially about the "*chutzpah*" (audacity) of the *Sabras* and their disrespectful attitude toward adults. For instance, an article entitled "Ignorance is not fitting for Tel Aviv":

> You will see a picture that is not worthy of our people, the people of the book. In one of the streets, hordes of youth, boys and girls, stride forth, their arms locked together, taking up the entire width of the street, singing and chanting in screeching voices, stomping with their feet in some sort of effort to accompany the singing that makes them seem like a lot of drunks reeling over their vomit.[60]

The criticism is dwarfed, however, by the general admiration of the "New Man" evolving in Palestine, so different from the "Diaspora Man." With great enthusiasm, the Jewish press in Poland reported on the cultural events in the Land; and first and foremost were the

---

59   *Ibid*, April 12, 1935.

60   *BaDerech*, October 23, 1936.

celebrations of the Jewish holidays. These holidays were described repeatedly: Chanukah, Purim, Passover, Shavuot, Rosh Hashanah. From the reporting, one gets the impression that the center of the celebration of all the holidays was almost always in Tel Aviv. During the holidays, young people from the *moshavim* and from other cities poured into Tel Aviv, and great joy broke out in its streets. On Chanukah, the first candle lighting ceremony was held in the presence of thousands of students. A cantor lit the candles; shop windows were adorned with menorahs, a torch procession was held, orchestras played, and the youth danced the hora. "A holiday atmosphere envelops everyone and penetrates the hearts!" Purim was celebrated for a whole week; with crowds arriving in Tel Aviv to celebrate, the city became a capital of laughter and joy. The town hall and the water tower were illuminated with unique lights, along the streets colored lanterns were lit, and "victory gates" were erected. On the streets, *hora* and *debka* dancers reveled throughout the nights, and the peak of the celebration was the carnival. On Passover, too, crowds of teenagers arrived in Tel Aviv. Public *Seders* were held in the city for tourists and residents; again, *hora* circles, singing and joy were evident everywhere.

Shavuot was celebrated as a holiday for children and youth. The holiday lasted three days and included a traditional parade of Tel Aviv children with flower garlands on their heads and flags and fruit baskets in their hands. At the central ceremony, the children submitted the produce of their school gardens to the JNF. *Tisha B'Av* was the only holiday that was centered in Jerusalem: Jews from all over the country reached the Western Wall and an atmosphere of gloom was felt everywhere: all the Jewish food houses and shops were closed; no shows and cinemas were held. Bus traffic halted, and the streetlights were not lit. On Rosh Hashanah, the center of festivities center returned to Tel Aviv. Again, the youth gathered from all over, and again, *hora* dances appeared in the streets. There were crowds of people, the sun was shining, and everything was bright and happy.

Not only during the holidays was Tel Aviv described as a cultural, educational, and recreation center, but throughout the entire year. Plays, films, concerts, sports and cycling competitions, as well as receptions of the mayor were presented almost daily. The city offered university courses, academic high schools and vocational schools, publishing houses and libraries.

> Tel Aviv is reminiscent of Vienna...Land and poetry have formed an alliance here. Those with more money hear concerts in the *"Ohel-Shem"* and *"Mugrabi"* halls; those with less – in *"Beit Ha'am."* Others hear concerts on the street, in the courtyard, wherever possible.[61]

Israeli dancer Rina Nikova, who visited Poland in 1930, said:

> In almost every home in Tel Aviv you can find a violin, piano or other musical instrument. Among the youth there is a real cult of music: concerts at the seashore in the presence of hundreds of *halutzim* (pioneers), workers and *moshavniks* (residents of the *moshavim*) are an almost daily occurrence. The opera in Palestine is on a very high level.

The *Shulamit* School of Music held recitals by its students. In

---

61 *N.P.,* March 20, 1934.

February 1934, the violinist Huberman, who in 1936 founded the Philharmonic Orchestra visited Palestine. The formation of a Philharmonic Orchestra was announced at the time of his visit. In March 1935, the construction of the *Habima* Theater and the establishment of the *Hamatate* Theater were reported. The Jewish press in Poland published articles critiquing the plays in Eretz Israel, including the old-fashioned repertoire of *Habima*. Reports about the vibrant cultural life were not limited to the performing arts. The newspapers also reported on important painters and exhibitions. The *Maccabiahs* and especially their festive opening ceremonies were described in great detail. Physical education was reportedly a mandatory subject in the schools, and various sports competitions were followed. There were also reports on the "Language Wars":

> There has been a war for the complete dominance of the Hebrew language… The recent large *Aliyah* resulted in an amalgam of foreign languages spreading rapidly. This has sparked fear in the hearts of the "language defenders," who have organized activities to strengthen the Hebrew language. In fact, a massive demonstration against foreign languages is currently being held in Jerusalem.[62]

The articles reveal a sense of dynamism, of rapid pace, of hectic economic activity. The pace of construction and expansion of Tel Aviv was repeatedly described. As described, the houses sprouted "like mushrooms after the rain" – the whole city became one big

---

62   *BaDerech* February 15, 1935. At that demonstration, Ben Zvi requested that immigrants Hebraicize their names.

building lot. "New houses are being built, new neighborhoods are sprouting, new quarters are being discovered, on the hill and on the seashore . . . Tel Aviv has already exploded beyond the German Colony."[63]

Industry and commerce also developed rapidly. *BaDerech* reported on the development of a silk industry in Ramat Gan, the production of large-scale packaging, the development of the rope and bag industry. Much was written about the Rutenberg Power Plant in the Jordan River, the development of the phosphate industry in the Dead Sea, the vast potential for chemical industry in the Land, the port being built in Haifa. Recurring headlines announced: "Prosperity in Palestine"; "The Situation in the Land is Good"; "People are Working, Earning, Satisfied, Enjoying Healthy Creativity and Personal Freedom"; "New Industrial Areas are Developing"; "Tens of Thousands of Acres of Orchards are being Planted"; "New Neighborhoods are being built in Tel Aviv, Jerusalem, and Haifa."[64]

From the beginning of 1935, the articles mentioning the problems associated with "Prosperity" proliferated: inflated prices for apartments and plots, the migration of workers from the village to the city,[65] and the lack of agricultural workers, which led to the mass entry of Arabs into the country. In early 1936, the beginnings of an unemployment problem emerged, but very little space was devoted

---

63   *Ibid*, March 16, 1933; May 25, 1933.

64   *N.P.*, June 3, 1934; July 7, 1934.

65   In a comparison that the newspaper made between the labor costs in a Tel Aviv building and the wages in European cities, the wages in Tel Aviv were higher than in all major European cities. Also noted is a rapid increase in the industry and crafts related to construction: doors, windows, cement, lime, paint. (*N.P.*, January 30, 1935).

to it in the newspaper pages.[66] "How to Manage in the Land" - a series of articles written by Miriam Wollman, was published in *N.P.* in response to reader questions. Here is a 1931 answer to a lawyer's request for the opportunity to practice his profession in Israel:

> You must know at least one of the official languages (Hebrew, English, Arabic). Based on a Polish lawyer's certificate, a government test can be taken once a year and costs £25. Those who pass the test will have to pass a three-year internship in a law firm without pay. In general, there is a surplus of lawyers in particular and free professionals in general.

In reply to another inquirer, who was interested in what could be done in the country with a £700 fortune, Wollman replied that he could be a candidate for settlement in Pardes Hanna.[67] Such answers were given to many interested inquirers: students (required education, tuition), architects (chances of finding work, recognition of Polish diplomas), physicians (there are only two vacancies in the entire country). Wellman specified the sought-after trades in the country: carpenters, builders, porters, and craftsmen in various industries. Along with livelihood options, the reader could learn about what is required for subsistence: food prices, cost of rent, and so on. A myth spread in the 1930s alleging that everybody can manage in Palestine and that money is "rolling in the streets." The newspaper presented a starkly alternative view: "We must counter the mistaken assumption that anyone can make it in Palestine,"

---

66   *Ibid*, February 21, 1936.

67   *Ibid* February 19, 1931.

wrote Wollman in December 1934:

> A person without a fortune and without a profession in
> demand, who does not want to work in agriculture - will
> not be able to manage here [. . .] In Palestine, there is
> no need for the intelligentsia, nor for officials, neither
> for editors nor for writers, but rather for young, healthy
> workers. A clerk or worker earns £10-12 per month;
> if he is married with children, he will not be able to
> support his family with this amount, and his wife must
> earn as well. In this case, they may have to hand their
> child over to an educational institution, which also costs
> money. They will not be able to afford a housekeeper
> or to attend a movie or the theater. The new Prosper-
> ity enriches people who previously bought a house, a
> lot, or an orchard. Industrialists, some businesspeople,
> and attorneys do well, but not the laborers in all fields
> except construction. Office workers, shopkeepers, and
> seamstresses are all forced to live very modestly. It is
> foolhardy to come to Palestine without proper training
> and preparation, both professionally and mentally.[68]

Wollman devoted several articles to immigrant women and repeatedly emphasized the need to prepare for immigration — to learn
Hebrew, to acquire professions that were in demand in Palestine:
cooks, nurses, hairdressers. Those with advanced education and
a non-service-oriented profession will find it challenging to find
work in Palestine. A spoiled girl who does not want to go to a

---

68   *Ibid* December 12, 1934.

kibbutz or work as a maid and who has no profession will not survive. About girls who come Palestine with the aim of finding a husband, Wellman writes: "Alongside the women pioneers, young women come here with the idea that they will easily find a husband; they arrive in an unfamiliar land totally unprepared, with only new dresses in their backpacks and hearts open for love. There are cases of men taking advantage of these women and stealing their money." Wellman described a case in which an immigrant woman fell prey to an Arab who disguised himself as a doctor and stole her money.[69] It also emerged that women who worked alongside men were earning lower wages (17 versus 25 qirsh per day). Regarding the danger to women immigrants, *BaDerech* published news about the rape of new arrivals who were unaware of what was happening in Palestine – they naively traveled in taxis and hitchhiked with Arab drivers and were attacked.[70] Benny Weinstock, one of the emissaries of *N.P.*, who tried all kinds of work, who met and talked with many of the inhabitants of the country, who visited many localities and whose writings reflected the difficulties of life in Palestine, described the life of the Jewish worker:

> Experts and professionals occupy the highest positions in Palestine and constitute the aristocracy. At the top of the pyramid are expert building workers... A worker can earn up to 35 qirsh per day, but there is no continuous work even for a month due to weather, illness, or the transition from project to project. No worker can build a house for himself. When there is no work, you

---

69   *N.P.*, December 2, 1934.

70   *Ibid*, January 28, 1934.

can contact the Histadrut Labor Office or the National Histadrut. In the first, you only have to pay dues; in the second, you also need to show ideological loyalty. The Histadrut sends you to a village where they really need working hands. You go to the village and very quickly return to town. The village only pays 20 qirsh a day, and there are many rainy days; even there, it is not easy to live on 20 qirsh per day. If you are sent to the village and return to the city, you need an official "release" from working in the village; otherwise, you will not be referred to any other work in the city. You are entirely dependent on your private employer. Every evening, on the corner of Allenby-Sheinkin streets, there is a kind of "workers' market," where private employers come looking for workers. They test you and your muscles as one would test a beast in the market. The main problem is that there are no permanent jobs. One day you carry bricks. The next you knead dough in a bakery, then you work in a printing press and more. Impermanence is distressing, and the future cannot be planned. There are very many disappointed and desperate young people in the country. Immigrants from Germany and America return to their countries. Polish immigrants have nowhere to return. That is why it is imperative to come here only with a profession in hand.[71]

---

71   *N.P.,* January 20, 1935.

He wrote about his work in the orchard:

> On the first day ... my hands are swollen and wounded,
> my lips are shaking, I seem to have been condemned
> to hard labor for my entire life, everyone around me
> is working fast, and I am lagging behind them, I am
> ashamed; the *torriya* (hoe) slides away, and I fall, my
> head is spinning, and I pass out. ... At the end of the
> workday, I fall down like a wooden board on my bed
> with only one thought in my head: "Tomorrow I won't
> go to the orchard" ... But I did go, and the next day
> again. In the first days of my work, I was physically and
> mentally broken; after five days I stopped cursing; after
> nine - I started to whistle, after three weeks, I stopped
> fearing the *torriya*.[72]

And about his work in the building: "Awful heat, *hamsin* (heat wave), a hot wind that throws sand in the eyes and will not allow you to breathe, the work manager drives his workers hard...It happens even in Palestine that the contractor is a bastard."[73] On that day, the workers rebelled and left the site in the middle of the roof construction.

Weinstock pointed out the divisions among the Jews of the Land, which are already apparent on the ship:

> Each of the passengers - tourist, capitalist, pioneer,
> student, or worker, represents a party, stream, group,

---

72   *Ibid*, November 21, 1934.

73   *Ibid*, November 28, 1934.

faction, or some other political color. There are as many delegates as the number of passengers. From morning and deep into the night, discussions, debates, and even hands-on discussions were held between the representatives of the various streams: Betar, Hapoel, Agudah, Al-HaMishmar, Menorah, and more.[74]

Upon arriving in Palestine, he encountered a street fight that was started because of a political argument:

I have concluded that those for whom it is the hardest to acclimate here are the few nonpartisan immigrants who come here as such. You have to decide quickly what side you are on and where you belong. If you go on a walk with a girl, she must know who you are. If you are looking for a job - the same. "You are a revisionist; very sorry, but you will not be able to work for us; you are Poalei Zion – get out of my shop right away!" You must decide on your ideological affiliation very quickly.[75]

On the night after the holiday, a group of Revisionists shouted and sang through the Rehavia neighborhood, throwing large stones in all the windows of the National Committee building of the Knesset. Twenty windows were shattered, and the stones were scattered on the floor of the rooms.[76]

---

74   *Ibid*, January 13, 1935.

75   *Ibid*.

76   *BaDerech*, June 8, 1934.

In March 1935, the "Sabbath wars" were reported in Tel Aviv. People marked the Sabbath in different ways: some in synagogues, some in cafes or on the beaches. But Tel Aviv had grown, and a need for public transport on Saturday had arisen. There were severe struggles around this issue with those who defined themselves as "Sabbath observers."

The writers' attitudes toward "others" - members of the Eastern communities and Arabs of the country - are intriguing. The Arabs were almost always portrayed as primitive, foreign to Western culture, poor, dirty, sick, and economically backward. Almost every mention of an Arab carries the term "dirty." The Arabs who transported immigrants from the ship to the coast were thus characterized, as were both the rural and urban Arabs. The writers did not know or did not want to know about the Arab aristocracy in Palestine and were not impressed by the beauty of the villages and agricultural areas cultivated by Arabs. Everything about the Arabs was seen as inferior and primitive. For example, in a child's impressions:

> The ship is approached by boats filled with Arabs. They scream to the skies, wildly grabbing us and the luggage and throwing us in boats. Darkness, storm, rain, and wild screams – this is our welcome in Palestine. ... In Jaffa, one sees Arabs in all colors: black, brown, yellow, and red ... Most are barefoot, and their feet are filthy. ... They are so dirty that many of the Arabs suffer from eye disease; many of them are blind.[77]

---

77   *N.P.*, May 8, 1931.

And impressions from a visit to a Bedouin village:

> The Bedouin send their wives and children to work
> while they sit, play backgammon or sleep. The little
> kids load the hookahs with tobacco or roll cigarettes.
> Their job - to collect cigarette butts from the sidewalks
> and sewers. At the same time, the girls are expected to
> collect dung used for heating. The woman is engaged in
> trade; she sells sabras, figs, or melons from a large bowl
> she carries on her head. The Bedouin live in densely
> populated tin shacks, eating with their hands, all from
> one plate. The women receive the leftovers; they do not
> join in the dinner at all.[78]

Regarding the attitude toward the Arab woman, a reporter for
BaDerech wrote: "Please go outside Jerusalem and you will see
sturdy Falakh riding alone, comfortably wide-legged on his horse,
while behind him the three wives he bought with his money are
trailing by foot, bent under the weight of the pillows and sacks
they are carrying on their backs."[79] The picture is sharpened when
comparing the Arabs to the Jews in the Land:

> The traveler on the Land sees on one side of the road
> an Arab plowing his land with an old-fashioned wooden
> plow, and on the other – a modern American tractor
> plowing the fields of a Jewish *moshav* (colony)...[80]

---

78   *Ibid*, November 26, 1934.

79   *BaDerech*, October 15, 1937.

80   *N.P.*, March 1, 1931.

With squinting eyes, the Falakh looks at the Jewish set-
tler, his home, his standard of living, and the education
of his children. Only a hundred meters separate his
village from the Jewish settlement, but the difference
between them is vast.[81]

In an article entitled "Our Cousins," Weinstock wrote:

On the way to Tel Aviv, we passed through Jaffa, an Oriental dream of a Thousand Nights and a Night, which
is suddenly shattered [...] is this the East? [...] narrow
alleys, crowds of beggars, children, and the elderly [...]
the stink, noise, dirt [...] After this Oriental *intermetzo*,
the traveler finds himself in Tel Aviv, and is in the West,
and can fully breathe again. The East seems, a priori,
to be an exotic fairy tale, but, after the fact, it proves
unbearable[...] The magic of the East has dissipated,
and the real East is revealed: dirt, poverty, blindness,
stinking huts, hungry villagers, depressing cemeteries,
black tents of Bedouin camps [...] the Arab man does no
work, sleeps most of the day or plays backgammon with
his friends; he will only work to collect the amount he
needs to acquire a wife and then his wives and children
will support him.[82]

At times, the writers viewed the Arabs in a slightly more positive
light. In August 1930, they reported on an agreement that was

<hr />

81   *BaDerech*, October 15, 1937.

82   *N.P.*, January 6, 1935.

signed between the Arab neighborhood of Beit Safafa and the Jewish neighborhood of Mekor Chaim.[83] On another occasion, the Jews and Arabs in *Wadi al-Hawarith* were noted for having good neighborly relations, and elsewhere it was written that modern development had reached the Arabs as well: they plant orchards, import tractors, and build houses. The Arab villagers learn from their Jewish neighbors and advance. Arabs understand that Jewish settlement raises the standard of living and brings progress to Palestine. Arabs willingly learn Hebrew (as opposed to Jews who do not learn Arabic), Jews are welcome guests in Arab homes and villages. Also mentioned is the rescue of *Gush Etzion's* Jews by their neighbors in *Beit Omer.*[84]

Additional "others" were Jews of Oriental communities. The Yemenite community received much attention. In many cases, they were described as manual laborers, shoe polishers, while the women were described as maids.[85] While there was sympathy and respect for the predicament of the Jews in Yemen and their dangerous journey to Palestine, their conduct was viewed critically: "In Eretz Israel, the Yemenites separated from each other. The landlords among them do not give jobs to their Yemeni brothers but rather to the Arabs.

Another argument dealt with their attitude toward their children's education:

> The Yemeni in his native land would take care of his sons
> and teach them Torah. Here in Eretz Israel, most of the

---

83   *Ibid*, August 18, 1930.

84   *Ibid*, October 7, 1937; 1934.

85   *BaDerech*, November 11, 1937; 1935

12-13-year-old children are sent out to sell newspapers in the streets; even those with affluent parents. What do these boys do with the money? They sit in restaurants, eat sausages, drink beer, and smoke cigarettes. This is how far the degeneration of the Yemenites has come.[86]

An article titled "Whole Industry Migrated to Israel" describes Jews from Salonika who were experienced fishermen. Thanks to them, fish was provided to the local residents. These immigrants were also experts in dock-working and served as the port workers in Palestine.

The immigrants from Germany were also "others" to Polish Jews, and since the rise of immigration from Germany in 1933, much has been written about them. Alongside a slight sense of satisfaction at the misfortune of the "privileged" Jews of Germany becoming refugees, one could feel a great deal of appreciation for the difficulty of their plight:

It is painful to see the masses of immigrants from Germany arriving in Haifa sad and depressed. They arrive exhausted and immediately encounter a new world. They are mute; they do not know Hebrew; all their culture and education is valueless. They were proud of their German culture and it was not pleasant for them to have to connect with the "Ostjuden." For years, they saw Palestine as a kind of "ostjuden madness," and suddenly the very same Palestine became a haven for them

---

86   *Ibid* December 7, 1934.

> [...] Now German is heard everywhere: on the streets of
> Tel Aviv and in cafes. An Association for German Jewish
> immigrants has already been established. These immi-
> grants are becoming part of Palestine."[87]

And in *BaDerech*:

> Many letters [from Germany] are now being received
> regarding *Aliyah*. Many are written in a tone as if they
> are doing us a favor by deciding to immigrate to Eretz Is-
> rael. They are willing to come but expect that in return,
> we will fulfill their desires, requirements, and habits.
> One writes from Berlin: "I was a big bank manager here
> and I got so and so a month, and now if you have a
> bank like that in Eretz Israel and can pay me in a similar
> manner per month, I am willing to come on *Aliyah*."[88]

Nevertheless, the diligence and willingness of the German immigrants to do any physical work aroused admiration. Writers noted
that the immigrants were careful, did not rush to invest their money,
and were willing to take on any work that was offered them. They
revealed a great deal of initiative: an industrialist moved an entire
factory to Israel with 10 German workers to teach the Palestine Jews
a new profession, a group of 12 families organized to sign a contract
with PIKA for agricultural settlement in Pardes Hanna, and German
immigrants set up poultry cooperatives. The Jews of Germany did
not reject any work, and they moved without complaints from one

---

87   *N.P.*, April 10, 1933.

88   *BaDerech*, May 11, 1933.

occupation to another. For example, stories were recorded about an older lawyer who worked in Palestine as a laborer,[89] about a group of doctors and scientists who founded a porter's organization, and another group that organized themselves as window cleaners – a new profitable profession. All these testify to the rapid integration of German immigrants.

> The Jews from Germany who came here, were dissatisfied at first: 'How will this Land, still in its early development, save us after the good life we lived in Berlin'? They complained of the lack of pleasures, the lack of luxury, [...] However, seeing the life of work and tranquility in Eretz Israel changed the minds of many. Now we see that German Jews have already entered many moshavim and kibbutzim and engage in agricultural work. On the streets of Tel Aviv and Jerusalem, Jewish boys from Germany can be seen working in buildings under construction with clay and lime [...] They are already visible in every printing house and factory [...] This is a wise and enterprising class of people who can be depended upon in every craft and industry and knowledge-based profession.[90]

The immigrants from Germany brought their traditions with them; they lived in remote places in Palestine, but their homes were furnished luxuriously. They even opened a cafe in a small town like *Pardes Hanna*. The writers highlighted the contribution of German

89   *N.P.*, December 3, 1933.
90   *BaDerech*, September 20, 1933.

immigrants: "Palestine is changing following the rise of German Jews. They brought elegance and chic that were unknown in the city. In the store windows, there is high-class fashion designer clothing displayed [...] one can see furs and monocles [...] German Jews bring high culture to the country and contribute significantly to industrial and commercial development."[91] Nevertheless, criticism intensified over time, and reporters also began to write about the negative consequences of German immigration that was changing the culture of Palestine: The German immigrants brought with them an appetite for luxury and a high standard of living. Every female immigrant from Germany needed a maid, and this fashion spread among other female immigrants as well. Many Tel Aviv women stopped looking for work; instead of cooking at home they ate at restaurants. Women from Poland and Russia, who heretofore worked in an office and ran a household at the same time, starting to emulate the lifestyle of their German immigrant sisters; the luxurious items displayed in the shop windows brought by German immigrants confused the workers' wives and an aspiration to purchase jewelry and expensive furniture developed. In the reports of the tourists and journalists from Poland, the same characteristics drew both admiration and condemnation.

Alongside an idyllic account of life in the country, the *N.P.* reported on conflicts between Jews and Arabs. In April 1931, the murder of three Nesher workers and the riots triggered by the Arabs during the Nabi-Musa holiday was reported.[92] In August 1931, they featured stories about the Arab strike and the great tensions that

---

91   *N.P.*, January 12, 1934.

92   *N.P.*, April 10, 1931.

caused Jews to flee mixed neighborhoods in the cities.[93] In March 1935, Arab gangs were reported attacking Jewish communities and travelers.[94] Jewish newspapers in Poland highlighted the outbreak of the Arab revolt in April 1936, and reported in great detail on the events.

From the wealth of articles and reports published in the Jewish press in Poland, one can conclude that the immigrants were exposed to a great deal of information about what was happening in Eretz Israel. Polish immigrants of the 1930s did not come to the "unknown." Although most of the information published in the press emphasized the positive and optimistic aspects of life in Palestine, readers could also become acquainted with the darker sides: difficulties earning a livelihood, price hikes, negative attitude toward new immigrants. The prevalent feeling regarding Palestine was that it was a dynamic, rapidly evolving, and changing place; a place that was continually improving thanks to construction, industrial and agricultural development, population growth, and rapid social and cultural development. This feeling was in sharp contrast to the sense of despair and hopelessness that reflected the reality of Polish Jewry at that time.

The chart below shows the distances between cities in Israel allowing someone in Poland to plan their trip in Palestine.

---

93   N.P., August 16, 1931.

94   N.P., March 15, 1935.

Spacer po Palestynie

Jak daleko z jednego miejsca na drugie?

Na podstawie podziałki można znaleźć odległość między wyliczonemi miastami i kolonjami. Podajemy ją w godzinach przy marszu pieszo. Odległość znajdzie się w odpowiednim kwadracie w miejscu, gdzie się przecina linja długości z linją szerokości. N. p. Jerozolima — Jafa = 16 godzin marszu.

	Jerozolima—ירושלים	Chebron—חברון	Bejr-Szewa—באר שבע	Gaza—עזה	Jericho—יריחו	Morze Martwe—ים המלח	Ejn-Gedi—עין גדי	Nablus—שכם	Betlehem—בית לחם	Moca—מוצא	Riszon Lecijon—ראשון לציון	Petach-Tikwa—פתח תקוה	Jafa—יפו
Chebron—חברון	9												
Bejr-Szewa—באר שבע	10	19											
Gaza—עזה	9	10	19										
Jericho—יריחו	28	26	17	8									
Morze Martwe—ים המלח	3	26	26	17	8								
Ejn-Gedi—עין גדי	10	13	27	21	11	14							
Nablus—שכם	29	22	22	33	34	24	15						
Betlehem—בית לחם	17	12	10	10	16	17	7	2					
Moca—מוצא	3	16	15	9	9	27	20	11	1				
Riszon Lecijon—ראשון לציון	12	15	16	28	32	32	12	20	23	14			
Petach-Tikwa—פתח תקוה	4	16	19	12	31	26	26	16	25	26	17		
Jafa—יפו	3	3	15	18	14	30	24	24	13	22	25	16	

A Trip in Palestine: Distance between Destinations in Hours of Travel
Source: Ilustrowana Palestyna, pismo zbiorowe http://rcin.org.pl,s.87

3

POLISH JEWISH MIGRATION IN THE 1930S

Increasing Jewish emigration fits the policies of the Polish government. ... The goal is to increase the number of Jewish emigrants to at least the level that will neutralize their natural increase or 30,000 emigrants per year.[95]

The 1930s were characterized by pressure to emigrate from all sectors of the Polish population. In addition, Polish authorities viewed emigration as a unique solution to the challenging economy, and thus greatly encouraged it. Emigration became one of the main issues on the agenda in Poland.

Along with the vigorous activity of encouraging the emigration of the general population, the Polish government made special efforts to encourage the emigration of minority members, first and

---

95   AAN-MS3-6270. A paragraph from a secret memo circulated by the consular division of the Polish Foreign Ministry in April 1936, which outlined the Polish government's policy regarding Jewish emigration.

foremost Jews. The potential for emigration from Poland was high throughout the years between the two world wars. When immigration restrictions were adopted by the United States and later by other countries, a significant gap developed between the number of those who wished to emigrate and immigration options. This gap manifested in the fight for visas, the pressure applied to foreign consulates, and growing illegal immigration.[96] The potential for immigration was estimated at between three to six million people, an estimate based on the number of "hidden" unemployed in the villages ("the superfluous people"), and the unemployed in cities and their families. Only 1.3 million succeeded in emigrating during the interwar period, meaning that only one in three to five potential immigrants was able to emigrate.

The central goal of encouraging emigration was to solve a structural economic problem in the Polish economy. However, there were other goals as well, the main one being the utilization of emigration to "repair" the multinational structure in Poland.[97] In order to encourage emigration, a system of operations was established: reducing taxes and fees related to emigration, the publication of information on immigration options and the state of the labor markets in different countries, the establishment of government and public companies to deal with emigration candidates and the search for new emigration destinations. In addition, new periodicals were formed to discuss emigration possibilities, such as *Glos Wychodzcy* (The Voice of the Emigrant), *Wychodzca* (The Emigrant), and others. A "League of Days and Colonies" was formed in Poland in 1930 to locate colonial territories. By 1931, this league had already

---

96   Janowska (1984) pp. 326-327.

97   Kicinger (2005) pp. 42, 63.

established eight units to explore emigration options. The results were almost zero: a few hundred people were sent annually to South America, but many returned. There were also attempts to establish Polish colonies in various places in America.[98] Despite the lack of success, attempts to obtain immigration territories continued until the Second World War.

The Polish government made a special effort to encourage Jewish emigration. In the early 1930s, with the rise in restrictions on Jewish immigration to Palestine, Polish authorities began to search for alternative destinations. With the aid of the Polish Government, Jewish organizations were set up to acquire territories for Jewish settlement in countries such as Angola, Biro-Bijan, Ecuador, and more.[99] The Polish government presented the emigration of Polish Jews as the only solution to the "Jewish problem in Poland." The Foreign Ministry ordered its overseas representatives to report on Jewish settlement options everywhere. A memorandum titled "Instructions on Increasing the Emigration of Jews from Poland," (a section of which was quoted at the beginning of this chapter) was sent to London, Moscow, Angola, Washington, Shanghai, Tokyo, Cairo, Mexico, Buenos Aires, Rio de Janeiro, Harbin, Istanbul, Jerusalem, Tel Aviv, Ottawa, Winnipeg, Chicago, New York, and to Pittsburgh.[100]

---

98   Landau, Tomaszewski (1982b) pp. 23-24.

99   For an in-depth discussion of Polish diplomacy in regard to Jewish Emigration in the second half of the 1930s, see Meltzer (1973) pp. 211-237 and Landau, Tomaszewski (1982b) pp. 24-27.

100   AAN-MSZ-6270, Instrukcja w Sprawie Wzmocnenia Emigracji Zydowskiej z Polski. April 10, 1936.

Give Land to the Jewish Immigrants to Palestine"
Source: National Military Archive - KRA 2096

On May 9, 1936, a conference of senior officials took place in Warsaw, dedicated to the requests by the government of Poland of the colonial powers to allocate territories in Africa to serve as a destination for Polish-Jew emigres. Additionally, the Polish government took exerted pressure on the Canadian authorities to accept Jewish immigrants with the argument that they too – not just Ukrainians and Poles – were suitable for agricultural work.[101] On February 8, 1936, the government declared that it would be

---

101   Reczynska (1986) p. 134

possible to solve the Jewish problem in Poland only after colonies would be established for them in Africa and America. The problem of Polish Jews was presented as an international issue whose solution must be provided by international elements. In October 1936, Polish Foreign Minister Jozef Beck presented to the French Foreign Minister the idea of Jewish settlement in Madagascar, and in early 1937 an investigative commission was sent there to explore this option. After its return, the issue "dissolved," but the Polish government's efforts to obtain colonies for the immigration of Polish Jews continued unabated. In 1937, Zarychta, head of the Polish Foreign Ministry's Immigration Department, gave an interview to a French journalist stating that the Polish government did not want to get rid of the Jews in the German way, that is, via persecution, but rather by seeking suitable colonies for Jewish settlement. However, the Polish authorities hinted that if the condition for international co-operation in solving the "Jewish problem" was for Poland to pursue similar cruel policies, Poland would adopt them as well. Zarychta also reached out to Jewish organizations for help in locating immigration destinations, but this, too, did not bear fruit.

The Polish government was interested in the subject of emigration to Palestine and tried to intervene. They worked in diplomatic ways to increase the quota of immigration to Israel, made an effort to include the issue of Polish Jews in international debates on refugee problems from Germany and Austria (the Avian Conference, July 1938), and even tried to influence the distribution of the certificates between the Jewish Agency and the New Zionist Organization. In April 1939, the Polish ambassador to London submitted a memorandum to the British Deputy Foreign Minister demanding that 45 percent of the immigration licenses be allocated to Polish immigrants. They also demanded that Jewish refugees who had been deported from Germany to Poland be included in the immigration licenses allocated to refugees from Germany. This, in turn, would increase the immigrant quota from Poland and thus allow a greater number of licenses to be handed over to Polish Jews. The ambassador also demanded an additional allocation of territories for the settlement of Polish Jews in the British Empire.[102]

Furthermore, the Polish government supported various initiatives among the Jewish public aimed at encouraging emigration. For example, the Polish Foreign Ministry supported Nahum Sokolov's 1934 initiative for the establishment of a "pro-Palestinian committee" in Poland aimed at disseminating information about what was happening in Palestine. The committee was set up and headed by Polish public figures and intellectuals.[103]

In 1938, there was an increased influx of returning migrants from Germany to Poland, most of them Jews. They returned destitute after their property had been confiscated in Germany. In order to prevent the phenomenon of repatriation, in March 1938, the Polish government summarily canceled the citizenship of those staying abroad for five years or more. The Director of the Consular Department of the Polish Foreign Ministry, Viktor Drymmer, went so far as to declare explicitly that the regulation is primarily directed against Jews.[104] In response, on October 28, 1938, Nazi German authorities deported thousands of Polish citizens to the border town

---

102 Meltzer (1982) pp. 318, 347.

103 The committee was headed by Z. Luwominski, a Pole who was chairman of the Foreign Relations committee of the Senate. The committee had a branch in Krakow. Miesiecznik Zydowski AAN-MSZ File 10546, January 1934.

104 Landau, Tomaszewski (1982b) p. 30.

of Zbaszyn. Herschel Grynszpan, one of those exiled to Zbaszyn, later assassinated the German diplomat Ernst vom Rath, an event that was used as a pretext by the Nazis to organize the Kristallnacht riots.

A protest in Warsaw against stopping Aliyah. June 11, 1930
Source: NAC – 1 – P – 2346 – 1

Members of the Warsaw Rabbinate at the Demonstration
against the cessation of Emigration to Palestine
Source: NAC 1-P-2346-3

Aid Organizations for Jewish Immigrants from Poland

In addition to the Zionist Office that dealt with *Aliyah*, other Jewish
immigration organizations operated in Poland, headed by the
Jewish Emigrant Aid Society (JEAS) – the Polish branch of a major

Jewish immigration organization, HICEM.[105]

JEAS was involved in providing information, granting travel loans, vocational training in agriculture, and the study of Languages. In 1931, the organization established a migrant hotel in Warsaw - the "Jewish Migrant House." They had branches in all the major cities in Poland.

In the second half of the 1930s, there was a sharp increase in the number of applications to JEAS for assistance, an increase that indicates the growing distress among Polish Jews as well as the increasing difficulty in obtaining a foreign immigration license. Based on the ratio of the number of JEAS applicants to the number of all Jewish emigrants from Poland (excluding emigrants to Palestine), one can conclude that only one in 40 of those who wished to emigrate managed to do so. JEAS was not the only organization to which Jews who were aspiring to emigrate turned. The Government Emigration Syndicate operated across all areas of Poland, and many Jews contacted it. In a 1937 study, it was found that out of 112 immigrants to the United States in September of that year, only 55 were assisted by JEAS, while the others sought help from the Polish "emigration syndicate." If we take into account that only a portion of those aspiring to emigrate turned to JEAS, while others turned to the Polish "emigration syndicate" and other immigration organizations - for which we do not have data - it turns out that the actual ratio between the number of applicants to those who emigrated was even less than one in 40.

---

105 HICEM is an Immigration Aid Society that was established in 1923 by a union of all the Jewish immigration organizations that existed separately until then (HIAS, registered in the United States; ICA, registered in London, and EMIGDREK in Germany).

The Bulletin *Emigracja i Kolonizacja* (published by the Jewish Committee for Colonization) is a source where one can learn about the "immigration fever," that encompassed both the Jewish public and institutions and the Polish establishment. Jewish and non-Jewish Poles, individuals and organizations, all desperately searched for possible destinations for Jewish settlement.[106]

Among other places, the suitability of the following destinations was examined: Kenya, Honduras, Paraguay, Rhodesia, Abyssinia (present-day Ethiopia), Colombia, Madagascar, Chile, Peru, Bolivia, South Africa, India-China, India, Cuba, Mexico, Tanganyika, Guiana, Alaska, Nicaragua, Guinea, East Africa, Java Island, Sumatra, Trinidad, Dominican Republic, Costa Rica, Ecuador, Angola, China, Mozambique, New Guinea, Congo, Venezuela, Cyprus, Syria, Jordan, and Lebanon.

The target countries frequently changed their requirements for immigration. A near-total freezing of immigration to South America was reported on, new difficulties in obtaining immigration permits for Rhodesia, a halt of immigration to Dutch India, Paraguay, Colombia, Trinidad, and Portugal, a harsh atmosphere against Jewish immigrants in Cuba, and a reduction of the quota for Polish Jews in Mexico. Immigration to Brazil was frozen for three months and limited to 1,230 migrants per year. 80 percent of Brazilian immigrants were required to be farmers, so the potential for immigration to Brazil for Polish Jews was reduced to only 250 people per year. Jewish organizations in the United States did not

106 The bulletin was published bi-weekly and included articles from Jewish and Polish journals on the subject of Jewish emigration. Professor Yisrael Gutman provided me with the collection of bulletins in his possession, which included the period of September 1938-May 1939.

support the emigration of Polish Jews due to concerns that a large immigration movement would cause anti-Semitism. Zionist Jewish organizations did not support the emigration of Jews to anywhere except Palestine. In February 1939, it was reported that a growing German influence in South America was causing the reduction of receptiveness to the possibility of immigration. The alliance between Germany and Japan caused a reduction of immigration options to northern China. In South Africa, too, the restrictions worsened. Despite hopes of raising immigration quota for the United States, the quota for Polish immigrants was not raised and remained within the framework of about 6,000 immigrants - Poles and Jews - per year, and limited to close relatives (first-degree) of American citizens.

*Emigracja i Kolonizat*ja reported on the hardships of immigration that were due to the difficulties enacted by the target countries and due to the proliferation of illegal immigration organized by various "Machers." For example, there were reportedly 16,000 illegal immigrants who came to Paris, resulting in the vigorous efforts of French police for their imprisonment and deportation. In another report, about 450 immigration candidates to Argentina were stuck in Warsaw; they had received all their documents but failed to get the visas they had been promised. In another case, a group of immigrants who came to Colombia with forged licenses were arrested. Yet another group of immigrants arrived in Kenya and were not allowed in because of the local immigration officer's demand to prove that they each had in their possession £200, while the amount that had been told that would be needed when they left Poland was £50. The group was transferred to Madagascar, but its entry was also banned there.

In different target countries, minimum amounts of capital were set which immigrants must bring as a condition of emigration, but the amount of the amounts changed from time to time, sometimes without notice. Australia set a minimum of 200 Australian pounds (about 10,000 zlotys); immigration to Canada was only offered to Jewish farmers who brought with them $1,000, and later the amount was raised to $1,200; Immigration to Bolivia was limited to those with 2,000 zlotys; in order to emigrate to Cuba, capital of $500 was required and later the amount was raised to $1,000.

The magnitude of "immigration fever" can be learned from the numbers presented in the Bulletin regarding the ratio between the immigration quotas of various countries and the demand for immigration to them. When Australia declared its readiness to absorb 5,000 Jewish immigrants (from all countries), 12,000 immigration applications were filed in Warsaw within three months. The quota for migrants from Poland to Brazil for 1939 was set at 2,100, but the number of those interested at the end of 1938 was already several times greater.[107]

The Paris Director of HICEM reported that only 10 percent of the quota for the United States was utilized because European consulates receive far lower than the official quota. For example, in the year between mid-1936 and mid-1937, only 1,200 visas were received, which were only about one-fourth of the official quota.[108] Despite the economic Depression in the target countries, the demand for immigration from Poland not only did not decrease, but it significantly increased. The sheer volume of inquiries to immigration organizations indicates that the desire of Jews to leave Poland did not diminish.

---

107 All data is cited from the bulletin Emigration and Colonization, September 1938-May 1939.

108 Letters from 14.12.1937 and 3.12.1937, YIVO RG 245.4

General Migration and Emigration of Jews from Poland[109]

From 1931-1938, 515,000 immigrants emigrated from Poland, approximately 119,000 of whom were Jews. The number of Jews among immigrants was 23 percent - more than twice their presence in the population. To compare Jewish immigration with non-Jewish immigration, one must differentiate between two types of emigrants. One type were seasonal migrant workers who have mainly emigrated to European countries, and the other type were immigrants who mostly wished to settle abroad. The number of Jews among those emigrating to Europe was almost nil, but their weight in overseas emigration overseas, even discounting those making *Aliyah*, was very high. The emigration of Polish Jews to Europe was relatively limited as compared to overseas immigration, with the scope dropping from 1,000-1,600 migrants per year in 1931-1934 to about 400-450 migrants per year between 1935 and 1938. This decline was due to growing immigration restrictions imposed beginning from the start of the second half of the decade. The extent of *Aliyah* was subject to sharp fluctuations that determined the volatility of Jewish immigration. There was a sharp increase in the first half of the decade to almost 25,000 in 1935, followed by a sharp decline in 1937-1938 until the outbreak of World War II. *Aliyah* accounted for a 57 percent of the total emigration of Polish Jews in the 1930s. Immigration to other countries overseas accounted for about 37 percent, while immigration to European countries accounted for only six percent of total Jewish immigration during these years.

---

109   This chapter is based on statistic data: Rocznik Statysyczny (GUS-RS); Maly Rocznik Statystyczny (GUS-MRS); Statystyka Pracy (GUS-ST), 1930-1939.

Chart 1: 1931-1938 Polish Jewish Emigrants by Destinations

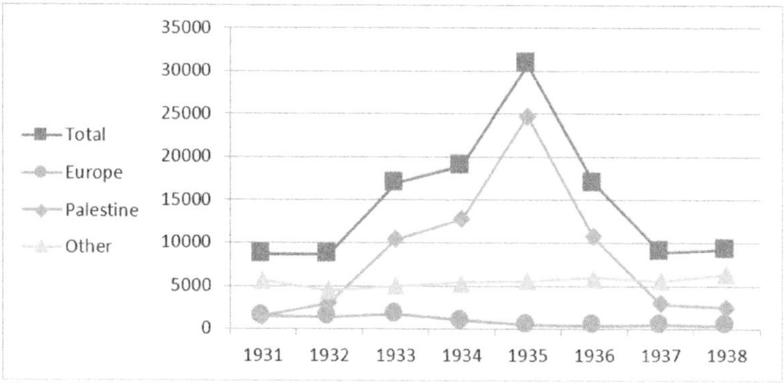

Source: Tab. A2 in Statistical Appendix

The fluctuations in *Aliyah* from Poland during the 1930s were dictated by conditions in Palestine rather than the motivations for departure from Poland, which were strong and steady. This can be learned from the comparison of the upward trend from Poland to the total amount of *Aliyah*. Had immigration from Poland been influenced by motivating factors unique to Poland, it would have been expected that the development of this immigration would be different and unique compared to the immigration from other countries, but as the following chart shows the extent of immigration of Polish immigrants was the same as that of immigrants to Palestine from all countries.

Chart 2: Total of Olim to Palestine from Poland
and other countries 1931-1939

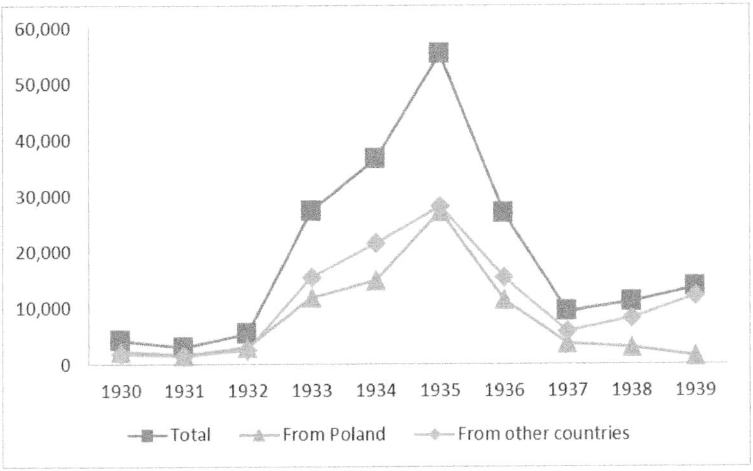

Source: Tab.13 in the Statistical Appendix

Destinations in Europe

The two main European destinations for Jewish immigrants were France and Belgium. These countries were also the primary destination for Polish seasonal migrant workers, who found increased employment opportunities in mines and industry with the emergence from the economic crisis. Although these sectors of employment did not suit Jewish immigrants, the Jews focused on these countries both because of their economic development and due to the fact that they were the only relatively developed countries open to Jews in Central Europe and the West, once Germany ceased to be an immigration destination. The Polish elite traditionally had a close relationship with France and its culture, and Jewish students from Poland vied for entry in French universities. However, the traditional employment sectors of Polish Jews - trade and crafts - were hit by the economic crisis in France and Belgium, in which legislation was enacted restricting entry options for middle-class immigrants. These regulations caused the number of Jewish immigrants to drop from 900 to 500 per year in 1931-1934, ped to only a few dozen in 1935-1938 in France. A similar progression developed in Belgium: the number of Jewish immigrants moved from around 300-500 per year at the beginning of the decade to only 120-170 per year in 1938-1934.

**Chart 3: Number of Jews Emigrating from Poland
to France and Belgium 1931-1938**

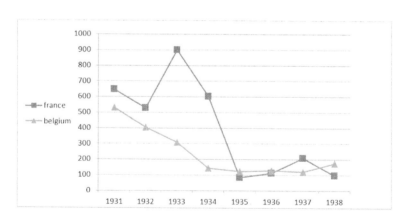

Source: Tab. A-8 in the Statistical Appendix

Destinations in Overseas Countries

Apart from Palestine, the leading immigration countries for Polish Jews from 1931-1938 were located in the Americas: Argentina (14,000 immigrants), the United States (7,800), Brazil (6,800), Uruguay (3,400), Canada (2,500), Cuba (1,200) and Mexico (1,000). Argentina became the central immigration destination after Palestine, in contrast to previous years when the central destination was the United States. It is possible that with the closure of the gates to the United States, the immigration to Argentina may be seen as the natural continuation of the great wave of immigration of Jews since the turn of the century, when Argentina was the destination of about 20 percent of all Jewish immigrants from Eastern Europe.[110] Immigration restrictions to the United States began in 1921. In 1924, the immigration quota in the United States was set at 6,500 migrants per year from Poland.

---

110   Alroey (2008) s.78.

**Chart 4: The number of Jews emigrating from Poland
to the America in the years 1931-1938**

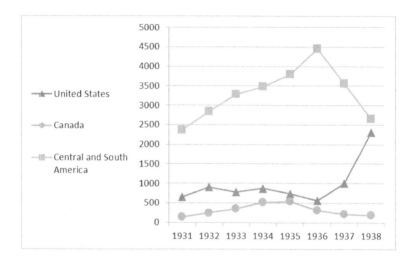

Source: Chart 8 in the Statistical Appendix

With the outbreak of the economic crisis and the massive increase in unemployment the restrictions in the United States were intensified; from 1930 the official quota became almost irrelevant. Due to concerns about immigrants becoming a burden, a new policy was introduced whereby US consulates in Europe were directed to limit the number of immigrants to 10 percent of the official quota, through the establishment of strict visa regulations. From 1931, the number of immigrants from Poland to the United States dropped sharply, such that in 1931-1937 it was approximately 1,000-1,600 migrants per year. The numbers rose to 2,500-3,000 in the last two years before the war.

Other American countries followed the lead of the United States and limited the number of immigrants. Brazil, for example, banned the entry of ship passengers who traveled in third-class, allowing entry only to migrants who could afford to travel in the expensive classes. From 1936, official immigration quotas were set in Brazil. The countries that either did not restrict or only partially restricted immigration were Argentina and Paraguay, which soon became major immigration destinations for Polish Jews.[111] In 1930, Canada began to allow immigration solely on an individual basis, and then only to relatives of Canadian citizens or to agricultural settlers. As a result, there was a sharp decline in the number of immigrants: the numbers dropped from tens of thousands per year in the second half of the 1920s to 1,000 to 2,000 per year in the 1930s. At the same time, the number of Jewish immigrants from Poland to Canada decreased - from about 3,000-2,500 per year in 1927-1930 to only 140-540 in the 1930s.

In addition to the tightening of immigration quotas and restrictive immigration laws and policies that burdened potential immigrants, the costs of immigration skyrocketed. The fee for immigration to Canada was raised to $170 per person, meaning that an average family needed at least $700 to immigrate. Brazil demanded a minimum of $2,000 per family, while immigration to Argentina cost $400-$600.[112]

An interesting issue is the differential tendency for emigration from the various districts in Poland. By examining the proportion of immigrants to the size of the Jewish population, it is possible to identify districts from which Jewish immigration was relatively large. These were mainly the districts of Bialystok and Polesie in

111 Kicinger (2005) p. 13.

112 Reczynska (1986) p. 189; Janowska (1984) p. 373.

Eastern Poland. One estimate speculates that the high rate of immigrants from Eastern Poland was due to the low economic status there, in which the Jewish urban component of the population (traders and craftsmen) was unable to earn a living. The rate could also be attributed to the continuation of a focus on emigration that had taken place in these areas earlier more than in other areas of Poland during the great migration period in the late 19th and early 20th centuries. Another notable factor especially evident in Bialystok district was connected to the strength of the far-right movements and the extreme anti-Semitic atmosphere that prevailed there.

Almost half of the Jewish immigrants from Poland came from the central provinces; one-third from the eastern provinces, and 20 percent from the southern provinces. Only one percent came from the western region. This data is instructive in understanding some of the linguistic-cultural characteristics of Jewish immigrants. The central and eastern areas were under Russian rule before World War I, so that the vast majority of Jewish emigrants from Poland had lived earlier under the sphere of Russian-Polish influence. Only about 20 percent of the emigrants- those from the southern and western regions - were subjected to Austrian-German influence before their emigration.

4

THE WORKINGS OF ALIYAH

While evil rules the world, even those who are not evil behave wickedly.[113]

After almost a complete hiatus due to the economic crisis in Palestine in 1927-1928, immigration from Poland resumed in early 1929. In this wave, which lasted until the outbreak of World War II, about 100,000 people emigrated from Poland, most of them officially and some illegally. The wave of immigration began on the order of 2,000-3,000 immigrants a year in 1930-1932, increased to 12,000-13,000 immigrants a year in 1933-1934, peaked at about 25,000 immigrants in 1935, and from there began to decline to 11,000 immigrants in 1936 and to 2,000-3,000 immigrants a year at the end of the decade.

Thirty-five percent of the immigrants from Poland during the 1930s came under two categories of relatives ("Referred" under the Workers' *Aliyah* and "Demanders" - Category D) and formed the largest group. The second largest group were the pioneers (*halutzim*) who constituted 22% of the immigrants. The middle-class

---

113   Agnon, Shira (1971) p. 13.

and craftsmen categories accounted for 18% of the immigrants, and about 10% came with significant capital. The rest came mainly as students and returning tourists. In the early 1930s, Polish Jews numbered about three million, so the number of immigrants in that decade accounted for only three percent of the total Jewish population in Poland, and the average immigrant rate per year was less than 0.3% of this population.

The Warsaw Zionist Office

The Warsaw Zionist Office was opened in 1918 and reached the height of its activity in the mid-1930s.[114] Its duties were: Representing the Jewish Agency to the local government and the British Consul, providing information to those interested in *Aliyah*, and assisting immigrants in all matters related to their move to Palestine. The Office acted as the executive arm in Poland of the Jewish Agency *Aliyah* Department and was also under the supervision of the Polish Immigration Office. The was in contact with the British Consulate in Warsaw, through which requests for immigration, visas for immigrants, and lists of claimants were received.[115] The Office was organized into two branches: one was administrative, headed by the Director of the Office, and the other – the "Office Committee" or "*Aliyah* Committee" – was an elected body of 13 representatives of the Jewish Agency. The key figures who operated the Office were A. Reiss, Chairman of the Office for most of the 1930s; R. Sheffer,

---

114   Barlas (1953) pp. 414-434.

115   Report on the Polish Aliyah Movement and activities of the Central Aliyah office in Warsaw from 1930-1931. Central Zionist Archives S6/3556.

Office Director throughout the 1930s, and I. Kashtan, Secretary of the Office from 1933. These individuals worked in the Office until the outbreak of the war. Other leading figures were Zerach Warhaftig, Moshe Kleinbaum, Av. Silon and Levin-Epstein. There was a high turnover rate among the leaders of the organization due to the fact that many of them made *Aliyah*. The office maintained a card index of data for all those who contacted the Office. In addition to objective information such as age, marital status, profession, education, and assets in Palestine and Poland, candidates were also examined about their party affiliation and Zionist background. The following is the questionnaire that the applicant was required to fill:

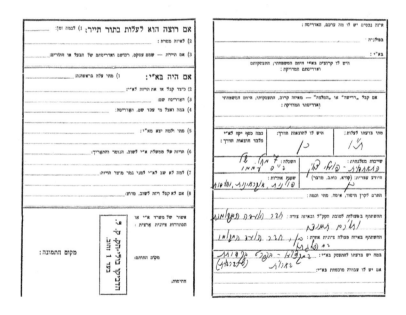

Chart 5 – Questionnaire for *Aliyah* Candidate, Palestine Office - Lvov

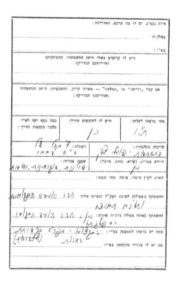

Source: CZA S6/2742

A letter and telegram exchange took place almost every day between the Warsaw Zionist office and the *Aliyah* Department. From Jerusalem, immigration licenses were sent to the Warsaw Zionist Office; directives, guidelines, lists of recommended candidates and relatives who were referred, as well as criticism of mismanagement of the *Aliyah* process. Reports, questions, requests for guidance, and many complaints about the excessive dominance of their *Aliyah* Department at the expense of the Warsaw Office were sent to Jerusalem from Warsaw. There were also mutual visits by officials from the *Aliyah* Department in Poland and activists from the Warsaw office in Palestine. Another connection between Warsaw and Jerusalem was created after the major activists of the Zionist institutions in Poland and the Warsaw Office came on *Aliyah*, when many of them continued their activity in the Jewish Agency, while remaining active regarding the offices in Poland. These included

Gruenbaum, Kleinbaum, Barlas, Dobkin, Levin-Epstein, and others. The Jewish Agency had full control over the choice of immigrants as part of the working *Aliyah*, which in the 1930s constituted about half of the Polish immigrants to Palestine. All the licenses allocated to Poland out of the total number of licenses for this category were decided upon by the Agency's *Aliyah* Department in Jerusalem. The internal division between immigrant types – pioneers, relatives, craftsmen and professionals – was also done by the Agency's *Aliyah* Department in Jerusalem. The number of certificates allocated to the pioneers was determined in Jerusalem, and the distribution of licenses among the *HeHalutz* (pioneering) movements was determined based on the relative size of the movements in Poland. The choice of who among the *halutzim* (pioneers) would go was determined by the *HeHalutz* movements. The distribution of licenses to craftsmen and relatives with recommendations was one of the few functions of the Warsaw Zionist Office, but even in this regard the criteria for the order of distribution were dictated by the *Aliyah* Department in Jerusalem.

These criteria were at the core of disagreements between the Warsaw Zionist Office and the *Aliyah* Department. In the middle of the decade, the right to *Aliyah* of craftsmen was conditional on their membership in Zionist organizations, and dozens of such were established. The Agency selected the organizations under which an immigration license could be obtained based on various parameters, most notably the extent of their commitment to Zionism. Industrial workers/experts were selected by industrialists in Israel and, similarly, agricultural workers were selected by the Farmers Association. The decisions regarding licenses for tourists who remained illegally in Israel and their families were also made in Jerusalem. The choice of immigrants based on the licenses allocated to political movements was made by these movements. Apparently, the authority of the Warsaw Zionist Office in Warsaw in the distribution of certificates was extremely limited and its main role was administrative-executive: checking the applicants according to lists sent from Jerusalem and arranging immigration licenses for owners of capital, relatives, and students whose eligibility criteria were not under the authority of the Office.

There was considerable tension between the Revisionists and the management of the Warsaw Zionist Office. Even before the Revisionists seceded from the Zionist Organization, the Betar representatives complained about that they were unfairly being deprived of licenses. At times they boycotted the *Aliyah* institutions, and there were even several physical assaults on the Warsaw Zionist Office, one in May 1934 and again in February 1937. Following the assassination of Arlozorov in Tel Aviv in 1933 and the establishment of *Ha Histadrut Haleumit* (National Employees Union), the Eighteenth Zionist Congress determined that from the beginning of 1934, the Betar movement's collective right to immigration would cease, a right that had allowed the movement independence in its choice of immigrants. From then on, the Betar licenses were granted on an individual basis only; however, in December 1934, its collective right to grant licenses to *halutzim* (pioneers) was restored.[116] Following the decision of the Revisionist Zionists in April 1935 to establish an independent Zionist Organization – the New Zionist Organization (*Ha-Tzach*) – Betar's collective right to receive immigration licenses was repealed again (in November 1935). Betar members received licenses on an individual basis proportionate to

---

116 Reports from the Warsaw Zionist Office, October 1933 – June 1935, Central Zionist Archives S6/5342, January 1935 – March 1937, CZA S6/4931.

the number of their members in *Hachshara* in the last census in which they participated. They received 4.5 percent of all licenses allocated to *halutzim*.[117] Revisionist representatives tried to organize a separate immigration route for their people by talking to the British Mandate government and by establishing contacts with the Polish government, but this was not successful. In their *Aliyah* as individuals they were assisted by Eretz Israel organizations such as the Farmers' Association, *Bney Binyamin*, and the *HaNotea* (Planting) Company.[118]

The criteria for selecting immigrants and determining the queue for immigration were primarily determined by the *Aliyah* Department of the Jewish Agency, and some by the Warsaw Zionist Office. Two critical criteria guided decision-makers in selecting immigrants from among the craftsmen: profession and ownership of capital. These criteria were intended to ensure the absorption of these immigrants into Palestine without the need for help from the Jewish Agency. The additional criterion was the commitment to Zionism of the immigrants. The *Aliyah* Department kept changing the financial criteria: in 1930, it was stated that applicants had to prove that they had £50 per family or £20 per single. In May 1932, a minimum amount of £150 was set, but since there were few candidates with means, by the end of that year, the amount was reduced to £100 and even to £80. Due to the *Aliyah* of many without means under the guise of a middle class, the amount was raised again to £150 per family, and applicants were also required to sign a statement pledging that they would not require assistance

117   Dobkin and Shapira, Executives of the Aliyah Department, to the Warsaw Zionist Office in Warsaw, 22.12.1937, CZA S6/3555.

118   Halamish (2006) s. 367.

from the Jewish Agency. In the fall of 1933, the requirement of a minimum amount from immigrants who were craftsmen was repealed.[119] The inconsistencies and frequent changes in criteria and regulations led to uncertainty and confusion among craftsmen who were considering immigration and prevented them from planning their future even in the short term.

The criteria for selecting immigrants from relatives with recommendations were the level of family closeness (son, daughter, brother, sister), age (mainly adults), Zionist credentials, and professional level.[120] In April, 1935, the leadership of the Warsaw Zionist Office in Warsaw decided to set a scoring method for determining the order of priorities in selecting immigrants from among the recommended relatives group, a method that was to ensure an objective choice and shorten the process of sorting. It is unclear how and if these criteria were applied at all, but it is possible to learn from the proposal that the decision-makers' considerations in Warsaw regarding the selection of immigrants were not the same as the considerations of the Jewish Agency's *Aliyah* Department. As determined by the Warsaw Office, the criterion with the greatest number of points (23) was Zionist activity; age was given 10 points, the family closeness level – four points, and the same number was given to seniority and to the situation of family members in Palestine. A candidate's profession was given only three

---

119   Memo from the Secretary of the Aliyah and Labor Department to the Warsaw Zionist Office, September 18, 1933, Central Zionist Archives S6/2519.

120   From the Warsaw Zionist Office to the Aliyah Department, February 4, 1931 and July 29, 1931, CZA S6/2514, Gruenbaum to the Zionist Office in Lvov, June 27, 1935, CZA S6/2523.

points.[121] Additional points were awarded based on how long the wait had been for *Aliyah*. These criteria, proposed by the Warsaw office, were largely based on the "needs on the ground" in Poland. It is doubtful whether this had any relation to the perception of the Jerusalem *Aliyah* Department, which primarily emphasized the potential benefit that an immigrant would bring to Palestine and their chances of successful absorption. In June, 1935, it was demanded of the Warsaw Zionist Office that they set as an absolute condition for the *Aliyah* of relatives that they be professionals, "because it is not desirable to increase the number of those without professions in Eretz Israel." The criteria set by the *Aliyah* Department for the order of priorities in the distribution of licenses to relatives with recommendations were:[122] Professionals – a necessary condition; those needed by farmers; police officers; Zionists; those who had been recommended for a long time.

According to the instructions of Gruenbaum, who was then head of the *Aliyah* Department, the criteria for distributing the licenses to farmers who came at the invitation of the Farmers' Association were as follows: three years of experience in agriculture – a necessary condition; priority for Zionists who contribute to Zionist Funds; anti-Zionists and those who fought against the Funds were ineligible for *Aliyah*; priority for young singles. Gruenbaum explained the preference for bachelors because they were suitable to replace Arab workers in the Farmers' Associations and their daily wages would be only 200 Palestinian Mil, which were not enough

---

121 From Kashtan, Secretary of the Warsaw Zionist Office, to the Aliyah Department, 8.4.1935, CZA S6/2523.

122 Letter to the Warsaw Zionist Office from the Aliyah Department, 21.6.1935, CZA S6/2523.

to support a family.[123]

Officially, a prerequisite for approving the *Aliyah* of members of *HeHalutz* (The Pioneer) was at least a year's training in working groups or training kibbutzim (Hachshara), so that their fitness for hard work in agriculture, building and industry was assured.[124] In certain periods, the minimum training period was shortened or extended according to the number of licenses available. The main element in the considerations of which immigrants to select among the *halutzim* (pioneers) was their conformity with the demands of Eretz Israel and the kibbutz, and accordingly, the *HeHalutz* institutions determined these criteria for the selection of immigrants: seniority in *Hachshara*; knowledge of Hebrew; social involvement; educational and cultural activities; on a conceptual level – the degree of likelihood that the candidate will join a kibbutz; and the amount of esteem that the member received from his team in training.

Analysis of the criteria for selecting immigrants from among the candidates indicates differences in the priorities of the various immigrant organizations. The primary considerations for the Jewish Agency were adjustment of professionals to the conditions of Palestine, minimum capital, and Zionist background. In contrast, for the Warsaw Office, the main priority was Zionist activity, followed by criteria such as age and family closeness to sponsoring inviters. While for the Jewish Agency needs of Palestine were at the center of their concerns, the Warsaw Zionist Office in Warsaw also sought to take into account the situation of the candidates themselves.

---

123 Gruenbaum's letter to the Warsaw Zionist Office, 7.12.1934, CZA S6/2522. Regarding the labor market and wage gaps between Jewish and Arab workers during the Mandate period, see Metzer (2002) pp. 123-137.

124 Addendum to circular No. 115, undated, S6/2514.

The main criterion for all types of immigrants in the framework of the Workers' *Aliyah* was Zionist party affiliation and activity. Nevertheless, there were still many complaints registered about the granting of licenses to non-Zionists. Agency officials in Palestine railed against the Warsaw Office for allowing the *Aliyah* of industrial enterprise experts who were members of non-Zionist and even anti-Zionist parties (mainly the Bund), and they demanded that they carefully examine the matter.[125] Warsaw Zionist Office officials claimed, on the other hand, that the non-Zionist "infiltration" was due to a reduction of the Warsaw Office's authority and the writing of immigrant lists by the *Aliyah* Department, which did not have the resources to check the political background of the candidates.

Belonging to Zionist organizations and parties served as a de-facto identity card for immigrant candidates. The forms that the candidates were required to complete included questions about organizational and party affiliation. The immigration licenses for *halutzim* were distributed along party/organizational lines, and the same method was also used to distribute licenses to craftsmen organizations, which in most cases had some party and movement affiliation. The political definition of relatives and experts invited from Palestine was more problematic. The Warsaw Zionist Office was required, in addition to clarifying the candidate's professional level, to investigate his Zionist and political background. In many cases, candidates were disqualified because of the "danger" of allowing the *Aliyah* of non-Zionists.

Internal struggles in the Zionist movement also wielded considerable weight in the allocation of immigration licenses. Right-wing members of the Zionist movement repeatedly complained about

---

125 Dobkin to the Warsaw Zionist Office, June 16, 1938, CZA S6/2739.

discrimination on political grounds. Thus, for example, wrote a resident of Netanya to Oved Ben-Ami, then the mayor of Netanya, about his sister-in-law not receiving an immigration permit:

> This is political revenge on the part of the left. As you know, I was active in the workers' union, but when the parties became unified, I left them... (Anon) was not ashamed to notify the envoy in Poland that since I had moved over to the "black" camp, there is no way they would let me get a license from the Agency ... I have no hope of obtaining the necessary license, and the only way is to demand one from the Farmer's Association of which I am a member.[126]

The emissary of the Farmer's Association to Poland, Issachar Sedkov, complained of harassment on his journey by Warsaw Zionist Office officials that was controlled, he believed, by leftists. He claimed that they arranged for newspapers to circulate calls to the Jewish public to refrain from cooperating with him, and the Warsaw Office openly came out against him. According to him, the former emissaries to Poland, Ada Fishman and Abba Hushi, avoided the obstacles that the Warsaw Zionist Office stacked against him, because Fishman and Hushi were associated with leftist movements.[127]

The distribution of licenses by party was an official and open policy, and reports sent from the Warsaw Zionist Office specified the party affiliation of the immigrants selected according to this

---

126 To A. Ben-Ami, August 16, 1935, Netanya Archive File A/23.

127 Report by Issachar Sedkov on his trip to Poland, May 1, 1935, Bustanai Booklet C, pp. 10-14.

criterion. Thus, a crucial "mediating factor" arose between the potential immigrant and the dual authorities of the Warsaw Zionist Office and *Aliyah* Department. The road to *Aliyah* via the schedules of quotas was closed to anyone who did not belong to a Zionist party or organization. This gave enormous power to the Zionist parties and organizations, which conversely grew and expanded as the plight of the potential immigrants worsened. The central goal of these political organizations was to increase their membership and share of immigration, and thus to increase their political power in the communities in which they operated. Management of these organizations required financial resources, and the primary source of revenue was from the immigrants. As a result, immigrant candidates were required to give money to the political parties and organizations in the form of taxes and various levies. The organizations collected travel expense funds long in advance, and used them to finance their ongoing expenses – including the purchase of the Zionist shekel (the purchase of the shekel represented an annual tax payment to the Zionist Organization and granted the right to choose the delegates to the Zionist Congress) – in an effort to increase their political clout. Power With the decline in the quotas of licenses, a situation was created where the organizations could not meet their obligations to the immigrants. A linkage was formed between obtaining an immigration license and the party's financial interest, and naturally, priority was given to candidates with means from whom funds could be raised to finance the organizations and parties. Furthermore, this method opened the door to corruption, an almost natural consequence of a situation in which unregulated bodies were handling large sums of money. Senator, director of the

Aliyah Department, called the situation "Rot."[128]

Polish Jews who aspired to immigrate to Palestine faced a series of hierarchical institutions, each of which reduced the possibility of *Aliyah*. At the top of the scale was the Mandate Government, after it – the Jewish Agency, followed by – the *Aliyah* Department, and then – the Warsaw Office. At the bottom of the scale were the movement, the party, or the Zionist organization – the only source from which it was possible to receive the much-awaited certificate. With the worsening of the ratio between the number of applications and the number of licenses, the conditions required of the applicants became more restrictive: Zionist cultural preparation, knowledge of Hebrew, and donations to the funds. These requirements, which in the early 1930s were required only of *halutzim*, began, from the middle of the decade, to be required of craftsmen and relatives as well.[129]

Officially, as stated, the main principle that guided the Jewish Agency on immigration was the absorption capacity of the country, the contribution of immigrants to its development, and their Zionist background. The official selection criteria for immigrants were in line with this policy. How the criteria were applied in "Polish Reality" can be learned from a report of Kashtan, Secretary of the Warsaw Zionist Office in Warsaw, about his visit to a pig hair processing cooperative in Mezeritch.[130]

---

128 Report of Senator to Ben-Gurion, May 8, 1936, Netanya Archives, file C/6.

129 Consul of Poland in Jerusalem to Foreign Ministry, 20.3.1935, AAN-MSZ, file 6269.

130 October 2, 1938, CZA S6/2740.

The thirty-eight members of the cooperative were put to the test of qualifying for *Aliyah*. Four candidates were disqualified following the medical examination; one was disqualified because he had parents in Palestine and it was suspected that upon his *Aliyah* he would leave the cooperative and join his parents; two were disqualified for incompatibility with membership in the cooperative, another was disqualified for past association with "extremists" (communists) and another candidate was disqualified because of his age (54) and his large family. The remaining 29 candidates were ranked according to their professional level and party affiliation. First priority was given to long-time members of "Po'alei Zion," followed by, in descending order: the "Union," "Mizrahi," non-partisans who recently joined "Po'alei Zion," former "Bund" members who joined "Po'alei Zion," and finally "extremists" who recently joined "Po'alei Zion." All the candidates had capital of between £120 and £400. The two guiding principles for selection of candidates were: fitness for employment in Palestine and the level of Zionist background. It is interesting to note the fear and concern of *Aliyah* institutions about the *Aliyah* of those with non-Zionist political leanings ("the Bund" and the Communists). The report also shows the rush to move from non-Zionist parties to Zionist parties in order to qualify for immigration certificates.

Chart 6 depicts the process of assigning immigration licenses. It is evident how small was the part that that the Warsaw Zionist Office played in the process of granting licenses relative to the dominant part played by the Mandate government and the Jewish Agency.

The Division of Authority for *Aliyah* Certificate Distribution

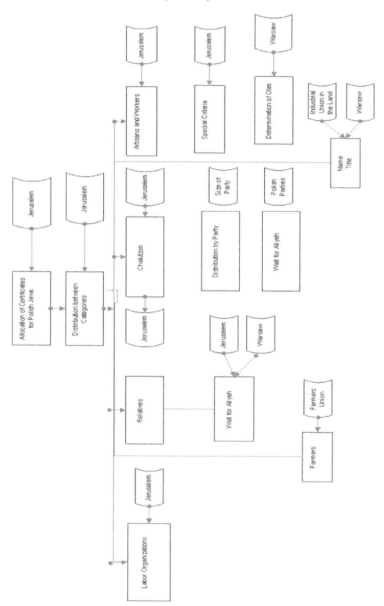

Chart 6 - Between Jerusalem and Warsaw:

The Ship Polonia
Source: Internet Website "Polonia"

Polish Immigrants on the ship Polonia, 1937
Source: PikiWiki_Israel_5694

The Journey to Eretz Israel

The Warsaw Zionist Office acted as a travel agency and organized the trip to Israel for most of the immigrants. The immigrants were concentrated in Warsaw, Lvov or Krakow and from there took trains to the ports of Trieste or Constanta. The transports included 600-700 immigrants. They were accompanied by a representative from the Warsaw Zionist Office up to the port of departure, at which point they were transferred to the Jewish Agency representative. Sometimes there was only a very short time from the day the immigrant received official approval for *Aliyah* until the time he had to leave. This made it very difficult to do all that getting organized for *Aliyah* required. The problem was particularly acute among the immigrants who were requested by sources within the Palestine through official lists of names. For example, the time interval between when the lists of names were sent from Jerusalem to Warsaw and the deadline for receipt of the visa was set for five weeks.[131] Given the time period required to transfer the lists by mail and the time required to prepare the letters and send them, candidates had little time to perform the required steps: Receiving the final decision regarding *Aliyah*, preparation of necessary documents, arranging for a medical examination, fundraising for travel, and visa arrangements. In one case, the immigrants were required to arrange the documents, raise the money for the journey, and transfer them to the Warsaw office in just six days; those who succeeded in meeting to the schedule and whose *Aliyah* was approved were then required to leave Poland seven days later.[132] Sometimes the immigrants were detained at the last minute after finishing their preparations for immigration. For example, the leaders of *HeHalutz* in Poland on 6.5.1931 wrote to the Jewish Agency:

> We were alarmed today with receipt of the telegram from the Warsaw Zionist Office regarding the delay in *Aliyah* of 41 certificate holders ... the date of immigration for most people was scheduled for May 25 – they have already informed people about this, and some of them are already in Warsaw; having left their homes

---

131 From the Secretary of the Aliyah Department to the Warsaw Zionist Office, 24.8.1933, CZA S6/2519.

132 Kashtan to the leaders of HeHalutz in Poland, March 16,1937, CZA S6/3551.

they are now waiting for transport ... These people have already severed their ties with home, with sources of livelihood and work, they are all set to go and then ... again, delays are declared. Even outside of the mantle of Zionist responsibility, there is a limit to the abuse that can be tolerated of human beings and their fate ... What special need of the Palestine, of Zionism, can compel and justify the taking away of certificates from people who are ready to go, backpacks on their shoulders? ... We demand a directive by telegraph eliminating all delays, so that the immigrants can embark on their *Aliyah* as scheduled.[133]

Aliyah candidate A. Krupel complained about the cancellation of his immigration certificate at the last minute:

I was told by the Zionist Office of Lvov ... that I have a certificate and that I must be ready for travel ... I was sure that it would be arranged by 10.10 or at the latest - 23.10. But since I didn't hear anything from them, I called the Director of the Zionist Office on the phone and he informed me that my *Aliyah* was postponed to the next schedule... I am very devastated by this because I have already liquidated my business, sold my home furniture, and handed over my apartment to someone else[...] The prevalent disorder in the Warsaw Zionist office here is now evident to me, and I see that

---

133 L. Levite, Director of the HeHalutz movement of the Histadrut in Poland, to the Directors of the Jewish Agency in Jerusalem.

without lobbying, goals will not be achieved here.[134]

The immigrants to Palestine, like all immigrants from Poland at the time, were exposed to the danger of theft and fraud on their way. This is how a bulletin of the Polish Immigration Syndicate described the dangers that lurked for migrants in Warsaw: "Warsaw is full of thieves preying on unsuspecting migrants. One should avoid all contact with strangers in the street, on buses, and in public parks. No documents or money should be given to any stranger." Immigrants were warned of thieves and fraudsters wandering around near immigration offices, consulates and ship offices, thieves offering housing, assistance with immigration, buying travel tickets, and the like. Sophisticated methods for robbery and theft from immigrants evolved. In the bulletin entitled *HaHagirah* (The Immigration), these methods were detailed and cases of fraud and theft by those "cheaters of immigrants" were reported. Immigrants were advised not to carry their money with them during their stay in Warsaw and were given the option to deposit the money in the Syndicate Office.[135]

The cost of boarding included the cost of sailing, the cost of a train journey from the place of residence to Warsaw, Lvov or Krakow, and from there to the ports of Constanta or Trieste; The cost of shipping the baggage, the cost of issuing the visa, entry fees, "download fees" at the port, "arrangement tax" and "immigration stamps." The costs varied according to the type of immigrants and

---

134 From the "Metal Artist" Cooperative in Tel Aviv to the Department of Industry and Commerce of the Jewish Agency, June 6, 1935, CZA S6/2522.

135 AAN-MOS File 105, Bulletin dated 13.12.1930; File 107, Bulletins dated 27.5.1933, 10.6.1933.

departments in the ships. Owners of capital sailed in the first class, the other - in the second and third wards. Travel expenses ranged from 300-500 zlotys per person. The cost for a three-person family was 1,200 zlotys, a very high amount relative to the income of most Polish Jews.[136] Discounts were sometimes given due to a difficult economic situation, to relatives of those who were killed as a result of events in the Palestine, to relatives of kibbutz members, and even to members of the Huberman Orchestra (the 1936 Philharmonic Orchestra).[137] The scope of the discounts was large, and sometimes tickets were given for free. A letter from Yitzhak Gutman, a policeman from Jerusalem, to the Agency's *Aliyah* Department, underscores the difficulties most encountered in raising the required funds for travel:

> Eight months ago, my parents came from Poland with your license and my sister remained in Poland ... I recently received an immigration license for her ... But the Warsaw Office wants 370 zlotys which is close to £15.5 and I can't pay it ... I ask that you take my situation under consideration ... and give a directive to the Warsaw Zionist Office to take it into consideration.[138]

An important parameter for screening candidates as part of the

---

136 For comparison: in the 1930s, income among small craftsmen and city traders fell to 30-60 zlotys a month.

137 Secretary of the Aliyah Department to the Warsaw Zionist Office, 23.7.1937, CZA S6 / 1512; Dobkin to the Warsaw Office, 27.6.1937, S6/1512.

138 Isaac Gutman to the Aliyah Department, undated, S6/1512.

Workers' *Aliyah* was their health status.[139] In the Workers category, people whose health was defined as type B were not allowed to come on *Aliyah* for fear of creating in the Eretz Israel "a class of disabled people who would become a public burden."[140] Applicants in the category of the Workers' *Aliyah* were examined twice in Poland: first before arranging for the passport, and the second on the eve of their immigration. To that end, the firm recruited dozens of physicians who conducted tests for candidates all over Poland. At the head of this medical system in Poland was the chief physician of the Warsaw Zionist Office, who was subordinate to the chief physician of the Health Department of the Jewish Agency in the Palestine. The head of the Health Department at the Agency set the criteria for medical examination and decided whether to allow the *Aliyah* of special problems. For example, the head of the Medical Department at the Agency, rejected the *Aliyah* of a yeshiva student with tuberculosis even though he had relatives in Palestine. Those with heart conditions, disabilities, and those who suffered from

---

139　Medical examinations were acceptable for all types of immigrants for all countries. For example, applicants for immigration from Poland to Canada were required to undergo a thorough medical examination based on which immigrants with contagious or ocular diseases would be disqualified, as well as people who were found unfit for physical work. Another medical examination was conducted for immigrants upon their departure from the ship in Canada. See Reczynska (1981) pp. 192-193.

140　Memo from the Secretary of the Aliyah Department to the Warsaw Zionist Office in which he complains about an immigrant who was defined in Poland as having type A health but was diagnosed upon his arrival with heart disease. August 29, 1933, CZA S6/2519.

ocular diseases were also disqualified.[141] A young healthy girl whose parents lived in Palestine was rejected because she had a history of syphilis. The explanation for the refusal sent to the physician in the Warsaw Office was worded as follows: "In my opinion, you should use all the means at your disposal to prevent her *Aliyah*. We do not need to bring in young women who are ill with such diseases and young women of this type." For their part, health authorities in the country complained that the medical examinations of the candidates in Poland were not sufficiently in-depth: Dozens of immigrants were found to be sick, mainly with mental illnesses and tuberculosis, and the health authorities in the country had to hospitalize and treat them.

Farewell at the Train Station 1929
Source: NAC 1-p-2348-1

---

141 Correspondence between Dr. Horwitz, Chief Physician of the Warsaw Zionist Office, and Dr. Dodson, Medical Supervisor of the Aliyah and Labor Department of the Jewish Agency, CZA S6/1502, S6/1514, S6/1525.

Over the years, a permanent ceremony of farewell to the immigrants has been established: The railway platform fills with people, and crowds accompany the lucky ones who leave for Israel. This is supplemented with cheers, dancing, tears, and singing of *Hatikvah*. Here's a personal description:

> The east railway platform in Warsaw looks like a square where a mass demonstration is being held by Jews. Each passenger is accompanied by at least 10 escorts who come in groups with flags and song. The sounds of *"Hatikvah"* are heard. A worried father gives final advice to his son the *halutz* (pioneer): not to forget his parents, to write, to write a lot, to be careful of malaria. Mama secretly wipes away her tears, hugs and caresses the son and looks at him with loving eyes. The train is moving. The young men have gone. Only the older adults remained on the platform.[142]

The ship is already a "piece of Eretz Israel": "The spirit of the Land floats across all the classes, and the songs of Eretz Israel seeps into the air of the sea and takes over all the passengers." The approach of the ship to the *Eretz* is very exciting among the immigrants. "We stand on the ship and urgently look to the East. The sun rises, and we know that the rising sun represents Eretz Israel. An emotion of anticipation overtakes us, and we keep our eyes afar off and long to finally see the Land before us."[143]

---

142 *N.P.,* March 24, 1934.

143 *BaDerech*, May 11, 1934.

As the ship is anchored and the descent to shore begins with its intrusive and annoying examinations, the mood immediately changes. In January 1930, the *N.P.* reported that at last the quarantine that was customary for third-class passengers was canceled, a procedure that had been very difficult for European passengers: "Dirty Arabs roughly unfurled luggage contents, the freshly pressed new clothes that had been painstakingly folded were shredded and ruined."[144] But even after the quarantine was canceled, entry into the country was described as unpleasant and even traumatic. According to immigrant descriptions, the first examination was conducted on the ship by sour-faced British officials and a useless cohort of Jewish Agency officials. The certificate check took many hours. The officials interrogated the newcomers about their relatives, their livelihoods, and who will help them to be absorbed in Palestine. The immigrants were then rudely thrown into boats and brought to shore by Arabs who are always described as "dirty" and "loud."

The trip to the Eretz Israel was rife with mixed emotions. On the one hand – longing and expectation of coming to Palestine, and on the other – great difficulty in obtaining the certificates, in preparing for the immigration, and an unpleasant first encounter with the d.

---

144 *N.P.,* January 2, 1931.

Figure 19 -- Dancing the hora on the deck of the ship
Source: Generously provided by Fundacja im. Professor M. Schorr

5

THE FIGHT OVER
IMMIGRATION LICENSES

For most of the 1930s, the demand for *Aliyah* was much higher than the supply of licenses. Naturally, therefore, conflicts persisted between groups, organizations, and institutions regarding their allocation and distribution. Struggles ensued between the Warsaw Zionist Office and its branches in Krakow and Lvov, between the Office and various Zionist organizations, and, in even greater measure, between representatives of Polish Jews and the Warsaw Zionist Office on the one side, and the Jewish Agency and its *Aliyah* Department in Jerusalem on the other. Although it is possible to indicate several points in time that saw a reduction in demand for immigration (months when tragic events occurred and periods of economic slump in the country), nevertheless, emigration in general and *Aliyah* to Israel, in particular, were seen in 1930s Poland as the only option to escape from an unbearable existential situation, and masses of Jews sought to come on *Aliyah*. As Barlas described in 1935: "The aspiration of *Aliyah* encompasses the masses of Jews from all sectors and all walks of life in Poland; the eyes of tens of thousands look to the institution of *Aliyah* as the anchor of rescue efforts from the life of poverty and hopelessness in which they are mired."[145]

The extent of the demand for *Aliyah* (which in our discussion is defined not only by the need or desire to come on *Aliyah* but also by actions to promote it), did not stand on its own but depended on the chance of obtaining approval for *Aliyah*. For example, there is a correlation between the likelihood of *Aliyah* and the number of *halutzim* in Poland; the number of registered members of the movement and of members being trained for kibbutzim increased during periods where the chance of obtaining an *Aliyah* license increased, and decreased in periods where this chance decreased. When the chances of immigration fell in 1936, after the boom of 1934-1935, the number of *HeHalutz* members fell by 25-30 percent, and the number of training kibbutzim decreased from 380 to 170. By the end of 1937, there were only 56 training kibbutzim in Poland.[146]

Similar phenomena were also evident among other immigrant groups, such as organized groups of craftsmen, which multiplied rapidly as soon as a window of opportunity to emigrate opened up for them. For most Polish Jews, emigration and *Aliyah* were not at all perceived as a possible realistic option, and consequently they were not among those applying to the Warsaw Zionist Office, nor did they undertake any other activity for immigration.

We do not have full data on the number of those interested in *Aliyah* who applied to the Warsaw Zionist Offices. The Warsaw Zionist Office, which was completely burned down at the beginning of the war, had a card file containing about 200,000 names.[147]

---

145   Confidential Memorandum, Nov. 10, 1935, CZA S6/1499.

146   Oppenheim (1993) pp. 480-481.

147   Kashtan to Barlas, January 12, 1940, CZA S6/1531/1.

It is unclear whether the list also included those registered in the provincial offices in Krakow and Lvov, and whether it included those who had already immigrated. Obviously, the number does not include those who had taken steps toward immigration but had not yet registered in the Warsaw Zionist Office: members of Zionist organizations, craftsmen organizations, *halutzim*, and training members. Many joined Zionist movements and parties, some at the same time abandoning non-Zionist political affiliations, for the sole purpose of increasing their chances of *Aliyah*. In June 1932, a writer from Poland reported on the "certificate rage":

> Who does not want to get a certificate? All the unemployed, all those who lack a means of livelihood, dream of immigration. Presently, when the doors to all other destinations are locked, there is no immigration other than *Aliyah* to Eretz Israel, and there is no *Aliyah* to the Palestine without procuring a certificate. There is therefore a rush to submit application forms to the Central Warsaw Zionist Office, and it has become urgent to register in one of the Zionist parties.[148]

The extent of the demand for immigration can be learned, among other things, from reports and correspondence on this issue between the Warsaw Zionist Office and the *Aliyah* Department. As an indicator of the demand for immigration, data can be analyzed for the number of applicants for Zionist offices, the number of those joining immigration organizations, the scope of requests for the *Aliyah* of relatives, the extent and depth of the struggles over

148   Sarid (1979) p. 419.

immigration licenses, as well as the assessments of the responsible officials in Poland and in Palestine. An important indicator of the volume of demand for immigration is the gap between the number of registered and interested candidates for immigration and the number of licenses available to the Warsaw Zionist Office at any given time. Throughout the period studied, there was a huge gap between the demand for immigration from Poland and the number of licenses available to the Agency, which could be shared among Polish Jews. However, the desperation for *Aliyah* greatly increased after mid-1935, when the number of licenses allocated to Poland was greatly reduced. This was due to the reduction in the total number of licenses and the allocation of many of the remaining licenses to Jews from Germany. In March 1931, representatives of the young East Galician youth claimed:

> Your decision to allocate only one certificate for us has embarrassed us. We simply cannot find rest in our souls. We now have about twenty *halutzim* who are fully qualified to immigrate ... [It is unfair that] from the other kibbutzim ... there are many *halutzim* who have been able to make *Aliyah*, but now from us – only one of us will come.[149]

In a report from the Israeli Land Office for 1933-1935 it was reported:

> Masses of Jews are knocking on the doors of the Warsaw Zionist Office and its branches. Hundreds of thousands

---

149   From the young HeHalutz and Hapoel HaMizrachi to the Directorate of the Jewish Agency, March 18, 1931, CZA 56/2514.

of Jews are looking for a refuge in Eretz Israel. Many
of them are not Zionists but consider Israel as the only
place of refuge for their rescue. In the training kibbutzim there are about 20,000 *halutzim*. Outside of the
training there are about 40,000 young people. Tens of
thousands of workers and craftsmen are registered with
Zionist workers' organizations and are preparing themselves for *Aliyah*. On top of that – there are thousands
of professionals and tiny industry owners – besides the
aforementioned organizations.[150]

In the category of "recommended" relatives, there was a gap between
the number of those holding recommendations as determined by
the Immigration Department in Jerusalem and the number of
certificates received for them: in August 1931, only 156 recommendations were received for 213 recommendation holders.[151] It
should be borne in mind that the "recommendations holders" are
people who (they and their relatives in Palestine) have already
passed the whole course of lobbying and bureaucracy in Palestine
and in Poland, before succeeding to be included in this category. In
September 1932, just a few months after the Zionist Office opened
in Krakow, the office's administrators reported that in this short
time they had transmitted information to several hundred people.
Of the 60 immigrant candidates who sought to come as *halutzim*,
the Office approved 37, and of the 100 "professionals," only 24 were
approved. For the "middle class" only 12 certificates were allocated

150   Report of the Warsaw Office, October 1933 June 1935, ETM S6/5342.

151   Kashtan from the Warsaw Office to the Aliyah Department, 5
       August 1931, CZA S6/2514.

although there were more than 100 applicants registered in this category.[152] On April 20, 1933, Dr. A. Stopp and Dr. Emil Shmorak, Chairman of the Executive Committee of The Zionist Organization in East Galicia, wrote to the Agency's management in Jerusalem:

> Day by day, in Lvov and other field cities, tens and hundreds of professionals and craftsmen are gathering on our doorstep. You cannot even imagine how many of these people flock to us and seek registration. So far, about 1,500 craftsmen have been registered ... and enrollment is continuing.[153]

They demanded to allocate to them a greater proportion than was set in the quota of certificates because of the preponderance of Galicia in the Zionist movement in Poland. On November 29, 1934, Kleinbaum and Reiss, heads of the Israeli Land Office in Warsaw, in their letter to Gruenbaum, head of the Immigration Department, complained about the minority of B-type immigrants:[154]

"There are 7,000 applicants seeking to apply of this type. Most applicants are Zionist activists as well as artisans. In the last quota only 130 certificates were allocated to this type." In early 1936, concurrently when the number of permits for immigrants to Palestine decreased, a particularly sharp reduction occurred for immigrants from

---

152   To the Jewish Agency from the Zionist Office in Krakow, September 21, 1932, CZA S6/5215.

153   Stopp and Shmorak to Jewish Agency Management, April 20, 1933, CZA S6/2519.

154   "Type B" - one of the designations for a sub-category of craftsmen in the framework of the "Working Immigration."

Poland, due to the large number of licenses granted to German Jews. This prompted A. Reiss and Dr. Schwarzbard, head of the Warsaw Zionist Office, to write to the Immigration Department in Jerusalem:

> There are tens of thousands of candidates, including thousands of veteran Zionist and dedicated activists registered in the Warsaw Zionist Office. ... We have no way to help them. The situation in "HeHalutz" is very dangerous because of the impossibility of arranging for the immigration of even small percentage of members who have been in training for years.[155]

Senator knew of 10,000 members of the "Haoved" organization for whom only 30 licenses were assigned during the winter 1935 schedule.[156] On November 9, 1936, the *HeHalutz* Federations in Poland - the General *HeHalutz* Federation, the General Zionist *HeHalutz* Federation and the Mizrachi *HeHalutz* Federation – jointly asked the immigration department to increase the scope of the *HeHalutz* immigration from Poland. The demand noted the country's needs (to recruit workers for the Jewish settlements, the port, the government and the police) and the strength, size, prominence, and contributions to Zionism of the *HeHalutz* movement in Poland.[157] With the increase in the number of immigrants arriving in Palestine, the number of requests to allow the immigration of relatives increased accordingly, and applications piled up in the offices

---

155 Reiss-Schwarzbard to the Aliyah Department, January 1, 1936, CZA S6/3552.

156 Senator to Ben Gurion, 8.5.1936, Netanya Archives C/6.

157 9/11/1936, CZA S6/3551.

of the Immigration Department of the Jewish Agency. There were 2,500 applications in 1932. By the summer of 1934, about 10,000 applications had accumulated, and by the beginning of 1935, they had reached 18,000, most of them referring to the Jews of Poland. In 1936, after the great wave of immigration in 1935, the number of applications decreased to 13,000.[158] Even if we consider that in order to obtain more licenses, immigration activists in Poland may have exaggerated data on the number of applicants, their very inquiries reflect the plight of immigration in Poland and the paucity of available certificates. With the drastic reduction in the number of certificates, beginning in 1937, complaints and referrals to increase the quota for Polish Jews also diminished, which may be more of an indication of despair than a reduction in the number of those who aspired to make *Aliyah*.

Representatives of Polish Jews often complained about discrimination against them in favor of German Jewry when it came to the allocation of immigration licenses.[159] The complaints highlighted the dire mental and economic condition of Polish Jews and the rights of the Zionist movement in Poland. The issue came up again in correspondence between the Warsaw Zionist Office and the Immigration Department. For example, at a meeting of the Warsaw Zionist Office on June 17, 1936, Reiss claimed:

> With this schedule, the number of certificates for Polish Jews again decreased by 30 percent. We do not want to

---

158 Halamish (2006) p. 285.

159 For a discussion of the distribution of certificates between Germany and Poland, see Halamish (2006) pp. 312-338 and Halamish (1994) pp. 289-293.

compete with the Jews of Germany, their sorrows pain
us as well, but the executive must note that Zionism is
fundamental and rooted here in Poland, which is where
a huge youth movement and the Halutz movement was
born here ... and to also take into account the harsh
predicament of the Jews in Poland.[160]

In a struggle to increase the share of Polish Jews in the quota for
immigration licenses, the plight of Polish Jews was highlighted. On
November 5, 1936, representatives of the Zionist Association of
Polish Immigrants in Palestine wrote in their appeal to Ben-Gurion:

The dangerous situation of Polish Jewry that has gone
on for years is getting even worse [....]. It has become
a daily occurrence that Jews are wounded – hundreds
gravely wounded –in the middle of the streets of central
Poland; we are being slaughtered and killed in the open
daylight, and no one is there to help and rescue us. ...
it is dreadful and horrific ... we are forced to demand
from you, our very honorable friends, to dedicate the
most substantial part of the current schedule -- about
a thousand licenses from the current quota -- in favor
of the Jews of Poland ... You must take into account the
injustice that the government has done. They reduced
from our already measly quota another 300 [certifi-
cates] in favor of the German capitalists who are living
in Palestine whose fortunes were not [yet]transferred
to Eretz Israel. This account is not for the Jews of Poland

---

160   17.6.1936, CZA S6/4791.

to pay![161]

Representatives of the Central Committee of the Zionist
Organization in Poland demanded an increase in the number of
certificates for Polish Jews because of the existence of a large and
high-quality Zionist population in Poland and due to the rights of
Polish Jews vested in the donations to Zionist funds:

> In the past year, Polish Jewry has been able to make new
> and increased efforts to build the country. The results of
> the last annual Keren Hayesod campaign, the KKL-JNF's
> special campaign, and more recently, the "Bitzaron cam-
> paign" are proof of this. Now, Polish Jewry is demanding
> its rights for immigration and Zionist fulfillment.[162]

The extent of immigration was of paramount importance; Zionist
leaders believed that the movement that offered the most opportunities for immigration would be the one that would attract the
most members from Polish Jews. They presumed that far more than
ideological background, the possibility of *Aliyah* was the one that
dictated the numbers of those joining the Zionist movements, and
thus according to Ben-Gurion in 1933:

---

161 November 15, 1936, CZA S6/3551. Several hundred licenses were
granted in 1935 to those with capital in Germany, on the condition
that the capital would be transferred to Palestine under the transfer
agreement. Since the capital was not transferred, the government
reduced 300 workers' certificates from the category of workers.
Halamish (2006) pp. 260-259.

162 To Jewish Agency Management, Nov. 22, 1936, CZA S6/3551.

They come to us because it seems to them that we are
the conduit for immigration. If we do not successfully
provide that conduit - they will flock elsewhere. In previous years, our ideology attracted the youth. At the moment, there is an entirely different factor: immigration.
They will go to the place that can control immigration.
The masses want to travel... *Aliyah* is the key to power,
and to life itself. Either we will be leaders of the Zionist
Organization and in control of the certificates or we will
not see, not certificates nor any budgets.[163]

The plight of Polish Jews and their desire to *Aliyah* was at the heart
of the struggles within the Zionist Organization. Jabotinsky proposed a plan for the mass evacuation of Polish Jews. The masses
of Polish Jews wanted to emigrate to any possible destination, and
this was the impression of representatives of various Jewish organizations who visited Poland. While it may be true that these representatives were sometimes interested in exaggerating the plight
and aspiration of Polish Jews to emigrate, similar impressions are
evident from other sources as well. For example, the director of
the JCA (Jewish Colonization Association), reported on his tour of
Poland in April – May, 1937:

Because of the economic and political situation of
Polish Jews, it is easy to understand that most of the
Jews in this country yearn to immigrate. I interviewed
many people, at different stages of life and professions
... all expressed a strong desire to leave Poland. Most

163   Quoted by Shavit (1978) pp. 73-72.

of them spoke about Palestine, the United States and Latin America because they had relatives in these countries. Others expressed a desire to emigrate anywhere ... which is better than staying in this hell ... the desire to emigrate encompasses the entire Jewish public.[164]

In a lecture on the emigration of Jews from Poland, which in May 1936 was presented to the "Jewish Immigration Examination Committee" in the Polish Ministry of Interior, the potential of large-scale Jewish-Polish immigration was presented, and therefore:

Under these conditions, every voice tells us that wherever it might be possible to go, you will find an attentive ear and a willingness to travel among the broad strata of Polish Jewry, even among those who, under other conditions, would have no desire for migration.

The speaker pointed to the phenomenon of frequent "discovery" of new places seemingly suitable for Jewish emigration, places that soon proved untenable after being properly examined. Among the places that arose as possible destinations for Jewish emigration were Birobidzhan, Ecuador, Angola, Bolivia, Uruguay, Paraguay, Chile, Colombia, Canada, Argentina, Brazil, and Cyprus.[165]

The paucity of immigration licenses considering the severe plight of Polish Jews and the desire for mass immigration caused severe conflicts between the Warsaw Zionist Office and Jewish institutions and organizations in Poland and in Palestine. The

---

164   YIVO RG 245.4.12, Poland 3.

165   AAN-MSW 1068, Lecture to the Committee, May 14, 1936.

most protracted and prominent conflict was between the Warsaw Zionist Office and the *Aliyah* Department of the Jewish Agency in Jerusalem. The conflict intensified, especially from 1936, when the number of certificates for Polish immigrants dropped abruptly. Representatives of the Warsaw Zionist Office again complained that their views were ignored, that the Immigration Department dictated all their actions, even though the policymakers at the Jewish Agency did not correctly understand the realities in Poland. The disputes mainly revolved around three issues: the limited number of licenses allocated to Polish immigrants, the distribution of powers between the Immigration Department and the Warsaw Zionist Office, and the allocation of immigration licenses to unworthy candidates at the expense of preferential candidates. Absolute compliance was demanded from the Warsaw Zionist Office to the instructions of the Immigration Department. Gruenbaum, head of the *Aliyah* Department, ordered the Warsaw office to follow the *Aliyah* Department's instructions without delay:

> [...] If an explicit order is transmitted from the *Aliyah* Department for the grant of an immigration permit to a recommendation holder who is not in the queue, or for an immigrant who is of some other type, this order should [nevertheless] be implemented without delay.[166]

In 1935, Barlas, Secretary of the *Aliyah* Department, prepared a severe report on the Warsaw Zionist Office following his visit to Warsaw in September of that year:

---

166 Gruenbaum to the Warsaw Office, June 30, 1935, CZA 56/2522.

The office is run by two entities: the presidency and the administration; the relationship between these two entities is bad ... The influence of the parties has penetrated both the presidency and the management. The office employs 75 officials, some of whom are incompetent and appointed solely for party reasons. The choice of who gets immigration certificates is also made under the influence of the party politics. As a result of disputes and disarray, there are even wasted licenses that remain unused.[167]

Barlas noted that the office should be "rejuvenated" and sent a special envoy to Warsaw for inspection. Dr. Senator, Director of the *Aliyah* Department, criticized the process of politicizing the ministry and the mixing of the political and administrative levels.[168] On 4.2.36 Kashtan wrote from the Warsaw Zionist Office to the *Aliyah* Department in Jerusalem:

We have approved your letter ... together with a list of 14 people you found to deserve urgent treatment ... We have to express our astonishment at your approach ... both from the context as well as a matter of principle in your attitude to our office ... if you come and give our committee an absolute order to arrange [a certificate] for these or others, we will execute that order without regard for all those whom [we regard] as more urgent. [However,] we will have performed an injustice

---

167   Barlas to Gruenbaum, CZA S6/1499.

168   Senator to Ben-Gurion, May 8, 1936, Netanya Archive File C/6.

to those whose *Aliyah* is more urgent and meritorious, but unfortunately did not have relatives in Eretz Israel that could exert as much pressure on the Jewish Agency as other. Besides that, by following such a policy you have in fact subverted every possibility of action by our committee and deprived it of any authority to perform its duties in a wise, fair, and just manner given the terrible lack of certificates.[169]

The conflict culminated in October 1936 when Reiss, President of the Warsaw Zionist Office, informed Dr. Senator that he refused to execute the instructions given to him and that he did not recognize his authority to give instructions on behalf of the *Aliyah* Department. Dr. Senator demanded from the administration of the Jewish Agency to "immediately put an end to the anarchy that has been created ."[170] The conflict also continued in the years to come. In December 1937, Reiss wrote to Yitzhak Ben-Zvi:

In connection with your request regarding the arrangement of your relative's immigration ... I find it necessary to disclose to you: The new custom of the Immigration Department is such that we only receive "heavenly" certificates and we cannot allocate a certificate to anyone who is not included in the Jewish Agency's list ... You should pursue your request in this matter directly with the immigration department.[171]

169   Kashtan to the Aliyah Department, February 4, 1936 CZA S6/3552.

170   Senator to Ben-Gurion, November 25, 1936, CZA S6/3555.

171   Reiss to Ben-Zvi, December 26, 1937, CZA S6/3555.

In June 1938, Reiss argued at the plenary session (The Plenum) of the Israeli Land Office: "The Immigration Department has taken over the privilege formerly held by the Commission [The Immigration Committee of the Warsaw Zionist Office] which is: Distribution of certificates in special cases. Because this distribution is decided from afar, it is quite obvious that mistakes are made." The clash over division of powers also continued in 1939. Reiss, who was leading the fight with the Immigration Department, argued against the Agency's preference for decisions of the Jerusalem office over those of the office in Warsaw, as the Warsaw office, being closer to the facts on the ground, had a more accurate picture of immigration needs. Reiss believed that this position did not constitute an insult to the honor due to the Agency, as the office in Warsaw was responsible for the Zionist public opinion in Poland and that therefore the office should oppose "this method of denying the right and possibility for us to fulfill our duty to the most urgent cases in the Zionist movement, while the Agency, at the expense of our quota, gives preference to those who have relatively no urgency for *Aliyah*." In the same manner, Reiss argued against the discrimination with which Poland was treated as compared to other countries: "Why is Warsaw different from Vienna or Berlin, where the local authorities are given free discretion to distribute certificates as they see fit?"[172] Despite these vigorous words, the Warsaw Zionist Office continued to follow orders from Jerusalem even in this case.[173]

The almost natural conflict between "field people" and

---

172 It is likely that the suspicious attitude of the Agency's staff in Jerusalem toward the immigration institutions in Poland was due, in part, to the large scale of fraud related to immigration in Poland.

173 Reiss at the presidency meeting of the Warsaw Zionist Office, January 12, 1939, CZA S6/3557.

policymakers who are far from the field manifested itself here. Those in the field felt that they understood the "real situation" better than those far way, but their impact on the policy was less than was appropriate. This was added to the frustration of being in the "front-line" position with the public and having to absorb the claims and complaints of the many disappointed people who were unable to obtain an immigration license. The field people are "between the hammer and the anvil." On the one hand, pressure is exerted on them from the field and on the other they encounter a lack of understanding of the situation and even complaints from management who sat far from the situation in the field.[174]

In addition to the ongoing confrontation with the *Aliyah*

---

174 This disparity between management and the field was also discovered in other Jewish institutions, one can learn more about if from the apologetic letter sent by L. Alter, JEAS director in Warsaw, to HICEM management in Paris, where he tried to explain the small number of Polish immigrants to the United States, noting that since the beginning of the economic crisis, when public opinion in the United States turned against immigration, conditions and attitudes in the United States Consulate in Warsaw completely changed. Agents were banned from entering, including JEAS representatives. About 75% of applicants were rejected as being in danger of becoming a "Public Charge," while others were rejected due to medical problems. The pressure of HIAS executives in the United States on behalf of relatives who demanded that their relatives be allowed to emigrate from Poland is understandable, but the branch in Poland was very limited in its activities. A similar tension between the "field" and the decision-making institutions was also extant within the Jewish Agency's institutions in Palestine: Thus, Senator's complaint that the Zionist Congress dictates the distribution of 80% of immigration licenses, leaving only a small minority of the certificates for distribution to the immigration department.

department, the Warsaw office was also attacked from other directions: the provincial Zionist Offices in Krakow and Lvov complained about the small amount of certificates they were allotted and of the control that the Warsaw office exerted over the distribution of licenses.[175] "Mizrachi" representatives complained about the lack of consideration of the public that they represent and of political protectionism in the work of the Office.[176] The Central Committee of the Zionist Organization in Poland appealed to the *Aliyah* Department, about the party politics that had taken over the Warsaw Zionist Office and of the ineffectiveness of its operation.[177] Representatives of the funds joined in the criticism of the Zionist Office as well. For example, the committee of the Jewish National Fund in Luboml approached the office of the Jewish National Fund in Jerusalem with a demand that contributions to the Funds be taken into consideration when decisions about the distribution of immigration licenses were made: "Eretz Israel is apparently for those who know how to ingratiate themselves with and bribe the officials of the Warsaw Zionist Office, but not for long-standing Zionists."[178]

The Office in Warsaw, as the main address toward which Polish

---

175 Letter from the Eretz Israel Committee in Krakow to the Directors of the Jewish Agency, September 21, 1932, CZA S6/2515; and from the Eretz Israel Committee in Lvov to the Aliyah Department, June 8, 1933, CZA S6/2518.

176 Letter of resignation from Blum, the Mizrachi representative, one of the Directors of the Warsaw Zionist Office, June 9, 1936, CZA S6/1499; Letter from Zerach Warhaftig, February 20, 1936, CZA S6/4823.

177 November 12, 1935, CZA S6/14.

178 April 5, 1938, CZA S6/1497.

Jews interested in *Aliyah* turned, became a bedrock of controversy and a "continual target" for all the competing interested parties. On the one hand, the Office was seen by Polish Jewry as responsible for all immigration issues, and on the other hand, its authority was limited, and to a great extent, it was powerless. To the institutions and organizations in Palestine, it represented the "field," and to some extent, the Exile with all its characteristics, which were then perceived as negative. At the same time, the institutions in Jerusalem were perceived in Poland as remote, and not tuned in to the real problems of Polish Jewry. In Poland itself, the Zionist Offices in Krakow and Lvov, as well as the various parties, movements and *Aliyah* organizations, were perceived as "the field," while the central Warsaw Zionist Office was perceived by these groups as an organizational entity distant from the field and its problems. The position of the central Zionist Office in Warsaw in the decision-making hierarchy and the objectively difficult situation of such a large gap between the number of applicants for *Aliyah* and the number of certificates led to incessant conflicts and between the Office and the other entities involved in *Aliyah*.

Trade in Licenses: Favoritism, Bribery and Forgeries

With the increase of the difficulties regarding *Aliyah*, rumors of trading with the certificates began to spread, and "*Aliyah* purity" became a full-fledged issue on the agenda. Heads of the Warsaw Zionist Office attributed the murky atmosphere and the wave of rumors about cheating, bribery, and corruption to the practice that existed among the *HeHalutz* movements to charge approved *Aliyah* candidates with "immigration taxes" that were earmarked for joint funds whose official purpose was to finance the *Aliyah* of indigent *halutzim.* The preference granted to members of the Zionist Histadrut organizations in the queue for *Aliyah* also contributed to the feeling, widespread in the Jewish community, that the *Aliyah* process was rife with corruption. In December 1932, Dr. Senator issued a circular intended for all immigrants and candidates for immigration:

> The Warsaw Zionist Office hereby announces that the distribution of the certificates depends solely on the Warsaw Zionist Office. Not one certificate has been granted to any of the parties participating in the Office's committees. Each questionnaire is personally examined, and the approval for *Aliyah* is given only when the suitability of the candidate for *Aliyah* has been considered without regard to party affiliation. Obviously, therefore, no party, institution or private person has the power to grant certificates to anyone. In connection with this, we warn all immigrants and candidates for immigration through any kind of certificate that they must not pay nor commit to pay any private person, institution or even to contribute to any Fund or party whatsoever with the intent of influencing the Warsaw Zionist Office to approve their *Aliyah*, whether it be at the time of submission of the questionnaire or after receiving approval.[179]

The circular failed to achieve its purpose, the procedure was

---

179 Circular of the Warsaw Zionist Office to all candidates for immigration, December 15, 1932, CZA S6/2517.

unfulfilled, and rumors of the negative phenomena of forgery, bribery, and favoritism continued to spread. The heads of the Warsaw Zionist Office admitted that there was some truth in these rumors; there were arrangements whereby amounts were charged that were higher than those approved for immigration. In quite a few cases, the federations of *halutzim* added "spouses" to holders of approved certificates of immigration for a fee. Many young people who were approved for immigration under Type B certificates or personal recommendations brought with them fictitious marriage partners in return for large payments. The editors of the report on the activities of the Warsaw Zionist Office in 1933-1935 wrote: "The dealings have become a malignant and contagious disease ... Many rabbis also cooperated in this area and issued fictitious marriage certificates."[180]

As part of the struggle between the Jewish Agency and the Warsaw Zionist Office against these phenomena, many reforms were instituted. These included the intensification of the supervision of Halutz training, the imposition of regulations and rules regarding the maximum payments that immigrants could be charged, and the prohibition payment in any form to all factions and parties by immigrants. In addition, they established a judicial system to hear complaints of fraud and corruption that included a Special Judge/Investigator to examine the Complaints, a judicial panel consisting of three judges, and above it - a Court of Appeal. At a joint meeting of the Directorate of the Immigration Department and members of the presidency of the Zionist Office in Warsaw, held in Jerusalem on February 18, 1935, a decision was again rendered to ban parties and organizations from accepting any payment

---

180   Report of the Warsaw Zionist Office, CZA S6/5342.

related to immigration licenses. However, the Halutz organization was allowed to collect from each Halutz a certain amount for travel expenses, the amount to be decided jointly by all the Halutz organizations. Furthermore, these funds were to be subject to full supervision and auditing. They also determined that any organization that would act contrary to these rules would not receive any licenses for its members who wished to immigrate. Any "professional" agents that would be caught will be handed over to the Polish police by the Zionist Office in Warsaw.[181] Dr. Senator demanded that all financial dealings with immigrants by the parties and organizations be transferred to the Warsaw Zionist Office in order to sever the unhealthy relationship between financial matters and immigrant selection considerations.[182] The large extent of this phenomenon is evident from the large number of files (72) regarding counterfeiting and bribery in the Warsaw Zionist Office division of the Zionist Archive.

Aliyah Taxes

The immigration taxes charged by organizations and parties ranged around a few hundred zlotys: a couple who immigrated in January 1935 paid, in addition to the fare, 600 zlotys to the "State Halutz" center. The "Mizrachi" imposed a tax of 300 zlotys per immigrant.[183]

---

181   Meeting of representatives of the Aliyah Department and representatives of the Warsaw Zionist Office in Poland, February 18, 1935, Jerusalem. CZA S6/5422.

182   Senator to Ben-Gurion, May 8,1936, Netanya Archives Case C/6.

183   The Main Bureau of the Mizrachi in Poland and the Mizrachi Committee of Siedlce, November 27, 1932. CZA S6/4815.

The "Zionist Youth" movement collected 368 zlotys above the amount allowed permitted to charge for the fare. In this case, suspicion was raised that the money found its way into the private pockets of the Halutz representatives.[184] The "Halutz Craftsmen" Federation, collected 200-150 from each individual approved for *Aliyah* for deposit into the "shared fund."[185] It was impossible to determine which part of the illegal taxes collected was allocated to finance the *Aliyah* of underprivileged members of the movements, how much funded the ongoing activities of the movements, and the amounts that found their way into private pockets

Forgeries: "Certificates Are Authorized by Money"

There was a great variety of forgery attempts; some perpetrated in Poland and some in Palestine. Professional certificates, industrial invitations, invitations from relatives, certificates attesting to age and/or marital status were all forged. In one case, an "invitation" sent to a certain woman allegedly from an aunt in Palestine was, in fact, arranged for by her husband, who had been in Palestine for three years as an illegal tourist.[186] A person who arrived at the Immigrant Home in Tel Aviv bearing a certificate professing that he was a professional Botanist was found to be lacking in any profession at all. Because of his ill health, he was unable to do any physical work, and thus the officials of the Tel Aviv Immigration Bureau

---

184   Report of the Investigating Judge, March 19, 1936, CZA S6/5314.

185   Representatives of the Jewish Agency's Craftsmen's Federation, September 29, 1937, CZA S6/2312.

186   Confidential letter, Warsaw Zionist Office to the Aliyah Department, October 10, 1935, CZA S6/1497.

were forced to refer him to the social services department. Another man bearing a locksmith certificate turned out to be a watchmaker, and after many hardships, found work as a cobbler. Yaffe, director of the Tel Aviv Immigration Bureau, noted:

> The details cited previously reveal only the bare surface of the problem. ... most of these "professionals" are either not professionals at all, or have professions that cannot be pursued in the current situation in Palestine ... Most of the single women who bear professional certificates are, in fact, seamstresses, and then not even of a high standard, a profession that has no significant demand in Palestine.[187]

The Zionist *BaDerech* reported:

> In the same way that there is much profiteering in real estate in Palestine, there is profiteering here in Poland trafficking in licenses and qualifications for anything and everything. Do you want to be certified as a locksmith, carpenter or other kinds of arts - go to the profiteer sitting in your city or in Warsaw, the capital city? For a certain amount, you will be transformed into an expert artist, as certificates are authorized by money.[188]

---

187 B. Yaffe, Director of the Immigration Bureau in Tel Aviv, to H. Barlas of the Immigration Department of the Jewish Agency, November 20, 1935, CZA. S6/1497.

188 *BaDerech*, February 27, 1935.

The immigration bureau in Haifa reported a case of a disabled seamstress who came as a farmer.[189] In another case, a grocer received his immigration permit in Tel Aviv as a rabbi.[190] In Palestine, there was an office called a "trust bureau" that dealt with arranging for a license – for a fee. Official professional government licenses, such as for drivers and electricians, were arranged through a bus company or industrial owners. Forged certificates carried a variety of price tags; 800-1,000 zlotys was the going rate for a Polish government license as a professional driver or electrician. A counterfeit passport would cost 45 Palestine lira (about 1,125 zlotys). Forging of the age in a passport for a Type D immigrant increased the price by 600-700 zlotys.[191] Arranging immigration in the clergy category (2B) required the provision of an invitation and commitment of a synagogue to employ the immigrant, which cost 25 Palestine lira in addition to the payment to the intermediaries.[192] There were cases where the forgeries were discovered by the Border Police, and then the immigrants were returned to Poland.

---

189 Haifa Aliyah Bureau to the Aliyah Department, February 26, 1936, CZA S6/1497.

190 Confidential letter, Ministry of Foreign Affairs to the Aliyah Department, December 4, 1934, CZA S6/2522.

191 Haifa Aliyah Bureau, January 23, 1935, CZA S6/2522; from Haifa Aliyah Bureau to the Aliyah Department. November 3, 1936, CZA S6/1512.

192 Confidential letter from M. Gurari to B. Yaffe, July 10, 1935, CZA S6/2522.

Fictitious Marriage

Men with a certificate could bring their wives with them (a right that was denied to women with certificates). A fictitious marriage practice thus developed that allowed for the *Aliyah* of many women, but also gave power to men with certificates. In the Halutz movement there were many women joined with male *halutzim* coming on *Aliyah*. There are also quite a few cases in which young men from Palestine went to Poland to marry women and bring them in. Many of the fictitious marriages – and probably most of them – were subject to a money payment to the certificate holder. In one case, 500 zlotys was paid to the Zionist Center of Lvov for a marriage certificate.[193] In another case, 1,500 zlotys were paid for a fictitious marriage and immigration license.[194] The Immigration Department opposed marriage for money, and Senator demanded that offenders be punished for participating in a fictitious marriage by rejecting their right to immigration or even canceling the right of immigration of the recommending certificate holder. Nevertheless, like many other provisions laid down in Jerusalem, this too was not followed, and fictitious marriages, which was a practical way to overcome the difficulties of immigration in that period, did not stop throughout the 1930s.[195]

Fictitious marriages are mentioned quite a bit in the literature dealing with this period. The book *Little Jew,* authored by Hanoch

---

193   Yaffe to the Aliyah Department, March 29, 1933, CZA S6/4815.

194   From Lodz, Nov. 23, 1934, CZA. S6/2522.

195   Senator for the Warsaw Zionist Office in Lvov, October 27, 1936, CZA S6/3572; Haifa Bureau of Aliyah to the Aliyah Department, January 16, 1936, CZA S6/1497.

172 | Irith Cherniavsky

Bartov, tells of the hero's uncle who went to Poland at the expense of a fictitious bride's family, but returned to Palestine with another woman.[196] Some believe that many of the deportations that took place in Palestine during these years were due to the large number of fictitious marriages that disbanded once the couple arrived in Palestine.[197]

Trading with certificates

The shortage of immigration licenses led to trading with the certificates. Immigrant applicants were promised assistance such as: assistance in obtaining a Type 3A and 2A certificate (a category of craftsmen who possessed a specific amount of capital); selling of certificates; lobbying in the Warsaw Zionist Office; lobbying in obtaining a certificate for a professional; and arranging a certificate for a professional in the British Consulate. There were reports of a case in which, for each license as an industrial worker, the factory owner in the country who allegedly ordered these immigrants received 1,500 zlotys.[198] In another case, a $50 tariff per certificate was reported.[199] In yet another case, $55 was paid for expediting a certificate for a young woman who threatened suicide if her immigration was not arranged.[200]

196   Bartov (1980) pp. 62-65.

197   See Bernstein's (2008) discussion of this topic pp. 102-105.

198   Report by Baruch Palevsky from his visit to Wolomin, September 8, 1935, CZA S6/2870.

199   S. Saltzman "Geula" Company Agency, May 24, 1933, CZA S6/2518.

200   Undated, CZA S6/4815.

Special Tribunal for Forgeries

Until 1935, a commission of inquiry into counterfeiting and cases of illegal money collection from immigrant candidates worked alongside the Warsaw Zionist Office. When the committee members found that there was a basis for the charge, they would bring the matter before the Histadrut party tribunal to which the suspect belonged. These party tribunals acquitted almost all suspects. In April 1935, it was decided to convert the commission of inquiry into an independent tribunal. By December, 15 cases had been discussed, and between January and June 1936, thirty additional cases were brought. The tribunal issued 15 judgments. As the tribunal was alleged to be acting too slowly due to the lack of judges it was decided to increase their number.[201] Beginning in October 1935, a special court of appeals began to operate in parallel with the tribunal dealing with forgeries. The composition of all tribunals was based on party affiliation.[202] The tribunal consisted of three members and a judge-investigator. The trials took place behind closed doors, and the defendant had recourse to a defense counsel. Possible punishments were: warning, reprimand, cessation of Zionist activity of the organization accused of counterfeiting for up to two years, denial of the right to distribute immigration licenses for one year (for party, group or organization) or denial of the right to obtain a license for up to 10 years (for the individual). Defendants had the right to appeal their case before the court of appeals.

---

201 Plenum meeting, June 17, 1936, CZA S6/4791.

202 Reports of the Warsaw Zionist Office, October – June 1933, CZA S6/5342; Reports of the Warsaw Zionist Office, January 1935 – March 1937, CZA S6/4931.

In March 1936, the Secretary of the *Poale Zion* Executive Committee in Lvov was prosecuted for collecting 250 zlotys in exchange for arranging *Aliyah* in the category of "recommendations" for a person who was not entitled to it.[203] 205 In Lvov, for two years, a trial was held against the *HeHalutz* Center for arranging *Aliyah* for a couple who had not had the requisite *Hachshara*, or training. The punishment was a rebuke.[204] Charges of another type were brought against an individual who was operating out of his Warsaw apartment and charging money for his help in arranging for the receipt of immigration licenses. He charged 2,600 zlotys for his services from immigrants who would be making *Aliyah* in the category of professionals (of which 800 zlotys were for travel expenses.) In another case, 1,700 zlotys were charged for similar services.[205]

From 1934 to 1936, the court dealt with seventy-five offenses. Of them, seventy were regarding money collected, while five were about forged documents. One complaint was lodged against a private expert who demanded money for a professional examination; while the remaining seventy-four investigated were members of Zionist parties or organizations. Regarding seven offenses of receiving money, it was noted that the defendant took money for himself; in seventeen cases it was stated that the money illegally collected was intended for a party, Histadrut or a Zionist fund. In the other cases related to the collection of funds, it was not specified where

---

203   Investigation Report against David Frenkel, March 25, 1936, CZA S6/2919.

204   Dr. Hoffman of the Krakow Zionist Office to the Aliyah Department, December 16, 1936, CZA S6/2938.

205   Indictment - Aryeh Zeitlin, June 8, 1936, CZA S6/2905.

the money was going. In some cases, the money was returned. At times, the courts were criticized by the Jewish Agency's administration. In a memo about the situation at the Warsaw Zionist Office, Barlas stated:

> The oversight institutions set up by the *Aliyah* Department in the battle against embezzlement and the trade in licenses did not work properly because judges were not courageous enough in fulfilling their role, which sometimes included indicting members and parties. Groups of judges were put together and disbanded frequently, and the work was conducted in a plodding manner. . . Contrary to our instructions, the Halutz organizations are charging unauthorized immigration taxes which we have forbidden to collect from the *halutzim*. The organizations of professionals affiliated with the political parties took the liberty of collecting taxes and donations in connection with the licenses approved by the Zionist Office. The leadership and the judges did not actually implement effective oversight measures to prevent such actions.[206]

It is likely that only a fraction of the fraud and forgery committed in Poland in connection with *Aliyah* came to court hearings, but the very need to establish courts and the extent to which the Zionist Offices and the *Aliyah* Department were busy dealing with the issue – even while their officials were overburdened with work due to the pressure of high demand for *Aliyah* – indicates the significant scope

---

206   November 10, 1935, CZA S6/1499.

of the phenomenon. As it turns out, the handling of this matter failed to achieve its purpose, and the Zionist establishment failed to enforce its policy. The phenomenon of counterfeiting and trafficking in certificates continued throughout the decade of the Thirties.

The Warsaw Zionist Office at the Outbreak of the War

Some information regarding the history of the personnel of the Warsaw Zionist Office at the outbreak of the war can be learned from a report that Kashtan, the secretary of the Office, sent to Barlas, the Director of the Agency's *Aliyah* Department, on April 21, 1940. According to this report, when the war broke out, a transport of 150 immigrants of various categories, arranged by the Warsaw Office, was ready and set to leave Poland on September 5; unfortunately, the transport never left. In the early days of the war, the Office still managed to operate despite the heavy bombardment on Warsaw. Afterwards, some of the activity continued in the private apartments of the Office Directors. On September 25, the Office was burned to the ground. At that time, there were about 380 immigration licenses in the Office, most of them for students. The British Consulate had several dozen more licenses. There were about 200,000 names on the Office tab. During the first weeks of the war, the Office staff dispersed: Three of the heads – Sheffer, Kleinbaum, Warhaftig – left for Vilna, and from there to Kovno, the capital of Lithuania, where many refugees from Poland were concentrated. The three established a temporary Zionist Office in Kovno and worked on arranging for the *Aliyah* of certificate holders and on finding clandestine ways to reach Palestine. Later, the three emigrated to Palestine. Anselm Reiss was in London on September 1, 1939. Other officials and activists from the Warsaw Zionist Office escaped eastward toward the Russian occupation area. Kashtan, Levita, Apolinary Hartglas and several other activists from the Warsaw Zionist Office went to Trieste. This was made possible with the assistance of H. Barlas. Eleven employees of the Warsaw Zionist Office remained In Warsaw.[207]

207   Kashtan to Barlas, January 12, 1940, CZA S6/1531/1; Barlas (1973) pp. 414-431; Warhaftig (1984).

6

CONDITIONS OF ALIYAH AND THE CHARACTERISTICS OF IMMIGRANTS

A group of immigrants before leaving for Palestine
Source: CZA GHP/3796101

The highest responsibility and authority over immigration issues was in the hands of the Mandate Government. Immigration policy was implemented through the Government Immigration Department and the Immigration Commissioner in Israel. They are the ones who defined both the categories and the number of immigrants. A Mandate document gave the Zionist Organization a statutory status on immigration matters. However, this status was limited only to immigrants slated to join the labor market (category "C, the working immigration"). The Mandate government determined the following categories of immigrants: A – Capitalists, B – Clerics and Students, C – Working Immigrants,[208] and D – Relatives of the Residents of Palestine. These groups were then divided into subcategories: The capitalist group was divided into several groups according to the scope of capital and the professional background of the candidates. Category B was distributed to clergy, orphans enrolling in institutions and students. The working immigration category was divided into several groups: Halutzim, craftsmen, relatives of the inhabitants of the country, and others. Some of the licensees could include family members dependent on the licensees, while other licenses were granted only to one person. From 1934, the agency's authority was also reduced in the category of working immigrants; only relatives and tourists remained in its authority. The agency has almost no authority over the other categories.

Characteristics of Immigrants

About a third of immigrants arrived alone, most of them single women and men. The rest came as married (some fictitiously), while others arrived as part of a family, mostly with an only child. The number of men and women was similar; children up to age

---

208   In the period documents, category C licenses were given different names: "schedule licenses"; "certificates"; "category G"; "category TZ." The sub-category of craftsmen and small industry within category C also received different names: " Type B"; "Craftsmen"; "middle class"; "professionals."

16 accounted for 18 percent of the immigrants. Most immigrants (more than 50 percent) were young and of working age (18-35). Comparison of the age distribution of Polish immigrants to that of Jewish immigrants from the Russian empire in the late 19th and early 20th centuries indicates similarities and differences. The majority of "Great Immigration" immigrants were also working age (58 percent), but the proportion of children up to the age of 16 was higher (30 percent) than their proportion among the Polish immigrants (18 percent), which indicates that the members of the "Great Immigration" were more of a family type. Nevertheless, the main characteristic of these two immigration movements is similar: those who immigrated were primarily younger and "stronger," while the weaker, older, and the poor remained behind.[209] People over working age had difficulty getting an immigration license. More than 76 percent of immigrants from Poland over the age of 45 immigrated as first-degree relatives of the Palestine residents, and another 10 percent as capitalists. It turns out, therefore, that for adults over the age of 45, virtually only those who had a fortune or had relatives in Palestine could immigrate.

---

209   Alroey (2008) pp. 76, 95.

Sons of Professor Moshe Schorr before
their immigration to Palestine, 1936.
Source: Fundacja im. M. Schorra

Scope of Aliyah

Three periods of Polish Jews can be discerned: in the years 1930 to
1932 there was a small increase (1,300-1,700 immigrants per year),
in 1933-1936 a dramatic increase in immigration (11,000 to 25,000
immigrants per year). In 1937-1938, the scale of immigration was
reduced to between 2,700 to 2,900 immigrants per year.

Table 2 – Number of Immigrants from Poland
to Palestine in the years 1931-1939

Year	Number of Immigrants from Poland
1930	2,504
1931	1,693
1932	3,429
1933	11,603
1934	13,180
1935	24,993
1936	10,762
1937	2,906
1938	2,713
Jan-Apr 1939	1,022
Total January 1931-April 1939	74,805

Source: Table A-14 in the Statistical Appendix

Table 3 – Number of Immigrants from Poland
by Category 1931-1939

Category	Number of Immigrants 1930-1939	Percentage of Total Number
Total	74,805	100
Relatives	28,411	38
Halutzim	16,707	23
Intermediate status, Type B, craftsmen, profession-al workers, experts	11,240	15
Capitalists	7,125	10
Students	4,377	6
Immigrants posing as tourists	2,777	4
Religious functionaries	2,263	3

Source: Table A-14 in the Statistical Appendix

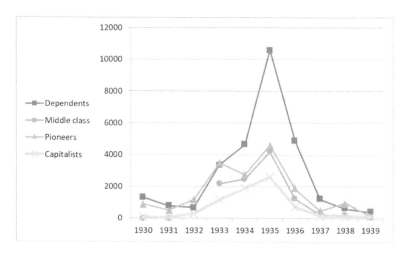

Chart 7: Immigrants from Poland to Palestine by Categories 1931-1938

Aliyah of Relatives

The largest group of immigrants from Poland in the 1930s were relatives of the residents of Palestine. These consisted of two categories. The first are those "with requests" (Category D); these were "dependent" immigrants who arrived based on their relatives' "request." The second are those "with recommendations" (one of the subcategories of the working immigration), those who came as a result of the "recommendation of a relative in Palestine." Immigrants in these two categories accounted for 38 percent of all immigrants. In addition, there were immigrants in other categories, such as industrial workers, experts, farmers, and capital owners, who also had relatives in Palestine. At least half of all immigrants were relatives.

Relatives 'with Requests' (Category D)

About two-thirds of the category of "Relatives" came with "requests": parents, women and children who were defined as "dependent" on their relatives in Palestine. Applicants in Palestine were required to prove that they were able to support the invited relatives, which was only possible for relatively high-income earners. A detailed definition of those who qualify to move within the "requests" category changed from time to time. From mid-1934, liberalization took place with regard to "request holders," and almost all requests were approved. As a result, from mid-1934 and even more so in 1935, the number of "with request" immigrants rose sharply. However, the number of requirements dropped significantly in 1936.[210] The reason for the decline was attributed to the economic situation in Israel, which worsened at the end of 1935, but it should be noted that at that time another difficulty was assessed in the process of approving relatives: the certificates came with a three-month time limit until immigration, as opposed to the previous policy of allowing up to a year to arrange the visa, followed by another three months until actual immigration. With the introduction of the stringent procedure, when candidates did not manage to arrange for immigration within the limited time, their licenses had to be returned to Palestine for their extension, and this cumbersome

---

210 According to the report of the Zionist Warsaw Office January 1935-March 1937 (CZA S6/4931) the number of licenses decreased from 5,773 in 1935 to only 1,107 in 1936. According to the statistical report of the Warsaw Zionist Office, the number of immigrants with requests was 7,771 in 1935 and 4,150 in 1936. It should also be noted that the licenses usually included several persons.

process made everything very difficult.[211] These two factors - the deterioration of the economic situation in Palestine and the bureaucratic hurdles – greatly affected the scope of the *Aliyah* of those with "requests." One might assume that the Arab revolt that began in April 1936 with a general strike also slowed the arrival of relatives, but the statistics show that the sharp decline in the number of immigrants in this category began only in October, and more so - in December - 1936 about six months after the outbreak of the revolt. In 1937 and 1938, the number of immigrant immigrants declined, and it began to rise again only in March and April of 1939 During these two months, which are the last to be known, the number of immigrants with requests increased significantly: from 15 and 22 immigrants for January and February 1939 to 121 immigrants in March and 214 in April 1939. This increase may indicate the sense of danger felt among Polish Jews after the events of Kristallnacht, and the increasing fear of the approaching war.

The bureaucratic hurdles and uncertainty about the possibility of realizing the immigration resulted in partial actualization and waste of licenses. The scope of the waste can be learned from the following considerations: From August 1937 to March 1938, 535 Type D licenses were received. 108 licenses, or 20 percent of the total, were not utilized for the following reasons: 67 claimants did not respond to the application or gave up on immigration, 36 claimants were rejected by the Warsaw Zionist Office, and three licenses were lost.[212]

Relatives who came with the requests were much older than other immigrants. Half of them were aged 45 and over, and they

---

211   Report of the Warsaw Zionist Office, CZA S6/4931.

212   Kashtan to the Aliyah Department, April 7, 1938, CZA S6/3555.

constituted an absolute majority of all immigrants of that age group. The rate of single and lone people was high - 54 percent. The number of immigrant women was twice that of men, a phenomenon typical of immigration of relatives - the "second wave" immigration - as the men who immigrated in the first stage brought their wives after settling in the new country. A large proportion of relatives who came as "requests" were the parents of the invitees, while about a third of the immigrants were younger than 18. Only 16% of the "request" immigrants were of working age (18-45), most of whom were women - the wives of the requesters. More than 80 percent of "request" immigrants were classified as unemployed, so immigrants in this category met the government requirements, i.e., immigration of first-degree relatives who are not of working age and are not a burden on the labor market.

Relatives of "with Recommendations"

The group called "Relatives with Recommendations" included relatives of residents of Palestine approved by the *Aliyah* Department based on the promise of a source of livelihood by their relatives in Palestine. A Palestine resident inviting immigrants in this category would have to fill out a voucher form accepting responsibility for their livelihood. The category included working-age relatives (who could not be included in category D), and, in particular: fiancées, daughters, sisters, and children of residents of Palestine aged 18 and over. These immigrants were included in the quotas allocated for the "working *Aliyah*," and the Jewish Agency had to divide the quota of licenses between relatives and others belonging to the working *Aliyah*: *halutzim*, craftsmen, professionals, and more.[213]

A relatively high number of licenses were allocated to relatives during times of economic crisis in Palestine and during periods when the Jewish Agency fund was depleted. This was because the Jewish Agency could not bring as many *halutzim* at that time, as their *Aliyah* entailed considerable expense. At other times, fewer licenses were granted for this purpose. Throughout the 1930s, the demand created by the "relatives with recommendations" applicants exceeded the supply of available licenses. In order to regulate the number of immigrants with recommendations, the definition of relatives entitled to be included in this category was frequently changed. In early 1934 it was decided that only requests from sons, daughters, brothers, and sisters should be accepted, while more distant relatives were rejected. Later that year, the definition expanded to include fiancées, brothers-in-law, and sisters-in-law. In 1936, once again, licenses for those with recommendations were restricted, this time only to sons and daughters age 25 and under. These frequent changes made it difficult for those who needed to make fateful decisions under conditions of uncertainty, when their inclusion or exclusion in the group that had the right to apply for *Aliyah* was unclear.

Those responsible for the *Aliyah* of those "with recommendations" faced two major problems: the limited number of licenses, and the criteria according to which the applications would be prioritized and the queue for the *Aliyah* of recommendation owners

---

213 Up until 1934, the number of immigrants in this category was exclusively determined by the Jewish Agency. In the autumn of 1934, the Mandate Government began to dictate to the Jewish Agency the number of relatives to be included in the upcoming schedule. Halamish (2006) pp. 277-278, 285-286.

would be determined. In order to receive a recommendation, relatives in Palestine had to apply to the *Aliyah* Department, which examined and sorted the applications. The candidates who passed the screening were referred to, as previously mentioned, as "holders of recommendations," and lists of men and women who were "holders of recommendations" were sent to the Warsaw Zionist Office. When the *Aliyah* Department would receive the overall quota, it would assign a quota of immigrants to this category in each country. Almost always, the number of recommendation holders was higher than the number of licenses received, requiring a prioritization of the queue for receipt of the certificates. Thus, requests for the *Aliyah* of relatives went through two sorting and appointment procedures: first, applications submitted to the *Aliyah* Department were filtered out, and second, the Warsaw Zionist Office, under the guidance of the *Aliyah* Department, established the candidate's place in the queue for *Aliyah*, rejecting some of the applications until some unknown future date.

This procedure caused heavy pressure on the Warsaw Zionist Office by relatives with recommendations, and at the same time – pressure on the *Aliyah* department in Palestine from the recommending relatives. The situation led to severe struggles between the Warsaw Zionist Office and the *Aliyah* department. The desperate situation of the inhabitants of Palestine in their struggle to obtain certificates for their relatives in exile is reflected in Agnon's description of Henrietta in his novel *Shira*:

> A great deal of trouble came on her relatives in Ashkenaz, and Henrietta's entire focus was to extract them from there and bring them to Eretz Israel. Her worries were etched on her face, with wrinkles appearing... She

ran from the offices of the Jewish Agency to lawyers,
and from them to the *Aliyah* Department, and from the
Aliyah Department to mediators and consultants and
pimps who acted unfairly with her, even though they
were not bad. When evil rules the world, even those
who are not evil behave wickedly. Henrietta shouldered
the burden of dealing with all this trouble, and spared
her husband the running and humiliations that many
Jews suffered in those days at the hands of English and
Arab officials, and at the hands of Jewish officials who
joined their brothers and were more difficult than the
Gentiles.[214]

In July 1931, a list of 152 female relatives with recommendations
was sent from the *Aliyah* Department to the Warsaw Zionist Office,
and at the same time, only 112 licenses were sent to the British
Consul in Warsaw. The Warsaw Office had to determine the 40
recommendations that would be rejected. The order of priority for
immigration that the Office sought to determine was: adults (not
older than 35) before younger women; brides and sisters before
other relatives; those with Zionist privileges before others.[215] This
priority reflected the needs of immigrants more than the needs of
Eretz Israel and the relatives living therein. In the spring of 1935,
there were 1,600 recommended men registered, but only 400 licenses were issued. This time, the main criterion for selecting
immigrants (as determined by the *Aliyah* Department and which
was passed on to the Warsaw Zionist Office), was the candidate's

---

214   Agnon (1971) p. 13.

215   Kashtan to the Aliyah Department, 29.7.1931, CZA S6/2514.

profession and that profession's suitability to the needs of Eretz Israel.[216] The second criterion for determining priority in the queue was the seniority of the recommending relative in Palestine. The third criterion was the potential contribution of the immigrant to the economy, and thus professions that were in demand, and candidates that were invited by farm owners, were given priority. The fourth criterion was the candidate's Zionist affinity, first and foremost – as illustrated by membership in the Zionist Histadrut and contribution to the Zionist Funds.[217] These criteria express the high priority that was given to the needs of Eretz Israel and the small consideration that was given to the situation of the immigrants themselves and to their needs.

216   Report of the Warsaw Zionist Office, CZA S6/5342.

217   Halamish (2006) p. 289.

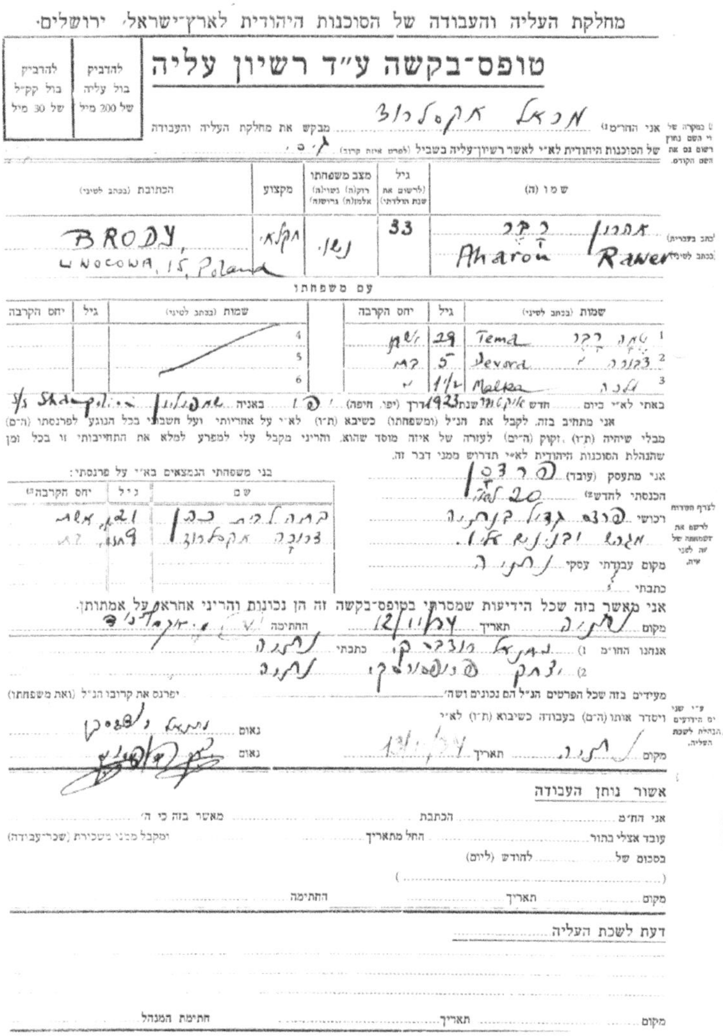

מחלקת העליה והעבודה של הסוכנות היהודית לארץ־ישראל, ירושלים.

טופס־בקשה ע״ד רשיון עליה

להדביק בול עליה של 200 מיל | להדביק בול קק״ל של 30 מיל

אני החו״מ ... מבקש את מחלקת העליה והעבודה של הסוכנות היהודית לא״י לאשר רשיון־עליה בשביל (לפרט איזה קרוב)

שמו(ה)	גיל (לרשום את שנת הולדתו)	מצב משפחתו רוק(ה) נשוי(ה) אלמן(ה) גרוש(ה)	מקצוע	הכתובת (בכתב לטיני)
Aharon Rawer	33			BRODY, ul Nocowa 15, Poland

עם משפחתו

	שמות (בכתב לטיני)	גיל	יחס הקרבה
1	Tema	29	
2	Devora	5	
3	Malka	1½	
4			
5			
6			

באתי לא״י ביום ... חדש ... שנת 1923 דרך (יפו, חיפה) ... באניה ... S/S Champollion

אני מתחיב בזה, לקבל את הנ״ל (ומשפחתו) כשיבא (ת־ו) לא״י על אחריותי ועל חשבוני בכל הנוגע לפרנסתו (ה־ם) מבלי שיהיה (ת־ו) זקוק (ה־ים) לעזרה של איזה מוסד שהוא, והריני מקבל עלי למפרע למלא את התחיבותי זו בכל זמן שהנהלת הסוכנות היהודית לא״י תדרוש ממני דבר זה.

אני מתעסק (עובד) ...

הכנסתי לחדש ...

רכושי ...

מקום עבודתי, עסקי ...

כתבתי ...

בני משפחתי הנמצאים בא״י על פרנסתי:

שם	גיל	יחס הקרבה

אני מאשר בזה שכל הידיעות שמסרתי בטופס־בקשה זה הן נכונות והריני אחראי על אמתותן.

מקום ... תאריך ... החתימה ...

אנחנו החו״מ 1) ... כתבתי ...

2) ...

מעידים בזה שכל הפרטים הנ״ל הם נכונים ושה... יפרנס את קרובו הנ״ל (ואת משפחתו) ויסדר אותו (ה־ם) בעבודה כשיבוא (ת־ו) לא״י

מקום ... תאריך ... נאום ... נאום ...

אשור נותן העבודה

אני הח״מ ... הכתבת ... מאשר בזה כי ה׳ ...

עובד אצלי בתור ... החל מתאריך ... ומקבל ממני משכורת (שכר־עבודה)

בסכום של ... להודש (ליום) ...

(...)

מקום ... תאריך ... החתימה ...

דעת לשכת העליה

...

מקום ... תאריך ... חתימת המנהל

Chart 8 - Application Form for an *Aliyah* Certificate for a Relative (Recommendation)

Source: Netanya's City Archive, File 32/A-502

The Warsaw Zionist Office operated a "recommendations committee" that sorted out the requests and set the queue for *Aliyah*. However, its authority was limited, and the *Aliyah* Department in Jerusalem would send from time to time lists of "urgent cases" whose urgency was in many cases at odds with the opinion of the members of the recommendations committee at the Warsaw Zionist Office.[218] Anselm Reiss, executive director of the Warsaw Zionist Office, protested to the *Aliyah* Department about the priority given to three holders of recommendations whom he felt were not appropriate for *Aliyah* – two were Revisionists who were involved in violent acts against Zionist institutions in Poland, and one was someone "with connections" who was not a Zionist activist. This protest by the Warsaw Zionist Office was rejected, and these applicants were granted permission to immigrate. How limited the number of licenses issued to those with recommendations was can be seen from the fact that despite the *Aliyah* of close to 3,000 holders of recommendations in 1935, there remained at the end of the year more than 2,500 recommendations that went unanswered. Dobkin informed Warsaw that due to restrictions on the number of licenses issued, it was decided not to include any licenses for relatives in the quota of Fall 1936.[219] Indeed, from then on the number of relatives with recommendations who came from Poland dropped sharply, and there were even long periods of complete cessation of this source of *Aliyah*.

---

218   Kashtan to the Aliyah Department, February 4, 1936, CZA S6/3552.

219   Dobkin to the Warsaw Zionist Office, December 15, 1936, CZA S6/3551.

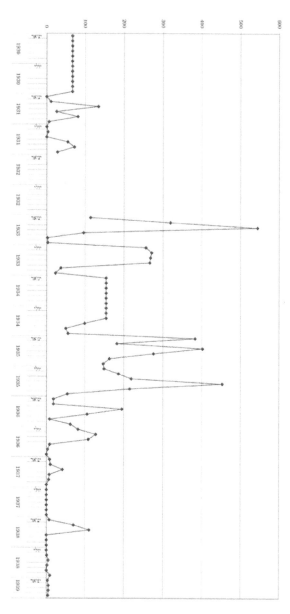

Chart 9 – Number of Recommended Immigrants by month, 1930-1939
Source: Cherniavsky (2010) p. 258

Procedure for the Aliyah of Holders of Recommendations

The *Aliyah* process for those in the category of holders of recommendations was complex and required the candidates to organize
all the requirements within a very short time frame, which made it
difficult for candidates and sometimes even prevented them from
emigrating. For example: On July 14, 1931, the *Aliyah* Department
in Jerusalem sent a list of 152 recommendations to the Warsaw
Zionist Office, for which 112 licenses were allocated. Ten days later,
a message was sent from the Warsaw Office to all the women on the
list that they had to adhere to a very tight schedule: within 20 days
they had to submit to the Warsaw office a number of documents:
(1) a notice of readiness for immigration and a declaration that they
had the necessary amount – 500 zlotys; (2) a medical certificate of
readiness for physical labor (prior to *Aliyah* the applicants were
re-examined by a physician on behalf of the Office at which point
they could still be disqualified from *Aliyah*); (3) a questionnaire and
a statement that the candidate would not make any demands of the
Jewish Agency; (4) application to the Immigration Office to arrange
the passport. Within five days of submitting the documents to the
Warsaw office, the applicant was expected to receive an answer as to
whether she was approved for *Aliyah*. The recommendation and the
receipt of an application from the Warsaw Zionist Office still did
not constitute a guaranteed receipt of the certificate. If the applicant
received a positive response, she was required to submit a passport
and the fare for the trip within a month. After obtaining the visa,
she had to leave Poland by the end of 1931 at the latest.[220]

Until the actual receipt of the recommendation, candidates had

---

220   Kashtan to the Aliyah Department, July 29, 1931, CZA S6/2514.

no reason to begin preparation. Even after they received the recommendation, they were still not guaranteed receipt of the desired
license for *Aliyah*. Once a candidate received a license, he would
have to arrange for permits and documents, raise funds for *Aliyah*,
arrange for a medical examination, etc. within just a few weeks,
and then liquidate all his affairs and connections in Poland within
a maximum of three months. If the recommendation holders were
excluded from the group of license recipients, they would have to
wait for the next quota in a state of uncertainty as to whether (and
when) they would be included among the license recipients. In this
situation, it is likely that some candidates looked for alternative ways
to immigrate to Palestine, while others gave up completely. Reports
sent from the Warsaw Zionist Office to the *Aliyah* Department indicate that out of the 644 recommended for the April – October
1932 quota, almost half did not complete their *Aliyah* (289).[221] One-
fourth of the licenses were "wasted" due to logistical difficulties.

---

221 List of male and female relatives recommended for Aliyah by the
     Jewish Agency according to the policy of licenses for relatives in
     April – October 1932 CZA S6/2515.

Table 4 – Reasons that Possessors of Recommendations Did Not Immigrate in the Apr-Oct 1932 Quota

Category	Men	Women	Total	Percent
Total Possessors of Recommendations	386	238	644	..
Possessors of Recommendations that chose not to come	185	104	289	100
Shortage of certificates	111	57	168	58
Did not respond to the office	30	26	56	19
Were unable to procure a passport	14	4	18	6
Wished to postpone immigration	9	5	14	5
Rejected for political reasons	2	2	4	1
Rejected due to age	1	-	1	-
Decided not to immigrate	1	-	1	-
Unknown Reason	17	10	27	9

Source: List of Relatives, CZA S6/2515

Aliyah of the Middle Class: Craftsmen and Merchants

The people of the middle-class – craftsmen and merchants – faced mainly two channels of *Aliyah*: one was the "middle class" within the quotas, and the other was a subcategory of capital owners: craftsmen and professionals with assets of £250 and £500. The *Aliyah* of the middle class within the framework of the "working *Aliyah*" began in the Spring 1932 quota; beginning in 1933 a separate category was set up for them in the statistical reports which was referred to as "type B" or "middle class." In 1934 another category was introduced: "organized craftsmen." In order to be included in this category, immigrant candidates had to meet, in addition to the conditions of professional expertise and ownership of a basic amount of capital, the condition of being involved in Zionist activity. In the 1930s, about 10,500 middle-class, type B, and organized craftsmen made up about 14 percent of all immigrants coming on *Aliyah* to Palestine, and a quarter of the "working *Aliyah*" from Poland. When the middle-class people began to be included as part of the 1932 quotas, several conditions were decided upon: they had to have at least £150 in capital and have expertise in professions that would be profitable in Palestine, and they had to pledge not to demand support from the Jewish Agency.[222] A "preparatory committee" was set up alongside the Warsaw Zionist Office to examine the candidates among the middle-class group and to recommend those worthy of *Aliyah*. In this category as well, there was a considerable gap between the number of those wanting to make *Aliyah* and the number of licenses they were granted. Considerations for distribution of the certificates among the middle class were the potential ease of absorption and political calculations.[223] Many demands were made of the Warsaw Zionist Office and the *Aliyah* Department to increase the number of licenses granted the middle class. Representatives of the middle class claimed that Palestine needed experienced

---

222   Instructions to the Zionist Offices regarding Aliyah licenses, supplement to circular no. 144, May 24, 1933, CZA S19/41; Halamish (2006) pp. 153-161.

223   For extensive discussion, see Halamish (2006) pp. 152-164.

craftsmen more than minimally trained *halutzim*.

> Our recognition of the idealism and efforts of the *halutzim* notwithstanding, we find it imperative to emphasize that the above, who received agricultural training or worked in some profession for only a few months before they came to Palestine, cannot take the place of the craftsman or professional, whose absence is now felt in all branches of industry in Palestine.[224]

With the opening of a designated route to *Aliyah* for the middle-class, many candidates were registered in the Zionist Offices. In eastern Galicia, a few months after the introduction of this route, some 1,500 craftsmen from all industries were registered in 1933. This is how the heads of the Lvov Zionist Office described the situation:

> Noting the strong push by craftsmen who are longing for *Aliyah*, we have instituted in our Office a registration procedure for immigrants with professions; these professionals flock to our doorsteps in Lvov and in the villages by the tens and hundreds daily. The extent to which these people flock to us and seek their fortune cannot be imagined. So far, about 1,500 artisans from various professions have been enrolled, and the number of enrollments keeps growing. We have recently prepared specialized spiritual training for them and

---

224 Levite, Chairman of the Poland-Palestine Chamber of Commerce in Warsaw, to Farbstein, April 6, 1933, CZA S6/2517.

consider them an essential element for building Eretz
Israel.

A list of 1,492 professionals was attached to the letter, including
a large number of electricians, painters, carpenters, locksmiths,
tinsmiths, and tailors.[225] In 1934, it was decided in the *Aliyah*
Department to give preference to would-be immigrants from the
middle class who belonged, for at least a year, to Zionist organizations engaged in cultural training, learning Hebrew, and fundraising activities.[226] In 1935, the Zionist General Council determined
that at least two-thirds of the licenses in the craftsmen category
be given to members of organizations recognized by the Zionist
Histadrut. In the Nineteenth Congress that year, it was decided that
15 percent of all quota licenses would be handed over to craftsmen
belonging to organizations.[227] In Poland, these two decisions were
not realized and organized craftsmen were given less licenses than
called for by these decisions.

---

225 Dr. A. Shmorak, Chairman, and Dr. A. Stopp, Secretary-General,
     Executive Committee of the Zionist Histadrut in East Galicia, to the
     heads of the Jewish Agency in Jerusalem, requesting an increase in
     their allocation of licenses, April 20, 1933, CZA S6/2519.

226 The *Histadrut Haboneh* to the Warsaw Zionist Office, May 3, 1934,
     CZA S6/2742. In the detailed reports of the Warsaw Zionist Office,
     this category was recorded separately only from 1936 and onwards.

227 Halamish (2006) p. 161.

Table 5 – Percentage of Licenses that were allocated to federations of craftsmen from Poland out of the entire number of licenses allocated to craftsmen, and percentage allocated to the Workers *Aliyah* out of the entire number of licenses, in the years 1936-1938

Year	Percentage of total licenses for Craftsmen*	Percentage of total licenses for Workers *Aliyah*
1936	30	9
1937	50	13
1938	35	4

Percentage of total licenses for craftsmen includes the following categories: Craftsmen type A2-A4, craftsmen belonging to organizations, professionals, and various Type B craftsmen.

Source: Chart N-14 In the Statistical Appendix

This is one of many examples of the gap between decisions made by Zionist institutions and their actual implementation.

Organizations of Zionist Craftsmen

The first organizations of Zionist craftsmen were established by organizations with a connection to the *HeHalutz* movement: "The Worker," "The HeHalutz Craftsman," and "Religious Professionals." There were other organizations that had an affiliation with political bodies: "the Builder" and "State Zionists." The pressure on demand for immigration can be learned from the fact that as early as 1935, several months after the decision to grant priority for immigration to artisans who were organized in Zionist frameworks, it was reported that these movements already encompass several thousand members.[228]

The "Haoved" Federation was founded in 1933 by the *HeHalutz* movement in Poland, under the direction of Mapai and the General Histadrut. This organization encompassed professionals of ages 27-36, too mature to receive *HeHalutz* training, but having a profession that was suitable for *Aliyah*. The organization was inaugurated with the help of the *HeHalutz* movement's institutions. Members of the Haoved were required to professionally prepare themselves for the needs of the country, learn Hebrew, join the General Histadrut organization and work for the Zionist foundations. The movement grew rapidly: in January 1934 there were 150 "Haoved" branches with 3,000 members in Poland. In May 1934 there were already 180 branches and 5,500 members. By early 1935 there were 371 branches and 12,000 members (including members' wives). By mid-1935, there were already 16,000 members in 400 cities and towns.[229] In addition, next to the *HeHalutz* organization, a teachers union requested recognition as an organization for the purposes of immigration.

The "*HeHalutz* Craftsmen's Federation" was founded in August

---

228 Report of the Warsaw Zionist Office, October 1933—June 1935, CZA S6/5342.

229 Sarid (1979) pp. 581-583. Generally, the data detailing the number of members and the extent of donations to Zionist organizations are presented as a struggle between organizations for their share of immigration, so the numbers are "inflated." Nevertheless, it is clear that as the possibility of Aliyah grew, the organizations also grew rapidly.

1934.[230] In 1935, over 4,000 members joined in this organization in dozens of branches.[231] The list of their professions included all the professions, notably: carpenters, tailors, shoemakers, bakers, plasterers and metalworkers. The organization engaged in Zionist activity, and according to the statement of their leaders collected in 1935 and 1936 large sums for the JNF (15,000-30,000 Zloty).[232]

In August 1934, in addition to the Mizrachi movement, a new "Center for Religious Craftsmen" was formed. In 1937, the organization had 120 branches and a membership of 4,000. From its formation until May 1937 only 330 immigrants succeeded to come on *Aliyah* from the Center for Religious Craftsmen. In 1933 in Western Galicia another organization arose (HaBoneh) with the aim of preparing craftsmen who were candidates for *Aliyah* by teaching them Hebrew, knowledge of Eretz Israel, history of the

---

230 Correspondence between the heads of the organization and Gruenbaum, CZA S6/3337; The Organization for the Administration of the Jewish Agency, September 29, 1937, CZA S6/2312.

231 Letter from the Executive Committee of the HeHalutz Craftsmen's Federation in Poland to Gruenbaum, January 24, 1935, CZA S6/2522.

232 In 1937, the organization ran into a financial crisis and applied to the Jewish Agency for a loan. The problem was caused by the procedure to collect from members who were approved for immigration, in addition to a tax for regular activities, an additional tax for "joint fund." Due to a cut in the number of immigrants, the organization remained indebted to members whose immigration was canceled. The amounts collected for the common fund ranged from 150-200 zlotys per member. May 3, 1934, CZA S6/2312.

204 | Irith Cherniavsky

Zionist movement, and the history of the Labor movement.[233] In May 1934, an application was made to Warsaw Zionist Office to certify the organization as a craftsman's organization. Membership totaling 1,800 in 30 branches was declared. A similar application was made to the *Aliyah* Department in August of that year, and by then it was claimed that the organization had grown to 2,300 members in 36 branches.[234] After the inquiries remained unanswered, another application was sent to the Immigration Department in January 1936, in which it was claimed that the number of members was 1,100 in only 23 branches. In this application the leaders of the organization claimed:

> You are kindly requested to take note of our just demand and answer us in the affirmative. If you do not do so, we will be forced to print a public letter in the press regarding how you treat a union with more than 1,100 members today and who fulfilled all the provisions in accordance with the rules of the Zionist General Council, but yet, in more than two years have not received even one certificate, nor does the *Aliyah* department even bother to answer our letters. Our delegates in Congress also voted for the current executive. We have the right to demand a little bit of honesty and a just a little bit of justice, that they do not steal (yes – steal!!) our *Aliyah* from us.[235]

233   HaBoneh Organization to the Warsaw Zionist Office, May 3, 1934, CZA S6/2742.

234   HaBoneh Organization to the Aliyah Department, August 26, 1935, CZA S6/2742.

235   January 20, 1936, CZA S6/2742.

Following conflicting reports regarding the number of members of the organization, suspicions of counterfeiting were raised, and it was decided to conduct a review in the Galicia craftsmen organizations. The review revealed that the number of members was indeed much lower than what was earlier declared.[236]

The certificates for organized craftsmen were distributed by party/movement allocation. Thirty percent of the licenses were given to Zionist Offices in Galicia, which showed some autonomy of the regional offices in the distribution of licenses. Of the license quota distributed by the Warsaw office, 80 percent was given to organizations related to the *HeHalutz* movement and 20 percent to organizations of religious and ultra-Orthodox craftsmen.

Independent Craft Organizations

In addition to artisan organizations established by the *HeHalutz* initiative and other political movements at that time, many attempts were made to establish independent organizations of artisans and professionals; some affiliated with organizations, parties or Zionist factions and some without such affiliation. The Zionist institutions rejected most of these initiatives, and the organizations were not included in the group of trade unions whose members were granted the right to immigrate. In Lodz, an organization was established called "The Association of Plumbers for Channelling and Related Work," that offered courses in these subjects as well as Hebrew,

---

236   Langsam, Head of Lvov Zionist Office, to the Aliyah Department, March 24, 1936, CZA S6/2742.

history, and Zionist studies.[237] In 1935, in the town of Borislaw (home to a government-sponsored school for drillers), a group was organized of thirty drillers who wanted to come on *Aliyah* as experts on mines and wells. Representatives of the Poalei Zion Association applied to the Jewish Agency on their behalf, but Dobkin, the director of the Jewish Agency *Aliyah* Department, responded that no drillers were needed in Israel.[238] Another group that organized for *Aliyah* and even sent a representative on its behalf to Palestine for lobbying activities was the "Mezeritch Cooperative of Brush Makers from Pig Hair," which we discussed in the introduction to this book. Despite the envoy's lobbying and efforts, dozens of meetings, and extensive correspondence with all relevant parties in Palestine and Poland, not one of the group members ever received permission to immigrate.[239]

Not only craftsmen but also independent professionals sought a way to immigrate by creating organizations: In Lvov, there was an active organization of engineers that numbered some three hundred members. Due to the economic crisis, in 1935, they applied to the Jewish Agency for a grant of immigration licenses.[240] In his negative response, Dobkin noted that special rights in the distribution of licenses were granted only to Zionist organizations and to organizations of professionals recognized by the Zionist Congress.[241]

There was a significant amount of exaggeration in the

---

237   Chairman of the Jewish Agency Plumbers Association, April 7, 1935, CZA S6/2522.

238   June 30, 1936; July 16, 1936; CZA S6/2742.

239   CZA S6/2740.

240   Lvov Engineers' Organization, CZA S6/2742.

241   January 7, 1936, CZA S6/2742.

organizations' reports on the number of their members and on the extent of their Zionist activities, which can be gleaned from the audits conducted in 1936 of several craftsmen organizations. The audits disqualified members who in fact were not professionals or not of the appropriate age (25-45). Additionally, the following activities of the various branches were reviewed: Study of Hebrew, the extent of branch, activities, the political affiliations of the members, the size of the branch, the extent that fraud was being practiced, the age and profession of the registrants, and the level of their professional expertise. As a result of the audit, many branches were disqualified, mostly "Zionist Professionals," "Religious Professionals," "HaBoneh," and relatively less branches of "Haoved." Due to a financial shortage, the audit was discontinued after a third of the branches were checked.[242]

The speed with which many groups of craftsmen organized as soon as the decision was made that only members of organized groups would be allowed to immigrate to Palestine; the large number of these groups; their wide variety; and the attempts to distort the data on their size and activity – all these testify to the desperate desire of Polish Jews to emigrate and their attempt to exploit all avenues – even the narrowest ones – to *Aliyah*. Despite the great efforts made by Polish Jewry in organizing craftsmen, the number of those who achieved *Aliyah* within this framework was tiny, not more than 1,000 immigrants, which constituted only one or two percent of all immigrants who were successful in coming on *Aliyah* from Poland in the 1930s. Contrary to official policy, those craftsmen who were selected individually accounted for a much higher

---

242   From the Lvov Zionist Office to the Aliyah Department, June 19, 1936, CZA S6/2313.

proportion (14 percent) of all immigrants to Palestine. Zionist artisan organizations had to compete for immigration licenses with non-Zionist organizations. Complaints about this were voiced, for example, by P. Steinwachs, a representative of the Association of Jewish Professional Organizations in the League for the Working Palestine, and a representative of the Executive Committee of the General Histadrut of the Workers in Palestine in their application to the Jewish Agency's *Aliyah* Department:

> Our members in Poland have often encountered the strange phenomenon that members of Bund professional associations receive named *Aliyah* licenses as invited workers by industry owners. There are also cases of direct inquiries from industry owners to these associations whose orientation is clearly anti-Zionist. These facts raise the prestige of these associations and humiliate the professional labor associations of Eretz Israel, not to mention the direct damage to our enterprise in Eretz Israel by bringing persons of dubious and possibly destructive philosophical leanings to our industries in Eretz Israel.[243]

Much can be learned from the statistical reports of the Warsaw Zionist Office about the characteristics of middle-class immigrants who came to Palestine within the framework of The Workers' *Aliyah*: About one-third of the licenses for artisans were given to bachelors, and about two-thirds – to men with families. The average family size was 3.1 persons, which means a typical family

---

243   April 27, 1938, CZA S6/2740.

was composed of two parents and one child. Almost all immigrant craftsmen (95 percent) were of working age, most of them aged 18-35, and a minority aged 35-45 years. The percentage of those older than 45 was negligible. The number of women was slightly higher than the number of men. Hence there were women, especially single women, who were granted licenses independently and not just as companions to men. About half of the adults who came on *Aliyah* in this category were defined as not professional; most of them were women, the wives of the certificate holders. A large majority of the professionals (about 80 percent) were craftsmen, and about 10 percent were farmers.

Aliyah of Professional Workers – "Experts"

Another category of middle-class members included in the working immigration were the "Professional Workers" and the "Experts," who were assigned unique immigration arrangements. Until 1933, the professional laborers were personally selected by the Warsaw Zionist Office according to the number of licenses received for this category. Beginning in 1933, more and more "experts" were workers commissioned by industrialists in Palestine on lists sent from Palestine.[244] Owners of industrial establishments in Palestine and farmers were given the opportunity to locate professional workers in Poland that would be useful to them, and to obtain

---

244 Report from the Warsaw Zionist Office on the Aliyah Movement, CZA S6/5342. Some of them were invited by employers through lists of names sent from Palestine (Part A), and some of them came due to specific requests by workplaces, but their names were not submitted on a list; instead, they were selected by the Zionist Offices (Part B).

immigration licenses for them. In retrospect, it turned out that this channel was utilized to a great extent in order to bring relatives to Palestine. Lists of names of workers were prepared in Palestine by the Manufacturers Association and by the *Aliyah* Department and transferred to the Warsaw Zionist Office, which examined the qualifications and handled the *Aliyah* of these workers. Again, regarding this issue as with many others, disagreements arose between the Warsaw Zionist Office and officials in Palestine. The Warsaw Zionist Office alleged that improprieties were rampant in the choice of immigrants due to the overwhelming preference shown to relatives. In a study conducted by the Office in which 1,981 candidates were examined, the results indicated that most of them were relatives of the inviters, and some of the invitees were not professionals at all.[245] A poll conducted in Palestine among 49 immigrants who arrived upon the demand from industrialists in 1935-1934 supports these claims. In another survey conducted in October 1935 that included 168 industrial workers it was found that 47 percent were never even employed by their inviter.[246]

The Manufacturers' Association involved in organizing the *Aliyah* of "the experts" appointed a representative on its behalf in Poland.[247] This lessened the influence of the Warsaw Zionist Office on the examination of candidates and gave control to the Manufacturers' Association in Palestine and their representative in Poland. The managers of the Warsaw Zionist Office attributed the

---

245 During the reporting period: January 1935 – March 1937, CZA S6/4931.

246 Department of Statistics, Aliyah Department, Census of Industrial Workers, December 1, 1935, CZA S19/49.

247 Report from the Warsaw Zionist Office, CZA S6/5342.

"infiltration" of non-Zionists into "the experts" category to the lack of their control over which candidates would be chosen for *Aliyah*:

> From the beginning of the allocation of special licenses to industrialists, we demanded that the Warsaw Zionist Office determine which experts would be assigned to the various trades, as requested by the industrial plants in Palestine, so that we could ensure that these people are proper Zionists. However, the Manufacturers' Association in Palestine opposed this. Even the request that the Zionist Office have the power to revoke an immigration license if it becomes clear that the candidate in question is not a Zionist – this, too, was rejected by the Manufacturers' Association.[248]

The procedure involved in the *Aliyah* of professional workers caused difficulties in full utilization of the license quotas because they were assigned by name, and thus non-transferable in cases where the original licensees did not make *Aliyah* or were found unsuitable. Indeed, many of those named on the lists were found to be inappropriate by the Warsaw Zionist Office. In 1936, 52 of the 360 experts named on a list sent from Palestine were disqualified by the Zionist Office, resulting in more than fifty precious licenses for *Aliyah* going to waste.[249] The list of *Aliyah* candidates in the category of experts, in the fall 1935 quota sent to Warsaw, included 404 names. Of these, 247 experts were approved for *Aliyah*, which means 157

---

248   Sheffer and Reiss to the Aliyah Department, June 28, 1938, CZA S6/2739.

249   Report from the Warsaw Zionist Office, CZA S6/4931.

candidates, who made up about 40 percent of the list, were found unsuitable. The primary reasons for this were lack of appropriate professional credentials, forgeries, and a lack of Zionist affiliation. Seventy-eight of the 247 eligible candidates failed to produce the passports or professional certificates required by the consul, and thus, although 256 licenses were obtained, only 169 could be utilized, and 78 licenses went down the drain.[250] In order to use all the licenses, lists much larger than the number of certificates that would be approved should have been sent from Palestine. However, this would have come at the cost of creating false hopes and unrest among the *Aliyah* candidates and their families in Palestine, due to the impossibility of knowing until the very last moment whether they could immigrate. Thus, the decision-makers found themselves trapped between two poor choices: losing a significant portion of the certificates or building up tension among the potential immigrants, their families, and their acquaintances in Palestine.

For industrialists in Palestine as well, arranging for the immigration of those with the expertise they needed was complex and prolonged. For example: an entrepreneur from Lodz was planning to set up a knitting factory, and to transfer capital and machinery to Palestine, for which he needed 10 expert workers from Poland. His case was discussed in the Industry and Commerce Department of the Jewish Agency, which contacted the *Aliyah* Department with a recommendation to assign 10 licenses. The *Aliyah* department allocated only six licenses. The entrepreneur had to choose the six candidates. He did so, and the names of the six were transferred to the Warsaw Zionist Office, which examined their suitability. The

---

250   Reiss to the Manufacturers' Association in Tel-Aviv, October 2, 1935, CZA S6/2737.

results of the assessment were forwarded to the *Aliyah* Department, which contacted the government representatives in Palestine with a request to arrange for them. Only five licenses were accepted, and these were sent to Warsaw. Visas had to be arranged at the British Consulate in Warsaw within 10 days, and permission of entry was limited to a period of only three months.[251] It is unclear how many of the five candidates were able to arrange their certificates in such a short time and to immigrate. The factory owner, in any case, had to settle for only half of the experts at best.

In another case, six weaving experts were required. The factory representative went to Poland to assess the applicants, and each of them was required to transfer £100-200 to the Jewish Agency in Palestine for investment in the plant, and another £100 to build a residential apartment for the would-be immigrant.[252] Apparently, the *Aliyah* of professional workers entailed, at least in part, payment to the industrialists who invited them. This is corroborated by an incident that occurred in the town of Wolomin in 1935. A factory owner from Palestine arrived at this town, who sold certificates to industrial workers who were applying for *Aliyah* as "experts." One of these candidates paid her 1,500 zlotys (£60), and another – 200 zlotys (£8). A representative of the Warsaw Zionist Office who was sent to investigate the issue received the impression that "the sale of certificates" by factory owners was acceptable practice

---

251 Correspondence between the Department of Industry and Commerce and the Aliyah Department of the Agency, the Immigration and Government Statistics Department, and the Warsaw Zionist Office, CZA S6/2738.

252 Conclusions of a conversation regarding licensing for experts – November 15, 1936, CZA S6/2738.

in Poland at the time.[253] In response to this report, it was decided in the *Aliyah* Department to no longer approve the requests of said factory for immigrant employees. Another complaint in this vein was made against another factory in Tel Aviv.[254] Figure 23 below outlines the complicated process of obtaining certificates of *Aliyah* for "the experts."

253 Report of the investigator in Wolomin, September 8, 1935, CZA S6/2870.

254 Senator to the Aliyah Office in Tel-Aviv, October 29, 1936, CZA S6/2738.

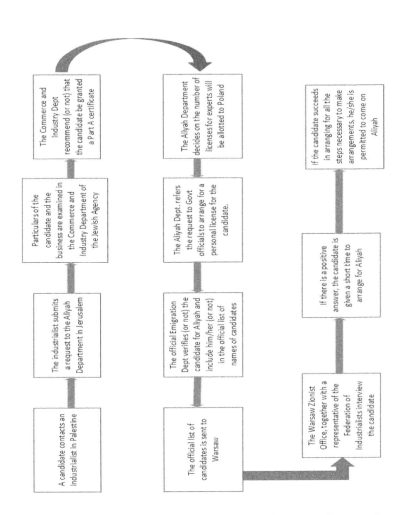

Chart 10: Process for receiving a certificate in the Part A framework

The *Aliyah* of Halutzim (Pioneers)

The *HeHalutz* movement, which trained young people for *Aliyah* and work, directed its members mainly toward agricultural work due to the central place of agricultural settlement in Zionist ideology, and to the agricultural needs of the country. Within the framework of agricultural settlement, the *HeHalutz* movement favored cooperative settlements, especially the kibbutzim. The world center of the *HeHalutz* movement sat in Poland, where 40-50 percent of all members of the movement could be found. The movement reached its peak in Poland in 1934, where it counted some 50,000 members.[255]

From 1930 to 1939, almost 17,000 *halutzim* immigrated to Palestine, representing 22 percent of all immigrants from Poland. The proportion of *halutzim* among all immigrants from Poland decreased during the 1930s from 35 percent in 1930 to 16 percent in 1937, and only in 1938 did the rate rise again. Why and how did this process occur? In 1929, the *HeHalutz* movement in Poland was still the main source of the Working *Aliyah*, but due to a lack of resources at the Jewish Agency, the Zionist Histadrut began to give a growing share of workers' licenses to relatives and later also to the middle class; thus, the proportion of the *HeHalutz* movement in the overall *Aliyah* decreased.[256] The demand for *Aliyah* among the *halutzim* also changed: The harrowing events of August 1929 initially created an atmosphere of "*davka* (retaliation)," when a relatively large number of *halutzim* came on *Aliyah* (about 1,100 in 1929 and close to 900 in 1930). The proportion of settlers in the kibbutzim

---

255   Sarid (1979) p. 478

256   Halamish (2006) pp. 164-165

was high (74 percent), and the absorption of these new immigrants went well. But after a few months the wave of enthusiasm faded. Parents tried to stop the *Aliyah* of their children, the candidates delayed their *Aliyah*, and thus the number of immigrant *halutzim* in 1931 did not exceed five hundred. Beginning in 1932, with the improvement in the economic situation in Palestine and an increase in the wave of immigration, the number of immigrant *halutzim* also increased and even peaked, as the overall *Aliyah* did, in 1935. In 1936 and 1937, the number of immigrant *halutzim* decreased, but in 1938, with the opening of indirect and illegal ways to immigrate, the number of *halutzim* rose again. The potential for *Aliyah* among the candidates of the halutz movement was strongest among the members of training groups – "*Hachshara*" – who formed the ideological and practical spearhead of the movement.

Throughout the period, the number of members in *Hachshara* in Poland was higher than the number of immigrant *halutzim*. In 1929-1931, the number of members in *Hachshara* was only twice as high as the number of immigrants, so the chance of *Hachshara* members coming on *Aliyah* was relatively high. Beginning in 1932, the gap grew considerably, and by 1934 it reached a point where there were five times as many *Hachshara* members as immigrant *halutzim*, meaning that only 20 percent of *Hachshara* members could immigrate to Palestine. This considerable gap continued in the years to come. The year 1937 was the most difficult for members of the *Hachshara* program in Poland. The chance of *Aliyah* dropped by at least 10 percent. In 1938, the number of members of *Hachshara* decreased, and the chance of *Aliyah* through unofficial means increased.

To qualify for training and immigration, the candidate had to invest time and financial resources in studying Hebrew and Zionist training, and when staying in training before receiving the immigration permit was extended from several months to years, the attractiveness of this path to immigration decreased. Sometimes a payment was required just to qualify for the training program.[257] *Hachshara* members whose *Aliyah* was postponed remained "suspended between heaven and earth," since they had severed their ties with their hometowns and their families during the long training period. When they returned to their towns destitute, an atmosphere of despair and resentment was created around them. They had lost years of earning a living and trying to build their lives. The more disillusioned *Hachshara* members were – the less the desire of the movement's members to join the *Hachshara* kibbutzim.

When opportunities for *Aliyah* opened up toward the middle of the decade, masses of young people sought to join the movement. The phenomenon caused much deliberation and controversy in the *HeHalutz* movement and the Zionist establishment. All concerned recognized that including the masses would come at the cost of lowering the level of the movement's Zionist idealism. Many of the newcomers saw the movement as a "springboard" or "rescue board" that would enable them to achieve *Aliyah* and they lacked the Zionist fervor of the graduates of the youth movements and the veteran pioneers.[258] Concomitantly, as the ranks of the movement expanded, the overall educational and intellectual level of the *halutzim* decreased. Instead of consisting of a majority of graduates of high schools, as was the case in the past, working class youth flooded the movement. The leadership of the *HeHalutz* movement

---

257   Sefer (The Book of) Yagur (1964) p. 281.

258   These halutzim were called "certificants"; "*stam halutzim*"; "emigrants." Oppenheim (1993) p. 35.

debated between opening the gates of the movement to all who approached, which could have ensured it hegemony in the Working *Aliyah* due to its size, and strict selecting of the candidates, which would most likely ensure its ideological strength. The Jewish Agency's management and the Histadrut (Federation) of Workers in Palestine also debated this issue. The policy changed from time to time: At the beginning of the decade it was decided to expand the ranks of the movement, but due to complaints in Palestine about *halutzim* who left the kibbutzim, at a time when the fulfillment of the kibbutz ideal was the main criterion for assessing the ideological strength of the "human material" of the movement, it was decided in 1932 and 1934 to apply strict norms, which the *halutzim* referred to as "decrees," as a condition for entering *Hachshara* and obtaining an *Aliyah* license. The ideological strength, social suitability, knowledge of Hebrew and familiarity with Zionism of each candidate were examined.[259] The number of members in the halutz movements and the *Hachshara* programs varied according to the severity of the "decrees" and the chance of achieving *Aliyah*: the number of members increased as the limitations on who could be accepted were relaxed, and decreased when the conditions for joining *Hachshara* and for receiving an *Aliyah* license became stricter.

The limited number of certificates caused fierce competition among those desiring *Aliyah*. Members within the training kibbutzim, the kibbutzim within the movement, and the halutz movements competed among themselves. They all struggled together against the other categories of the Working *Aliyah*: relatives of residents of Palestine, craftsmen, experts and veteran Zionists. One of the arguments against stopping the *Aliyah* of *halutzim* was

---

259   Oppenheim (1993) pp. 206, 208.

that they were in a special and more difficult situation than other candidates for *Aliyah*: some had already given up Polish citizenship, those who were of military age could very likely be called to enlist, and many others had cut off contact with their families and did not have the means to subsist because of their long stay in *Hachshara*.[260] Many claims about the discrimination against the pioneering *Aliyah* as opposed to other pathways to *Aliyah* were referred to the *Aliyah* Department from Palestine and Poland, both from political parties and from the pioneering organizations. On November 9, 1936, the pioneering organizations in Poland – which included the "*HeHalutz*," the "General Zionist *HeHalutz*," and the "*HeHalutz* HaMizrachi" – jointly contacted the *Aliyah* Department, demanding an increase in the *Aliyah* of *halutzim*. They justified the demand by explaining that it would help meet the needs of the Jews of Palestine (recruitment of workers for the rural settlements, the port and police) and by citing the strength, size, importance, and Zionist contribution of the "*HeHalutz*" movement in Poland.[261] A similar request was sent to the Jewish Agency's management from the Executive Committee of the Workers' Histadrut, claiming that the Spring 1937 quota should be given in its entirety to the *halutzim*.

The decisive element in selecting those eligible for *Aliyah* among the *halutzim* in the training kibbutzim was their conformity with the requirements of Eretz Israel and the kibbutz.[262] The main criteria for selecting candidates among the members that were in training were seniority in training, knowledge of Hebrew, social involvement, educational and cultural activities, and a level of

---

260   Shefer to the Aliyah Department, January 14, 1931, S6/2514.

261   CZA S6/3551.

262   Sarid (1979) p. 524

idealism indicating a strong chance that the candidate would join a kibbutz and stay there. The distribution of certificates among the movements was done by a quantitative measure in accordance with the relative number of each movement's members in *Hachshara*. The Betar movement was in a special position among the pioneering movements. The movement was founded in 1924 and started to implement programs of *Hachshara* beginning in 1929. The movement expanded rapidly: Within a year the number of members of Betar's *Hachshara* reached 450, and at the height of its activity in the early 1930s, the movement's *Hachshara* numbered 1,500-2,000 members, who made up about 15 percent of all *Hachshara* members of the pioneering movements in Poland. The number of Betar members reached 70,000 at the time. The kibbutz training formula did not match the character of the Revisionist movement which advocated individualism and the development of the country on the foundation of urban-bourgeois elements, and not necessarily pioneering-agricultural ones. The Revisionist movement participated in the kibbutz *Hachshara* enterprise as a means of increasing its share of *Aliyah* opportunities, and not as an end in itself; its kibbutz training program kept dwindling until it was liquidated in the mid-1930s, with the secession of the Revisionists from the Zionist Histadrut. It was replaced with vocational training – "*Hachshara solelet* (paving)," the scope of which was limited.[263] The distribution of licenses among the movements and the number of licenses allotted the *halutzim* were not exempt from party and political considerations.[264] Small pioneering movements such as Mizrahi

---

263 Oppenheim (1993) pp. 205, 295-395.

264 For an extensive discussion of the political aspects of the distribution of licenses see Halamish (2006) pp. 190-219.

and Betar complained of discrimination vis-a-vis the *HeHalutz* movement. In response, the *Aliyah* Department in 1931 issued a disclaimer detailing the allocation of licenses. According to this publication, the share of the "*HeHalutz* HaMizrachi" was seven percent, and a similar percentage of licenses was also given to the Betar movement.[265]

Leaving for *Hachshara* involved being disconnected from home. Home was perceived by the leadership of the *HeHalutz* movement as a "rotten environment" that the *halutzim* needed to disengage from in preparation for the disengagement from family that *Aliyah* entailed.[266] In one of the *hachsharot*, the *halutzim* were not allowed to travel to their homes during the holidays, and only prior to immigration was it customary for the *halutzim* to return to their parents' home, partly to raise funds there to cover their travel expenses.[267] Despite the risk of disconnection, many parents sent their sons and daughters to *Hachshara* nonetheless, in the hope that their children would receive an immigration certificate, and be able to bring the rest of the family to follow in their footsteps to Palestine.

Unlike Germany, where the Zionist management participated in the travel expenses as part of the special mechanism that was established for German immigrants, in Poland all the expenses were shouldered by immigrants. Travel expenses to Palestine were sometimes a real problem, and many could not immigrate to Palestine because they could not finance it. With the expansion of the "*HeHalutz*" ranks and the entry of working youth into the movement, the number of parents who were able to finance their

---

265   Circular No. 137, July 25, 1932, CZA S6/2516.

266   Sefer (The book of) Yagur (1964) p. 292.

267   Oppenheim (1993) pp. 138-139, Sefer Yagur (1964) pp. 300-303.

children's expenses decreased, and there was in increase in the number of *halutzim* who had completed years of *Hachshara*, received permission for *Aliyah*, but could not actually go because of financial problems. A situation was created that favored those with means and discriminated against those without, and this caused much resentment. This is how, for example, one of those without means expressed his frustration: "I worked for three years at the kibbutz. I wasted my energy and now they come down to my life and demand money. From where should I get it? Yankel, he has money, and he will immigrate even though he has been in *Hachshara* for only a few months, and I will have to sit here for years."[268]

In order to reduce the discrimination, joint funds and foundations were established in the various movements. It is not clear to what extent the funds were used to help needy members and to what extent they funded the movement's functioning or found their way into private pockets, but it is clear that the procedure for raising money for the joint funds and foundations helped fuel rumors that spread among Polish Jews about the mechanisms of bribery and corruption involved in *Aliyah*. This is how Shalom Dovrat, a key activist of the *HeHalutz* movement in Volhynia and Lithuania, described the state of the *HeHalutz* movement:

> What should a *halutz* do who receives the permit to immigrate, the permit so longed for, if his parents do not have the means to finance his travel? We were forced to impose a higher fee than necessary on those with means, in order to finance the *Aliyah* of those with little or no means. It is our moral duty to ensure that not one

---

268   Oppenheim (1993) p. 202.

candidate for *Aliyah* who was approved by his kibbutz and by the central authorities be left in the Diaspora due to his family's precarious financial situation. Against this backdrop, innumerable frictions popped up with regard to the wealthy; suspicion and resentment emerged. The one with wealth did not always understand or want to understand, that the amount demanded of him was not sent to the central authorities but was dedicated to help his poor friend...The problem became especially complicated due to the fact that the wealthy were a minority of the minority while most of the candidates for *Aliyah* were destitute... One of the options for funding was to authorize a wealthy woman as a spouse who was willing to pay a huge sum for her right to immigrate without doing any *Hachshara* at all ... and in this way – to finance the *Aliyah* of the poor; yet in this way the poorer girls' right to accompany the immigrants as their "wives" was unfairly taken away. We got into a vicious circle that was hard to break. Well do I remember unto death the cruel joke: "You have money – you are a pioneer; you have no money – you remain in exile."[269]

The *HeHalutz* movement was more active in the eastern provinces of Poland than in central Poland. The proportion of *HeHalutz* members in relation to the size of the Jewish population in the relevant ages (19 to 26) ranged from seven percent in central Poland to 28 percent in its eastern districts. With the decline in the number of certificates, starting from 1936, many members remained in

---

269   Dovrat (1993) p. 143.

Hachshara for three to four years and some even more than five years. The phenomenon led to an increase in the age of the *halutzim*. In 1938, about 45 percent of members were aged 25 and over, 13 percent were aged 27 and over, and this included 30 – 34 year-olds.[270] Female *halutzot* made up only 20 to 30 percent of all members of the training kibbutzim, and most of them were employed in households, in the kitchen and as maids.

The immigration licenses were granted separately to male and female *halutzim*. About 40 percent of the licenses for male pioneers were given to singles and 60 percent were given to families, many of which were couples (average family size: 2.1 persons). Since the leadership of *HeHalutz* did not look favorably upon the building of families in the *Hachshara* kibbutzim, and was generally opposed to accepting married couples and parents of children, it would seem that most of the couples from among the *halutzim* who immigrated to Palestine were in fictitious marriages. As mentioned above, the possibility of attaching a spouse to an immigration certificate was given only to men, and therefore all the women *halutzim* who came to Palestine came as singles. The number of women and men among the *halutzim* arriving in Palestine was similar. Almost all these pioneering immigrants were 18-35 years old. Contrary to what one might have expected, only 10 percent of pioneers were registered as farmers, and most were craftsmen (or at least they were registered as such).

---

270   Oppenheim (1993) p. 493.

Aliyah *of* Agricultural Workers

During the 1930s, there were several initiatives by the Farmers' Association in Palestine and by independent activists to bring settlers and agricultural workers from Poland to Palestine. In this context, the activities of Zvi Lieberman and Issachar Sedkov should be noted.[271] Lieberman's activities in 1934 and Sedkov's in 1935 were carried out during a period of economic boom in Palestine, when a shortage of agricultural labor could be claimed. It is difficult to determine to what extent the Farmer's Association initiative to bring workers from abroad came to answer a real shortage of workers (even before the outbreak of the Arab revolt), and to what extent the activity's purpose was to strengthen the farmers' political power through creating another channel of immigration, unique to them.

Zvi Lieberman, one of the founders of Nahalal, came to Poland several times to recruit candidates for immigration that were suitable for agriculture. In his first trip to Poland in October 1934, Lieberman organized two immigrant groups: The first consisted of several dozen families for agricultural settlement on lands of the Jewish National Fund. Each family paid £500 to the Jewish Agency, and their licenses were allocated as part of the Working *Aliyah*. The second group that Lieberman organized was that of 100 East Galician youth, who, it was planned, would immigrate and settle on Jewish National Fund land. Each of the youth put in £80 and committed to agricultural work for at least three years. These young people were also assigned licenses under category C. By mid-1935, licenses were given to 47 young people from the group, and they

---

271   His name is also written: "Zadkov"; "Sitkov."

all immigrated.[272]

At the beginning of 1935, four hundred immigration licenses for farmers that had been jointly chosen by representatives of the Warsaw Zionist Office and the agent of the Farmers Association, Issachar Sedkov, were sent to the British Consul in Poland. The certificates were designated for men: 360 for ages 18-35 and 40 for ages 36-45.[273] The immigrants committed to at least three years of agricultural labor as farmers or agricultural workers. The innovators of this immigration pathway hoped it would open up wide as a source of *Aliyah* that would solve the labor shortage and strengthen the political power of the farmers. The agricultural committees of the rural villages of the Farmers' Union were asked to help absorb the Sedkov immigrants by offering them jobs, living arrangements and assistance with their initial absorption. They also participated in funding Sedkov's campaign. In choosing immigrants, priority was given to relatives of the Farmers' Association members, provided they had the ability to do agricultural work and were experienced. Sedkov's trip, his schedule and itinerary were published among the residents of the rural villages so that they could inform their relatives abroad about the new opportunity to obtain a certificate.[274] In Poland, Sedkov selected 350 families, all from eastern Galicia and the eastern districts of Poland, from which 250 immigrated. According to his testimony, Sedkov preferred neither to choose people who, in addition to their agricultural experience, were peddlers, "lest they be drawn after other opportunities in Palestine," nor

---

272   Reports of the Warsaw Zionist Office, CZA S6/ 4931, S6/ 5342.

273   Gruenbaum to Warsaw, February 21, 1937, CZA S6/2522.

274   Circular of the Farmers' Association of Eretz Israel, January 13, 1935, Netanya Archives, File 23/1.

did he prefer agriculturists who had another profession, all because of the danger that due to a lack of professionals in Palestine, these immigrants would move to the cities. He also avoided choosing wealthy farmers for fear they would not adapt to work as day laborers, which proves that the purpose of bringing these immigrants was that they serve as laborers in the rural villages.[275] Thus wrote Eliezer Schiff of Even-Yehudah in his memoirs, about his attempt to immigrate as part of the *Aliyah* organized by Sedkov:

> I wrote to my brother-in-law to help me get a certificate. He requested me as an agricultural worker, but I was not a member of any party and I had no chance at *Aliyah*. He wrote to me about the *Aliyah* emissary Sitkov who was in Warsaw. I traveled to the Jewish Agency office and saw who he was choosing – sturdy country guys wearing boots, and I...a yeshivah student. Sitkov asked me to show him my hands and of course I was disqualified. I went to *Hachshara* because the truth was that I really wasn't used to manual labor. I got a certificate and immigrated. My *Aliyah* was difficult for my parents, as if I were converting to Christianity. The Rabbi of my yeshivah told me before I left: "It's not for you, you won't be able to work and tolerate the high heat there." Out of the whole *Hachshara* group, we – the brother of A., Chaim, who was the brother of Y., and myself – were saved from the Holocaust.[276]

---

275   *Bustanai*, 3, May 1,1935, p. 10.

276   Gara (1988) p. 141.

Even among Sedkov's people, the number who wanted to immigrate was greater than the number of licenses, and a group of 24 families remained in Galicia that were not included among the immigrants. According to the directors of the Lvov Zionist Office, "these unfortunate people" came day in and day out to the *Aliyah* Office in Lvov, and "the cries and screams could not be borne."[277]

In Poland, groups who were interested in agricultural settlement organized themselves by their own independent initiative. In Warsaw, a company called "Avodat Yisrael (Work of Israel)" was organized, which purchased 3,500 dunams in the village of Atta (Kfar Ata). The company sold lots of various sizes to a group of Jewish families in Warsaw, and based on this purchase, the settlers requested immigration licenses from the government's Immigration Office and from the Jewish Agency.[278] Another cooperative that was involved in immigration was a cooperative of gardeners ("export-import") who operated in Warsaw and organized courses in agriculture and horticulture. A group of 17 gardeners organized for immigration and applied to the Jewish Agency through the Farmers' Association in Palestine.[279] About six months after the appeal, Gruenbaum instructed the Warsaw Zionist Office to check the applicants before approving their immigration. The immigrants were assigned to work in the properties of the Farmer Association's members, and thus to replace the Arab workers in these places.

---

277   Dr. Stopp and Dr. Shmorak to Dr. Senator, CZA S6/3572.

278   Barlas of the Aliyah Department, August 14, 1934; Gruenbaum to the Supervisor

Of Immigration and Statistics, October 8, 1934; from the Zion American Community to the Aliyah Department

November 15, 1934; CZA S6/3100.

279   June 11, 1934; June 16, 1934; CZA S6/2521.

Their wages were set at £200 per day, wages that were too low to support a family, and therefore only singles could immigrate within this framework. The licenses were to be granted under the framework of the four hundred licenses allocated to the Farmers' Association. The immigrants were required to have a minimum of three years of agricultural work experience.[280] Another example of a private immigration initiative was the "Pardes" savings cooperative, which operated in Warsaw in 1933, and which organized a group of middle-class settlers who were supposed to establish orchards in Israel.[281] The company signed a contract with the planting company "Yachin" regarding the planting of 20 orchards for the first 20 members of the group. The Jewish National Fund and the Department of Settlement allocated 400 dunams in Wadi al-Hawarith (Emek Hefer) to 20 farms: In each farm, 10 dunams were allocated to orchards and 10 dunams to other branches of the farm's enterprise. The cost of the initiative was estimated at £580 per member, and the cooperative members deposited sums of £300-500 in the banks in Palestine.

The activities of private groups with regard to agricultural settlement sometimes ended in grave disappointment. Rabbi Taub of the town of Jablonna initiated a registration for agricultural settlement. Two hundred and fifty families paid a part of the required amount, and he promised to arrange their settlement on the lands of the "Hachsharat Hayishuv (Settlement Training)" company. The relationship with Rabbi Taub was cut off and it was later discovered that the "Hachsharat Hayishuv" had no knowledge of any details

---

280   Gruenbaum to Warsaw, December 7, 1934, CZA S6/2522.

281   Gruenbaum on behalf of the "Pardes" cooperative in Warsaw to the Jewish Agency's management, May 25, 1933, CZA S6/2519.

regarding this venture, so the money paid went down the drain.[282]

In the mid-1930s, another route was opened for the *Aliyah* of agriculturists. It was a "tourist-worker"[283] route designed for relatives of farmers in the rural villages who received a temporary license from the government for a three-year period to employ relatives in their farms. In order to ensure that the invitees did not stay in Palestine, the inviter had to deposit a guarantee of £100. The immigrant received a one-year certificate which was renewed every year until the end of the three years allotted to him. The renewal of the license was contingent upon the tourist being employed in the farm of the inviting relative.[284]

Aliyah of Owners of Capital

The Capital Owners category included several subcategories: capital owners of £1,000 and above (A1), who were the only ones who could practically freely obtain immigration licenses; independent professionals and capital of £500 (A2); craftsmen with capital of £250 (A3); Steady income earners (A4); specialized professionals and capital between £500 and £1,000 (A5). The vast majority of immigrants from Poland who were members of this category had £1,000 or more in capital, a minority of them were craftsmen with £250 capital, while the number of immigrants in the other subcategories of equity holders was negligible. The share of capital holders

---

282   *N.P.,* December 10, 1932.

283   In the statistical reports of the Warsaw Zionist Office, this category was called H/C.

284   Ariav, Secretary General of the Farmers' Association, to the Agricultural Committees, July 28, 1935, Netanya Archives File A/23.

in the total immigration from Poland in the 1930s was nine percent.

People who could prove to the British authorities that they could transfer at least £1,000 worth of capital (money, machinery or property) to Palestine allegedly received free immigration licenses, but the procedure for obtaining the license, which was changed from time to time, was complex and led to only partial realization of the potential for *Aliyah* in the category of equity owners.[285] In the 1920s, approval was required from the rulers of Palestine for each immigrant. In the early 1930s, candidates had to submit applications through the Warsaw Zionist Office and the immigration arrangements were carried out by the British Consulate in Poland. In early 1933, the procedure was changed: Those interested in *Aliyah* as an owner of capital applied to the consul through the Warsaw Zionist Office and declared his capital. The consul forwarded the request to Palestine. After a while, the candidate received a one-year entry permit and had to transfer his capital to Palestine even before obtaining the visa. The complex procedure meant that from the time the application was submitted, eight to 10 months passed until a response was received. During this time, economic and security conditions in Palestine and Poland could change and immigration considerations could change with them. Beginning in April 1934, a new procedure was introduced that made the process even more difficult: Capital owners were required to first transfer their capital to Palestine and wait for an answer. This required them

---

285   The class of owners of capital of £1,000 among Polish Jews was very small. Common opinion among Polish government officials was that some of the capital presented was fictitious: The same £1,000 under which the immigration was approved returned to Poland and served additional immigrants (Polish Consul in Palestine to the Polish Foreign Ministry, May 4, 1936, AAN-MSZ File 6270).

to liquidate their businesses and fortunes in Poland and wait for an uncertain answer. This difficulty caused some equity holders to give up on the possibility of *Aliyah* in this way. Four hundred out of six hundred applicants in the pre-April period gave up on *Aliyah* in 1934, and only two hundred of them transferred funds to Palestine under the new procedure. In August 1934, the procedure was changed again: instead of transferring the capital to Palestine, people who were interested in *Aliyah* were to deposit their capital at a bank in Warsaw in an account under the name of the consulate. The licenses were received within four to six weeks. During this period, the number of applications increased by 30 percent. In April 1935, there was further relief, such that the consul's reply was given within a week to four weeks after the deposit of the money in the bank. Under these favorable conditions, the number of immigrants with capital rose, despite the deterioration of the economic situation in Palestine toward the end of 1935. In early 1936, the conditions of *Aliyah* for capital owners changed, and this time, worsened again: most of the applications filed in January-April 1936 were delayed in the British Consulate in Warsaw, and at the end of April, the "Foreign Currency Restriction Act" was made known, which limited the amount of foreign currency allowed to be taken out of Poland. Based on this law, which was approved on April 26, 1936, the maximum amount allowed to be taken out of Poland was 500 zlotys (£20), an amount that was relevant to students and tourists but not to people with major capital.

ידידים ציונים לרגלי עלית חבריגו ד"ר מרדכי ופנינה קוימפמאן לארץ ישראל תרצ"ו

1936 Przyjaciele - sjoniści z okazji wyjazdu tow. Dr. Markusa i Pany Kaufman do Palestyny

Zionist friends in the group picture on the occasion of the *Aliyah* of their friends Mordechai and Pnina (Dr. Kaufman was honorary president of the local Zionist Committee) Source: Beth Hatefutsoth, Photo Archive, 39122, Courtesy of the World Federation of Polish Jews, Tel Aviv

From that date on, only capital owners who already had property of the required amount in Palestine could immigrate. These were not many, and thus the opportunity for *Aliyah* of owners of considerable wealth from Poland was eliminated. The Foreign Currency Restriction Law canceled the *Aliyah* of 160 wealthy families who were already prepared to immigrate and prevented new applicants from obtaining licenses. The number of licenses for capital holders arranged by the Warsaw Zionist Office fell sharply from 808 in 1935 to only 186 in 1936. In the period from January through March

1937, only 17 licenses were issued, and those, too, only to owners of equity in Palestine.[286]

When the legislation restricting foreign currency was enacted, contacts began between the Jewish Agency leaders and the Polish government with the aim of eliminating the injustice. In May 1936, a special delegation of the heads of the Agency went to Poland, with the participation of Dr. Senator, Dr. Rottenstreich, and H. Farbstein, for discussions with the authorities about the FCRA, but these efforts were unsuccessful.[287] In the Warsaw Zionist Office, a select committee was established for the FCRA and "Clearing" (a method of financial accounting based on mutual payments, in this case – creating a balance in the volume of foreign currency transferred from Poland to Palestine and from Palestine to Poland).

The committee tried to get permission to transfer money out of Poland in various forms, for example, to get a permit to spend 1,000 zlotys (£40) per immigrant – but the Polish authorities did not comply with these requests.[288] The FCRA Law severely hampered *Aliyah*. In an article in *BaDerech*, Landman pointed to a sharp decline in the number of immigrants with capital at the end of 1936. "Among the reasons that led to the decline in the number of immigrants with property and especially in the number of those coming from Poland – the FCRA law was first and foremost, as it prevented the ability to move capital abroad." Doubts and property owners had to stay in Poland because they could not transfer their

---

286 Reports of the Warsaw Zionist Office, January 1935 – March 1937, CZA S6/4931.

287 Confidential, Consul General of Poland in Palestine to the Polish Foreign Ministry, May 4, 1936, AAN-MSZ File 6270.

288 From Sheffer to Dobkin, September 5, 1938, CZA S6/1519.

236 | I CHERNIAVSKY

money to Palestine." Landman theorized that while owners of capital had always been wary of transferring their assets to Palestine, "when the FCRA restrictions arrived, those doubts ended and the capital owners felt compelled to remain in Poland because of the impossibility of transferring their wealth to Palestine."[289] The FCRA Act also hampered the possibility of the *Aliyah* of craftsmen. In September 1935, the British Consul in Poland received seventy licenses for craftsmen who possessed capital of £250. After the law came into force, 13 of these families, who were already granted an immigration license, were forced to stay in Poland since they could not transfer the £250 to Palestine.[290]

The clearing contract that replaced the FCRA Law was an agreement in which it was decided to balance the volume of money transfers from Poland to Palestine and from Palestine to Poland. The law was supposed to solve the problems created with the legislation of the FCRA. On March 5, 1937, a "Clearing" contract was signed between the government of Poland and the Jewish Agency representative, but this law was also ineffective in solving the problem of the ability of capital owners to immigrate.[291] The exchange contract was based on the goal of balancing the capital transferred from Poland to Palestine and back. The agreement included all types of capital transfer from Poland to Palestine and from Palestine to Poland: foreign trade, tourism, transfer of capital of immigrants, transfer of funds from Poland to Palestine, transfer of funds from

---

289   *BaDerech*, March 18, 1937.

290   Reports of the Warsaw Zionist Office, January 1935-March 1937, CZA S6/4931.

291   See Halamish. (2006) pp. 261-267 for an extensive discussion of an exchange contract from the point of view of immigration policy.

Poland to Palestine (to students, students and family members) and transferring funds from Palestine to family members in Poland. Landman, as reported by *BaDerech*, thought that the FCRA Law was the primary cause preventing the *Aliyah* of many capital holders and reckoned that nullification of the FCRA and the signing the clearing contract would solve the problem:

> Due to the signing of the clearing agreement between the Jewish Agency and the Polish government, the restriction of the removal of capital from Poland no longer hinders the transfer of the property wealthy Jews from Poland to Palestine. It has thus removed one of the most significant factors that have hindered the *Aliyah* of owners of capital.[292]

The lifespan of the clearance agreement was short. Merely one year later, on May 1, 1938, the Polish government canceled the settlement due to the excess foreign exchange transfer from Poland to Palestine. The volume of foreign exchange transferred from Poland to Palestine was much greater than that transferred from Palestine to Poland. In that year, a million and a half zlotys of the clearing money accumulated in the clearinghouse awaiting disbursal, but the disbursal sources in Palestine were blocked. The sum that accumulated and awaited transfer was comprised primarily of monies from tourists, immigrants, tuition for academic institutions for advanced studies in Palestine, and scholarships for students. The imbalance caused problems. Tourists arriving in Palestine could not access their money, and a problematic situation was created

---

292   *BaDerech*, June 18, 1937.

in educational institutions where students from Poland studied. The Warsaw Zionist Office was forced to advise applicants not to deposit money into the clearing account:

> In recent weeks there has been unrest for this kind of *Aliyah* [of owners of capital in excess of £1,000]. These people appeal to us daily and unfortunately, most of them, who had no previous property in Palestine, leave us as they came, with no way of giving them any clear information regarding if and when they will have a legal option for capital transfer and for *Aliyah*. The unrest and movement of the aforementioned type is proven by the movement of tourists from these circles from Poland who traveled during the spring season to Palestine in an extent unseen for the past two years. . . Obviously, if not for the problem of the transfer of wealth, we would be witnessing a large increase in the *Aliyah* of capital owners.[293]

In the situation that was created, organizations outside the Jewish Agency – the Revisionists, Agudat Yisrael, the Poland-Palestine Chamber of Commerce – tried to reach separate agreements with the Polish government and gained some cooperation. However, this effort also did not produce results.[294] The number of capital owners immigrating rose to a peak in 1935, a year that saw more than 2,300 capital owners immigrate. In 1936, only 564 capital owners made *Aliyah*, and in 1937 their numbers dropped to 153.

---

293   Kashtan to the Aliyah Department, May 11, 1938, CZA S6/3555.

294   Halamish (2006) pp. 264-265.

As mentioned above, the immigration of capital owners who owned £1,000 and above was not limited in principle by the Mandate government. That is why those who were working with immigrants in Palestine and Poland were interested in uncovering the reasons for the decline in the number of immigrants with capital after 1936. At the time, the decline was attributed to two major factors: the Arab revolt in Palestine and the restrictions on foreign currency withdrawal from Poland. Both reasons were raised simultaneously by different activists and even by the same activist himself under different circumstances. In September 1936, Reiss, chairman of the Warsaw Zionist Office, argued that the Arab revolt in Palestine did not affect the desire to immigrate: "Despite the revolt, there is still great pressure from those who want to immigrate. All the certificates were utilized, and even those with [unsatisfied] requirements were not deterred from coming to Palestine."[295] In the report of the ministry's activity for the period from January 1935 to March 1937, the author noted that as a result of the FCRA, the *Aliyah* of those with significant means and other immigrants with property who already held entry permits was almost completely halted because of the inability to transfer the capital to Palestine. He noted, however, that it is possible that capital owners might be additionally deterred by the troubling events in Palestine. On June 8, 1938, during an internal plenary session (the plenary session of the Warsaw Zionist Office), Sheffer, the director of the Warsaw Zionist Office, noted that the reduction in the *Aliyah* of capital holders was caused, in particular, by the FCRA restrictions. At that meeting, Reiss said:

---

295   Plenum Session, September 23, 1936, CZA S6/1505.

> The *Aliyah* of capital owners has been completely dev-
> astated due to the FCRA … The interest of capital own-
> ers in immigration is great, and if we could have opened
> a wider opening for this *Aliyah*, we would have brought
> about an improvement in the situation in Palestine.[296]

A few weeks later, in his letter to the Immigration Department on
July 26, 2008, Sheffer attributed the cessation of the *Aliyah* of capital
owners to the Arab revolt:

> The events that took place in Palestine for the past few
> weeks, and are still happening, have had and continue
> to have a negative impact on the immigration move-
> ment from Poland. The requests of capital owners that
> previously was overwhelming, to the point of 15-20
> daily requests, has virtually ended.

It is likely that in contacts with external parties, it was more con-
venient for the officials of the Warsaw office to blame the cessation of *Aliyah* on events in Palestine rather than on the situation
in Poland, for which they had some degree of responsibility. The
assumption that the Arab revolt was the main factor that deterred
capital owners from immigrating was acceptable to many in the
1930s. It was adopted in contemporary research, mainly based on
newspaper reports in Palestine and the positions of officials in
the *Aliyah* Department.[297] Thus, for example, data is presented to
allegedly prove that with the signing of the exchange contract

---

296   CZA S6/1515.

297   Halamish (2006) pp. 265-267.

following the Clearing Law, the Warsaw Zionist Office appealed to 160 capital owners whose *Aliyah* had been prevented by the FCRA, and with the enactment of the Exchange Law they would now be able to immigrate. However, only 15 of those shareholders responded positively to the Warsaw Zionist Office.[298]

At an executive meeting of the Warsaw Zionist Office on February 21, 1939, Dobkin, director of the Immigration Department, noted that there are no capital owners who want to make *Aliyah*. It is unclear what Dobkin's impression was based on at a time that only those whose property had already been transferred to Palestine could immigrate. It is more likely that given the negligible chance of obtaining an immigration permit, more capital owners did not contact the Warsaw Zionist Office in this regard, which might have created the impression that they were not interested in *Aliyah*. It is important to note that the agency's Immigration Department did not encourage the *Aliyah* of capital owners who had already transferred their wealth to Palestine. According to Dobkin in the same meeting: "We might have considered those capital owners who already have assets in Palestine, but what is of first and foremost importance to us is the *Aliyah* of capital owners who will transfer funds from here, and in this area, nothing has yet been achieved."[299]

A detailed examination of the fluctuations in the number of immigrants with capital from Poland supports the view that what prevented their *Aliyah* was not necessarily the fear of the Arab revolt: The decline in the number of immigrants with capital began as late as 1935, a few months before April 1936, when the revolt broke out. In fact, the decline in the number of immigrants with capital

---

298   *Ibid*, p. 265.

299   Executive Session, February 21, 1939, CZA S6/1523.

began in the months when the economic boom in Palestine ended. It is, therefore, difficult to determine the influence of the revolt relative to other factors - the deterioration of the economic situation in Palestine and the severe restrictions on transfer of capital from Poland – such that there is no certainty that the rebellion was the only or major cause of the decline in the number of capital owners who immigrated to Palestine.

The *Aliyah* of capital owners was mainly comprised of families. Only about a quarter of capital owners' licenses were given to bachelors, all of whom were men. The average size of a family was 3.1 persons. Contrary to what one might expect – given that this *Aliyah* was virtually the only one available to those aged 45 and over – the rate of adults among immigrants with capital was only slightly higher than the average of all immigrants during this period. Professionally, the capital owners were characterized by a high proportion of merchants, who accounted for 64 percent of those among them who were working. The second largest group (21 percent) was craftsmen.

According to a survey conducted by the Jewish Agency's Statistics Department among the capital owners who immigrated from 1933 to 1934 - about a quarter of Polish immigrants had exactly £1,000 in capital. An additional 23 percent brought in capital of £1,000 to £2,000. About 39 percent of the immigrants brought a fortune of over £2,000. It is noteworthy that among the immigrants from Germany, those that brought wealth in excess £2,000 was slightly smaller – 34 per cent.[300] As mentioned, the only group among cap-

---

300   Department of Immigration Statistics, January 29, 1936, UM S19/51. This survey only covers the years 1934-1933. The ratio of capital of immigrants from Germany to that of immigrants from Poland may have been different in other years.

ital owners in Poland who could allegedly enjoy free immigration was the group with capital of £1,000 and above. However, in the end *Aliyah* for this group was also limited because of the restrictions on capital transfers from Poland and the bureaucracy that it entailed.

Student Aliyah

Between 1939 and 1930, some 4,400 students and students immigrated to Palestine. At the beginning of the period, licenses for this category were granted by the Mandate Government without the participation of the Warsaw Zionist Office. In the opinion of the officials at the Office, some of the licensees had no intention of studying and did not fit into the category of the Workers *Aliyah*. The Office endeavored to increase its control of this immigration channel and also reached agreements with educational institutions in Palestine, according to which those recommended for immigration as students would be examined and approved by the Warsaw Zionist Office.[301] Indeed, from 1934, the Warsaw Zionist Office began to handle the immigration of students and students in Warsaw. In the summer of 1934, in preparation for the academic year of 1934, an unusually large number of immigrant licenses were received for young people to study in various educational institutions. In that year, almost 1,000 scholars and students immigrated, and in 1935 the number increased to 1,100.

Most of the immigrants in the student category were enrolled in higher education institutions - the Hebrew University and the Technion. Others enrolled in various high schools: The

---

301 Report of the Warsaw Zionist Office, CZA S6/4931, S6 5342. Plenum meeting, June 8, 1938, CZA S6/1515.

Realy School in Haifa, The Herzliya Gymnasium in Tel Aviv, the Hebrew Gymnasium in Jerusalem, The Agricultural School for Girls in *Nahalal, Mikve Israel*, A Teacher Seminary in Jerusalem, Haifa Professional School, Technion Heinrich Hertz in Tel Aviv, The Agricultural School *Ben Shemen*, Max Payne School in Tel Aviv, Religious Youth Villages, *Mishmar HaEmek* Institute, *Talpiot* Education Farm in Jerusalem and Nursing School in Jerusalem. In addition, students came to Yeshivot and religious schools, such as the Mizrachi school for young women in Jerusalem.[302]. The Council of Workers in Eretz Israel was awarded dozens of licenses for female agricultural students. Ada Fishman, the founder of the female worker agricultural industry, was sent to Poland and selected over a hundred students for this route.[303]

The studies involved tuition, and the registrants were required to prove their ability to bear the cost. Tuition ranged from about 15-30 £Palestine per year in higher education institutions, and as much as 50-80 £Palestine per year in boarding schools. Parents were required to pay, and in order to secure the payments, they were required to deposit a guarantee of 40-100 £Palestine and declare that they could afford the cost of tuition.[304] According to estimates

---

302   Kashtan to the Aliyah Department, May 11, 1938, CZA S6/3555; Sheffer to Dobkin, May 5, 1939, CZA S6/1519; Details of tuition fees, undated, CZA S6/3398; Henrietta Szold to Prof. Rashish, head of the Youth Aliyah Association in Warsaw, August 4,1938, CZA S6/3347; The Warsaw Zionist Office to the Warsaw Rabbinical Committee, October 17, 1935, CZA S6/3552.

303   Reports of the Warsaw Zionist Office October 1933 June 1935, CZA S6/5342.

304   £40 for Technion registrants, £100 for Heinrich Hertz School registrants, CZA S6/3398.

by the Polish Ministry of Finance, the amount of foreign currency required for a student in Palestine amounted to 100 £per year.[305] The immigrants in the student category, almost all of whom were students in higher education institutions, were required to have a recognized high school diploma and be part of families who had sufficient financial means to finance their studies and life in Palestine.

An important source of information about the immigrant students is the *Book of Certificate Immigrants*, which contains stories about 116 immigrants, almost all from Poland.[306] A large part of the immigrants graduated from schools of a Zionist Jewish character; in eastern Poland, mainly schools from the "Tarbut" network, and in other parts of Poland - Hebrew-Polish bilingual schools. Some of the immigrants attended Polish general schools. The great majority of these immigrants, especially those from the central and southern districts of Poland, had a deep background in Polish language and culture. Thus, Haim Brewer described it: "Poland, Poland; no Polish friend did I leave behind, only the love of romantic Polish literature still pines in my heart." Historian Joshua Prawer noted: "We spoke Polish and sometimes German. With my friends in the Gymnasium we spoke in Polish. . . I loved Polish, and composed poetry in that language. Another writer: "I learned Hebrew in Poland from the age of 7, but my mother tongue was Polish because in my home we spoke only Polish and read a newspaper in Polish." Memoir writers noted that the Polish language was common in the university and in the streets of Jerusalem, and the students spoke with each other in Hebrew mixed with Polish.[307]

The Polish Consul in Tel Aviv estimated that since the middle

---

305   Protocol from, August 17, 1938, AAN-MS file 5014.

306   Leichter and Milkov (1993).

307   *Ibid*, pp. 86, 91, 202, 212-213.

246 | IRITH CHERNIAVSKY

of the decade, younger and more educated immigrants arrived in Palestine than in the previous wave of immigration. The immigrants who came from circles of the intelligentsia were associated with Polish culture and language and differed from the Yiddish world of the previous generation immigrants.[308] Even before this wave of immigration, it was possible to point out the cultural connection of the immigrants to Poland. This was indicated by the large number of Polish translations into Hebrew. Prior to 1932, major works of Polish literature were translated into Hebrew by Mickiewicz, Sienkiewicz, Prus, Konopnicka, Slowacki, Reymont, Orzeszkowa, Zeromski, Tuwim and more.[309] In 1933, the Polish Consul in Jerusalem reported to the Foreign Ministry that much of the Jewish youth who had been thoroughly educated in Polish culture not only did not sever his cultural ties with Poland but also nurtured them by maintaining a spiritual connection with the "homeland." The consul also reported that in cities such as Jerusalem, Tel Aviv and Haifa there are private libraries with a large number of books in Polish. In contrast, in smaller settlements where many young people from Poland concentrated, there was a lack of books in Polish. The consul also initiated the establishment of a mobile library of books in Polish.[310] The connection of Immigrants to Polish culture is seen in a fascinating way in the works of these second-generation immigrants, for example in the books of Hanoch Bartov, Amos Oz,

---

308   Consul of Poland in Tel Aviv to Foreign Ministry,, January 20, 1938, AAN-MSZ file 10547.

309   Miesiecznik Zydowski (1931, 1932) pp. 183-184; 92-93.

310   Consul of Poland in Palestine to Foreign Ministry, June 1933, AAN-MSZ File 894.

Avraham Hefner and Yaakov Shabtai.[311]

Many of the student immigrants noted the high level of the schools in which they studied in Poland. For example, here is a description of the Biala elementary school:

> A large modern school, equipped with a laboratory, a workshop, and a gymnasium, at which the students studied Polish, German, arithmetic, geography, chemistry, history and more. Most of the Polish teachers had diplomas and had pedagogical talent. At the Jewish Humanist Gymnasium in Lublin Latin, German, World and Polish History, Hebrew, Bible, Mathematics were taught ... all at a very high level.[312]

One of the conditions for obtaining a student certificate was for students to be proficient in Hebrew, and indeed - most of the immigrants knew Hebrew, some even at a high level. However, some of the writers indicated that it was difficult to pass the test for all applicants administered by the Jerusalem University representative, Dr. Poznansky. Acquisition of a High school education, and particularly from private schools like those of the "Tarbut" network and the dual language schools was expensive. That is why it was mainly children from financially well-off homes who received certificates as students. The immigrants were required to deposit in the Friends of the University offices the sum of £10 in addition to the annual tuition as a deposit to be returned after completing one school year. Most probably, this was why many dropped out after the end of

---

311   Schenfeld (1997).

312   Leichter and Milkov (1993) pp. 40, 89-91.

their first year of study, others did not start school at all, and only a few of the certificate immigrants graduated from the university. Apart from the Zionist ideology, many students indicated the hopelessness in Jewish life in Poland, the harsh anti-Semitism and the Numerus Clausus as the main reasons for seeking another venue to acquire their education and for immigration to Palestine:

> I concluded that there is no future for Jewish youth in Poland. Many of the Jews who graduated from Gymnasia in Poland wandered aimlessly, as they were unable to be accepted into a university in Poland. ... I applied to the Hebrew University of Jerusalem and was accepted, ... I decided to immigrate. I knew that to arrive in Palestine I will be met with great difficulties, so I applied to the University of Padua ... The situation in the land in which we were born and raised became stressed and the future did not bode well. Anti-Semitism was on the rise, there were rumors about Hitler, and anyone who thought that going to France or Italy was not a complete solution chose to travel to Palestine ... Jews had a feeling that there was no future in Poland. The Universities closed their doors. I was admitted to the law faculty but did not go to study. There were faculties, such as medicine, that were completely closed to Jews. A new decree was enacted whereby Jews had to remain standing during the lectures; I realized that I had nothing more to do in Poland and that I had to leave. Some of my friends went to France to continue their studies, some went to Prague. ... I decided to immigrate to Palestine. It was a

bold decision. My parents saw in my *Aliyah* a route [for their own] rescue.[313]

Reading through the memoirs of the immigrant students raises a feeling of deep despair and hopelessness for Jewish life in Poland, especially concerning young people. The same feeling emerges from the autobiographies written by young Jews in Poland in an essay competition held there in the 1930s. In many homes, the young people debated whether study in Palestine or at one of the universities in Italy or France. At times it was the young people who pushed for *Aliyah*, sometimes in rebellion against the parents who feared the security situation in Palestine. In contrast, at times it was precisely the parents who influenced their sons or daughters to go to Palestine in the hope that the family could then follow. Uriel Akbia followed his father's advice to immigrate to Palestine after exploring other options for his studies: "After graduation, these options were available to me: A. Studying medicine in Paris; B. for the Rabbinate - Germany; C. Agronomy - California; or D. Literature, history, philosophy, sociology in Jerusalem. My father convinced me to immigrate to Eretz Israel."[314]

Some of the writers described their absorption in the country and in the university. Prawer believed that most of the students in the humanities were immigrants, and in these circles, an intellectual elite was created consisting of German immigrants who were equipped with knowledge of languages and in-depth knowledge of European culture. According to his impression, the Polish immigrants split according to their region of origin: Most of the immigrants from

---

313   Leichter and Milkov (1993) pp. 40, 89-91, 117, 131, 212.

314   *Ibid*, 204.

Eastern Poland, who mostly were proficient in Hebrew, applied to Jewish studies, Jewish history, Talmud and Bible. In contrast, the immigrants from Central and Western Poland applied for general studies. Those from the Central and Southern part of Poland had a broad education, most of them had difficulty speaking Hebrew and continued to speak in Polish among themselves.[315] Many of the authors cited their financial difficulties, the difficulty of finding a permanent job, and the constant race for work. This situation hurt their ability to learn. Many mentioned the help the university provided to these students; Among other things - subsidized meals and regular work on campus cleaning services.

The FCRA Laws introduced in Poland in 1936 and 1937, which stopped the transfer of funds from Poland to Israel, caused great hardship to many of the students. The Technion manager complained to Gruenbaum that many students suffer from actual famine and are unable to pay their tuition. The Technion manager was subsequently informed that the deficit in the clearing account was due to the *Aliyah* of 11 capital owners who transferred their money to Israel, thus "clogging" the sources of the clearing account. He asked: "What is more important to us from an ideological point of view of settlement - the *Aliyah* of 11 families or having hundreds of students establish their roots in the Land?"[316]

All immigrants in the various student categories arrived with bachelor's licenses. The number of men who immigrated in this group was twice that of women. The number of boys up to age 18 who came as students was scant; the vast majority of immigrants in category B were students enrolled in higher education institutions in Palestine.

---

315   *Ibid*, 214.

316   April 27,1938, CZA S6/3398.

Aliyah of Religious Functionaries

"Religious professionals" - as rabbis, religious service providers, and other religious functionaries were called- immigrated as members of category B2. Candidates for these certificates required an invitation from a religious institution in Palestine. There were instances in which applicants had to pay in order to be considered for a possible invitation. In late 1934 and January 1935, several hundred type B2 licenses (rabbis) were obtained by the Chief Rabbinate of Jerusalem and Agudat Yisrael. In 1934, some 170 religious professionals immigrated, and in 1935 about 1,500. 1935 was a record year for immigration in general and for rabbis from Poland in particular. However, in 1936, only 537 rabbis immigrated, and in the following years, this *Aliyah* stopped almost entirely.[317] Over the 1930s, about 2,260 clerics from Poland immigrated. Occasionally, people who did were not "religious professionals" immigrated in this category. For example, the Warsaw Zionist Office reported on a grocer who was licensed as a rabbi while lacking any rabbinical education. The license was obtained by the efforts of his relative in Palestine.[318] The *Aliyah* of "religious professionals" was the most "family-oriented" *Aliyah* - 95 percent of them immigrated as a family. The family size in this category was the largest - an average of 3.9 people. The percentage of those aged 45 and over was also relatively high - 20 percent.

---

317 Reports of the Warsaw Zionist Office, CZA S6/4931, S6/5342.

318 Warsaw Office to Aliyah Department, December 4, 1934, CZA S6/4931.

Aliyah of Zionist *Askanim* and Veteran Zionists

The most deprived group of aspirants to emigrate appears to have been adult Zionist "askanim." They were not assigned a separate category, and most of them could not be included in any of the other categories, mainly due to age restrictions. A report on the activity of the Warsaw Zionist Office in 1935-1933 showed hundreds of askanim who said that they wanted to immigrate. The professionals among them who were at a relatively young age were given the right of way, but no solution was found for the others. In the previous two schedules, a few special certificates were received for the veteran class, but their numbers were far from what was needed. From January 1935 to March 1937, only 50 licenses were received for the hundreds of veteran Zionists who wanted to immigrate.[319]

The minimal allocation of certificates for veteran Zionist activists caused severe feelings of deprivation among them. Thus, members of the local committee of the *Keren Kayemet* in the town of *Luboml* wrote to the chief bureau of the *Keren Kayemet* in Jerusalem: " "It is known to everyone what happens to veteran Zionists, after many years of Zionist work. When they come to the authorized institutions to try to arrange for their *Aliyah* ... and have a chance to immigrate, they are met with laughter ... Eretz Israel is not for long-standing veteran Zionists these days, not for them is the Land." The author complained about protectionism and the practice of giving and receiving bribes in the context of distributing the certificates. They demanded: "to claim the right of Zionists to immigrate.] ... [the ones extended a right to obtain certificates are those who have a wallet full of money that can offer a holy bribe to

---

319   Reports of the Warsaw Zionist Office, CZA S6/4931, S6/5342.

the office workers in the Warsaw Zionist Office"[320] Attached to the letter were the funds that had been collected by the writers for the Keren Kayemet. Many special requests for immigration by groups or individuals were sent from Poland. For example, a request was sent from the Warsaw Zionist Office for certificates to be issued to office workers who had been laid off because of budget cuts.[321] And then there was the request of the Jews of Przytyk – after a pogrom had taken place in the town – to receive certificates for the small group of 23 Zionists activist survivors.[322] An example of a request - or rather a plea - for immigration approval was made by a man named Naftali Zigel to Gruenbaum:

> Dear Sir, please do not be angry with me! I come to you once again with my long-standing request, the same request -- that is based on your promise to me at the time -- that you will send to me the very first certificate as a "veteran Zionist." ... Truth has always been the candle at your feet. ... Your promises are sacred because they are based on knowing the reality and a desire to keep your word. For this reason, I almost entirely closed all my businesses and am ready to move on. I must make *Aliyah* now, during the summer vacation, so that I can arrange for a position as a teacher in the next school year [in Palestine]. Therefore, I very much ask you, please use your influence on those who will decide these matters, as your promise remains open and demands

---

320   April 7, 1935, S6/1497.

321   Warsaw to the Aliyah Department, August 5,1936, CZA S6/3549.

322   May 10,1936, CZA S6/3550.

fulfillment... I am a courteous "Galician," polite and try
not to bother people, perhaps you noticed this about
me, but for the sake of the certificate, I must act like a
nagging wife - because I have no rest and I will not have
any until I receive the certificate. Please, dear sir, Stand
at my side!

With gratitude and blessing,
Naftali Zigel.[323]

In May 1939, a member of the Plenum at the Warsaw Zionist Office
asked Dobkin to fast-track his immigration. Dobkin's laconic
answer was: "As for your immigration to Israel - I think this is not
a relevant matter until after the [Zionist] Congress; why, therefore,
all the early steps in this regard?" ... forgive me for the lack of letters
from me and for the shortness of this letter."[324] The style of the
answer illustrates the hierarchy in the Zionist establishment and
marks the inferior status of Zionist movement activists in Poland,
and in particular - the older ones.

Aliyah in the Guise of Tourism and via Illegal Immigration

In the 1930s, a major upturn in tourism from Poland to Palestine
arose. Part of the tourism movement was, in fact, "*Aliyah* in the
guise of tourism," as many "tourists" remained in the country
illegally. A small portion of these "tourists" received afterward a
permit to immigrate afterward and became legal immigrants, but

---

323   Naftali Zigel to Gruenbaum, July 2, 1936, CZA S6/2793.

324   May 15, 1939, CZA S6/3557.

the vast majority of them continued to stay in Palestine illegally. These immigrants joined the number of official immigrants who came from Poland. Various sources present different data on the extent of tourism to Palestine and the number of tourists who stayed there. According to statistics from the Jewish Agency, almost 18,000 tourists from Poland entered the country in 1932-1939 and 3,500 of them were permitted to settle there.[325] The Polish Consul in Palestine reported to the Polish Foreign Ministry that by October 1933, 10,000 illegal immigrants remained in Palestine, out of a total of 15,000 illegal immigrants.[326] According to this estimate, two-thirds of the tourists that remained in the country illegally were from Poland. According to the State Commission of Inquiry (the Peel Commission), there were about 18,000 illegal immigrants living in Palestine at the end of 1933 who had arrived as tourists. Assuming that two-thirds of them came from Poland, then that year, there were about 12,000 illegal immigrants from Poland, a number close to the estimation of the consul. According to the estimate of Gurevich, from the Dept of Statistics of the Jewish Agency, about 17,000 tourists remained in Palestine during 1929-1933, but only 2,000 received an immigration license.[327] The estimates of Sicron were lower. According to his estimates, from all the immigrants from 1932-1933 there were about 10,000 illegals who stayed in Palestine. Out of all the tourists who arrived in Palestine from

325   GGB (1945) Tables 17 and 18.

326   Letter from Dr. Bernard Hausner, Consul of Poland in Palestine, to the Polish Foreign Ministry, October 28, 1933, AAN, Embassy of London File 902.

327   Department of Statistics, Immigration Department, January 15, 1934, CZA S19/41.

1934—1939, 9,000 settled illegally, and in all of the 1930s, about 19,000.[328] Assuming that half to two-thirds of those who stayed illegally came from Poland, the number is estimated at 10,000-12,000. In 1935, the Polish Foreign Ministry appraised the total number of immigrants, both legal and illegal, at 31,000.[329] From the reports of the Warsaw Zionist Office of that year one can learn that there were 25,000 legal immigrants (see Table 14 in the Statistical Appendix) and therefore the number of illegal immigrants non-waves in that year is estimated at 6,000, which is about a quarter of the number of legal immigrants.

Based on these figures, the total number of immigrants from Poland in the 1930s can be estimated as follows: By the low estimate - the number of tourists from Poland who settled in the country in 1930-1939 ranged from 15,000 to 18,000 (according to the other estimates, the number was higher). Added to that were more than 7,000 immigrants from Poland entered Palestine illegally in other ways (Ma'apilim). Therefore, the number of illegal immigrants in the 1930s amounted to about 25,000, which can be added to the 75,000 who immigrated legally during those years, so the total number of immigrants from Poland in the 1930s is estimated to be 100,000.

The Warsaw Zionist Office helped arrange tourist visas and mediated between potential tourists and the British Consul but did so only for "real tourists." The Warsaw Zionist Office was aware that much of this tourism was, in fact, immigration, and thus performed the initial sorting and receipt of applications, and registered only

---

328   Sicron (1957), Statistical Appendix.

329   Session Report of the Office of the Director of the Consular Department of the Foreign Ministry (undated), AAN-MSZ file 9578.

those who were appropriate applicants under the immigration laws, namely those with capital, and relatives.[330] As a result, only a small number of tourists to Palestine were treated by the Warsaw Zionist Office. For example, the ministry officials estimated that in the years 1932-1933, several tens of thousands of tourists traveled on tours arranged by various tour companies, while the office handled only a few hundred tourists during these years.[331]

Two statistical sources indicate the characteristics of tourists and the differences between the tourists who subsequently received an immigration license and the tourists who did not receive such a license. One source is a survey conducted by the Jewish Agency's Statistics Department among all immigrants who came to Israel as tourists. From this survey, one can learn about the characteristics of all tourists, including those who did not receive an immigration license.[332] According to this survey, most tourists were men: some single and some married who came without their wives. Among women, the majority was single. About three-quarters of the tourists were of working age - 18 to 45. According to Gurevich, the agency's statistician, 50-60 percent of the tourists who stayed in the country were employed, and 30-40 percent were owners of capital. Only ten percent were "dependent" on others for support. This profile fits the conditions demanded of immigrants to Israel: These immigrants needed financial means to finance the journey and the

---

330   Reports of the Warsaw Zionist Office, October 1933—June 1935, CZA S6/5342.

331   Reports of the Ministry of Land-Israel, January 1935, March 1937, CZA S6/4931.

332   Department of Statistics, Immigration Department, January 15, 1934, CZA S19/41.

initial period of stay in the country. Therefore, they had at least basic means among Polish Jews - most of them were single, working-age men – who fit into the categories of working immigration.

The second source of information regarding the tourists are the statistics compiled by the Warsaw Zionist Office, including tourists who received immigration licenses. The majority of them, as well, were single (over 80 percent). The number of men among them was twice the number of women, and the number of children was low. A high proportion - more than a third - of tourists who received an immigration license were adults aged 45 and over. Prominent among the occupations among the tourists were merchants, who made up 54 percent, and the freelancers (21 percent). A link can be drawn between this occupational structure and the economic means that were required of candidates for immigration. It should also be remembered that the license was granted only to those who managed to set themselves up in the Land. These were primarily merchants who brought merchandise along with them, enabling them to make a living in Palestine or freelance, those who were relatively older, relatives of veteran residents of Palestine

Additional information about the profiles of the tourists can be gleaned from the reports of the Polish Embassy in London. According to these reports, a large proportion of tourists had Type 1A capital, another group were relatives with recommendations, and only a small minority were from other categories. Of all the tourists reported by the Embassy who came to Palestine from Poland in the years 1935-1936, 62 percent fit the category of capital holders with £1,000, and over 27 percent fit the category of relatives with recommendations.[333]

---

333   Polish Embassy in London, AAN Case 271.

In Poland, many different groups were involved in arranging tours to Palestine: There were tourist agencies such as Orbis, Lloyd, Francophile, Polthor; there were newspapers like *Haynt, Moment, Gazeta Gospodar*cza.; and there were Zionist organizations such as the "Executive Committee of the Zionist Federation of Eastern Galicia," "Poalei Zion," "State Zionists," "Time to Build," the Chamber of Commerce of Palestine-Poland. Some of the private tourist companies were operated by past officials of the Jewish Agency.[334] Representatives of the minority parties in the Agency tried to create separate routes of *Aliyah* for their people through tourism. Farbstein, the representative of "the Mizrachi" at the Agency, arrived in Warsaw and conducted negotiations with the Polish authorities for the issuance of 2,000 discounted passports for tourists, mainly for people of the middle-class and recommended relatives. The Polish government agreed to this, but the *Aliyah* Department opposed it.[335]

Most of the immigrant-tourists remained in Palestine without a license and without citizenship because, according to immigration laws, they had to fit into one of the categories – having a capital of £1,000, students, clergy, or relatives of a permanent resident. The tourists who did not fit into these categories did not apply at all. While it was possible to obtain a permanent resident's license

---

334 The Central Bureau of HaMizrahi Federation of Poland to Gruenbaum, CZA S6/2911; Report of the Warsaw Zionist Office, CZA S6/4931; CZA S6 / 2911; Report of the Warsaw Zionist Office, CZA S6/4931.

335 Sheffer to Jerusalem and Jerusalem's response, July 12, 1932, August 2, 1932, CZA S6/5436.

For an extensive discussion of Farbstein's activities, see Halamish (2006) pp. 347-349.

through the category of the Workers' *Aliyah*, due to the fear of being deported in the event of a negative answer, few applied for this. The tourists who nevertheless applied to the Agency for certificates were mainly family members who required citizenship in Palestine in order to be able to facilitate the *Aliyah* of other family members,[336] or those who were freelance professionals who could not work in their profession without a permanent residence permit, or those who wanted to work in British commercial companies, or merchants whose work required that they leave Palestine from time to time. The tourists who were unable to obtain a permit had to live illegally in Palestine, and if they were caught – they were expelled. By the fall of 1932, the Mandate government began to take measures against the phenomenon of would-be immigrants arriving in Palestine under the guise of tourism: the Zionist Offices were required to explain to tourists and warn them that they should not hope to get certificates in Palestine, tourists were required to leave a financial guarantee that they would leave Palestine, and the number of tourists who were refused entry increased. In late 1932, visas were no longer issued to third-class tourists, and a guarantee of £40 was required of second-class tourists. In 1933, the quota was reduced as a fine for the phenomenon of tourists who remained in Palestine, and in November 1933, aggressive steps began to be taken to expel tourists, and searches were initiated to expel illegal

---

336   As a result of the Aliyah of immigrants under the guise of tourists, several hundred families remained in Poland for years, some without livelihoods and without the opportunity for Aliyah. There were many cases of "agunot" (women "chained" to a marriage whose husbands left on a journey and did not return), and family members who were neglected by those who should have been supporting them. (Warsaw Zionist Office Report, CZA S6/5342).

aliens. A £60 deposit was imposed on all tourists on ships across all classes, and they were required to present a return ticket to Poland. The hunting for tourists and deportations continued in the following years as well.[337] In 1935, the immigration authorities in Palestine issued a directive prohibiting the employment of tourists. In unusual cases, tourists could be employed, but only after obtaining permission from the authorities and depositing a financial guarantee of the tourist's departure before his visa expired.[338] With the intensification of the government's struggle against tourists remaining in Palestine illegally, incidents of exploitation of tourists spread, through false promises to arrange their affairs, informing on them, and the like. The Jewish Agency tried to assist tourists with legal advice and with obtaining licenses.[339] The cost of the trip to Palestine, and in addition, the cost of the guarantee, meant that most of the tourists were relatively affluent. This was also the common assumption among the *Aliyah* activists. Members of the Palestine-Poland Chamber of Commerce, moreover, believed that many of the tourists brought in capital that they invested in Palestine.[340] The Jewish press in Poland carried details about the danger inherent in an attempt at illegal *Aliyah* under the guise of tourism. On April 13, 1933, it was reported on the front page of *N.P.* that tourists who were suspected of being illegal immigrants were denied entry to Palestine. In November 1933, tough regulations

---

337 Halamish (2006) pp. 351-354.

338 Polish Consul to the Ministry of Foreign Affairs, AAN-MSZ, 11.6.1935 File 6269.

339 Halamish (2006) p. 353.

340 Palestine-Poland Chamber of Commerce, December 1933, CZA S6/5436.

262 | Irith Cherniavsky

were issued against tourism to Palestine: A brutal campaign by the Mandate authorities against illegal immigrants began. Many immigrants were apprehended and incarcerated – the men were sent to the Acre prison, the women – to Bethlehem, and the children – to an orphanage in Haifa. Arabs helped British police officers locate illegal immigrants.

In many cases, the tourists' journey was difficult and dangerous. In April 1935, a group of 61 tourists arrived on shore after a difficult six-week voyage on a small ship, without enough food. They were dropped off on shore in a disorderly manner and left there, and after arriving without proper direction to Tel Aviv, they were described as "destitute and depressed people wandering around in Tel Aviv."[341] In order to organize *Aliyah* disguised as tourism, it was necessary to deceive the authorities and the passengers. Thus, for example, in August 1932, several organized groups of tourists from Poland arrived in Palestine. The groups numbered from a few dozen to more than 200 tourists. Some of the tourists arrived on shore at the port of Haifa, and some continued to Beirut, disembarked there, and were transferred to Palestine via the border crossing. At the border crossing, the passports were stamped with a three-month permit, even though visas were granted for only 60 hours. It was clear to all that these "tourists" did not intend to return to Poland.[342] On August 20, 1937, the newspaper *Zman* (*Czas*) reported on a person "known as a criminal type" who organized a group of middlemen who, in exchange for 150 zlotys, pledged to provide passports and arranged trips to Palestine. On December 21, 1937, the newspaper

---

341   Lerman, Director of the Haifa Aliyah Bureau, to H. Yaffe, April 29, 1935, CZA S6/2911.

342   Correspondence between Sheffer and Barlas, 1932, CZA S6/5436.

Kurier Warszawski reported about the closure of a travel office that arranged trips to Paris, and from there – with the help of fake passports – to Palestine. In another instance, it reported that an official of the "Argos" office together with "Maher" ("Macher" – in the Polish source) organized the smuggling of Jewish immigrants under the guise of tourists to Belgium.[343]

There were cases in which "tourists" were apprehended and immediately expelled from Palestine. In March 1933, a group of 23 tourists was captured and deported to Marseille. On March 30, 1933, Senator wrote to the in Warsaw Zionist Office: "The attempt to move people through Syria has failed, and 23 people are still imprisoned. The *Aliyah* Department opposes giving priority to the people that were sent back to Marseille." Later, these people were transferred from Marseille to Warsaw, and on April 24, 1933, Kashtan wrote from the Warsaw Zionist Office to the *Aliyah* Department: "Twenty people from the group of 23 tourists, who were imprisoned at the start and returned to Poland tormented and depressed, have come to the Warsaw Office. They ask that we immediately allocate licenses to them, and they do not intend to return to their cities but will wait in Warsaw for the license."[344] These tourists were not the only ones sent back to Marseille during that period. At that time, 95 other deportees who were returned from Syria were staying in Marseille. The members of this group belonged to various Zionist organizations: Revisionists (39), the Zionist–Labor Party "Hitahdut" (39), Mizrahi (7), Time to Build (6). Another example of a failed immigration attempt was a group of women organized by the Department of Tourism, which operated alongside the Central

---

343   Wieczor Warszawski, February 16, 1938, AAN-MS File 5013.

344   CZA S6/2517.

264 | I<small>RITH</small> C<small>HERNIAVSKY</small>

Bureau of the Eastern Federation of Poland. Each paid from 1,600 to 1,800 zlotys for this adventure. The group was expelled from Palestine and sent to Athens, where the organizer abandoned it, and the women were left destitute. Later, a representative of Mizrahi was sent to Athens to rescue the group.[345] Regarding the fate of illegal immigrants captured in Palestine, H. Justus reported in *BaDerech*:

> A few days ago, I spoke to an immigrant who had just come out of the Acre prison told me all about what he had been through ... The hair stood up on my head and I still cannot shake off the terrible impression it made on me. Torments of Hell! Awful shaking and wanderings in small boats over the sea ... hunger ... and then imprisonment. "They beat us," the man tells me, "and forced us to do hard labor. I paid the one who handled our trip 1600 gold, everything I took with me, all my belongings were lost in the depths of the sea... I was left naked and destitute."[346]

Members of the Warsaw Zionist Office and *Aliyah* Department officials related negatively to the *Aliyah* disguised as tourism. This channel bypassed the immigration authorities, and so many immigrated who did not fit the set criteria. Furthermore, this *Aliyah*, at least in part, came at the expense of the orderly and supervised *Aliyah*, because the immigration authorities had to issue certificates

---

345   Central Bureau of HaMizrachi Federation of Poland to Gruenbaum, Gruenbaum to the Supervisory Board of the Mizrachi in Warsaw, November 18, 1934, CZA S6/2911.

346   *BaDerech*, March 22, 1935.

to tourists at the expense of more qualified immigrants. Members of the Warsaw Zionist Office warned every so often of the damage caused by this *Aliyah* channel. In the Plenum meetings and in correspondence with the *Aliyah* Department, the heads of the Warsaw Zionist Office repeatedly argued against *Aliyah* in the guise of tourism, and against the issuing of licenses retroactively to these tourists.[347] Senator, Director of the *Aliyah* Department, wrote to the directors of the Jewish Agency:

> The tourists who stay in Palestine apply for licenses. Responding even partially to these requests results in a significant loss of licenses (every certificate that is issued to a tourist "costs" the Agency two certificates since another certificate is deducted from the next quota) and encourages further illegal immigration. This process is negatively affecting the labor market in Palestine.

In Senator's view, the number of licenses provided to tourists should have been as few as possible.[348] There was even an attempt on the part of the Warsaw Zionist Office to intervene with the British Consul in Warsaw to stop this wave of immigration, but the attempt failed.[349]

---

347 Plenum meeting, June 17, 1936, CZA S6/4791; Report of the Warsaw Zionist Office, CZA S6/5342.

348 Gruenbaum to the Executive Board of the HaMizrachi Federation of Poland, July 2, 1934, CZA S6/2911; Senator to the Directors of the Jewish Agency, November 20, 1932, Senator, confidential memorandum, November 21, 1932, CZA S6/5346.

349 Sheffer to Jerusalem, August 3, 1932; the Aliyah Department to the Executive Board of the HaMizrachi Federation of Poland, July 2, 1934; CZA S6/2911.

In addition to illegal immigration as tourists, "*Ha'apalah* (illegal immigration)" took place, mainly by sea. Unlike tourists who arrived in Palestine with a residence permit for a certain period, these immigrants arrived without any permit. The illegal immigration began in 1934 in four voyages: In July 1934, some 340 illegal immigrants arrived on the ship *Wallace* and came ashore without interference in an operation organized by *HeHalutz* with the assistance of the Haganah. In August of that year, about 100 members of the Betar movement successfully immigrated in a similar manner, arriving on the ship *Union*. Two more voyages that followed the first successful voyages failed: In its second voyage in September 1934, the "Wallace" was captured by the British, and the immigrants returned to Poland. The second voyage, organized by Betar on the ship *Wanda*, also failed. After these two failures, the illegal immigration movement ceased until 1937. In September 1937, the United Kibbutz decided to renew "*Aliyah* B." Even earlier, in the spring of 1937, the illegal immigration of Betar members on ships that were called "*Af Al Pi Chen* (Nevertheless)" began. By the summer of 1938, five such voyages were carried out, each with a few dozen "*ma'apilim* (illegal immigrants)". In January 1938, *HeHalutz* in Poland organized an illegal immigration on the ship *Poseidon* with several dozen immigrants. From the end of 1938, the illegal immigration movement grew under the leadership of the "*Aliyah* B" enterprise, which included the "Center for *Aliyah*" of the Revisionist movement and the "The *Aliyah* B initiative" of the Haganah. From the end of 1938, until the outbreak of the War, some 17,000 immigrants arrived in Palestine. Twelve thousand of them were brought by the Revisionists and by various private groups, and 5,000 by the "*HeHalutz*" movement and the *Aliyah* B initiative. Most of those who immigrated illegally through the

HeHalutz movement and 20 percent of the Revisionist illegal im-migrants came from Poland.[350] According to these calculations, the total number of illegal immigrants from Poland in the 1930s can be estimated at approximately 7,000 persons.

For Whom among Polish Jews Was Aliyah a Real Option?

Only those Polish Jews who met the immigration criteria truly had the option of immigrating to Palestine. As we shall see below, they were a small minority among Polish Jewry before the Holocaust. The most important factor in determining immigration options was the candidate's economic situation. Only those with "major capital"— £1,000 and above — were able to immigrate freely, and even their *Aliyah* was limited in the last few years of the decade. Other immigrants were also required to have financial means: vari-ous groups in the capital category had to prove that they had £250 or £500 per person. Others were required to prove that they possessed "steady income" in the form of rent or pensions. Craftsmen were required to prove they had at least £150 in capital. Those who im-migrated as relatives of residents of Palestine had to prove that these relatives had sufficient means to support them. *Aliyah* for students was open only to those with a high-school education and knowl-edge of Hebrew, or children of families who could finance their studies in Palestine. In addition, this required the sum of £60-80 a year plus another £100 deposit. Furthermore, like all immigrants, the students were required to pay the fare for their journey in the amount of 300-400 zlotys. The *halutzim* were also required to bear the cost of the trip to Palestine. A pound sterling was then equal to

---

350   Ofer (1988) pp. 11-35.

25 zlotys. The amounts required from the immigrants were: 25,000 zlotys from the "major capital" holders, 12,500 zlotys or 6,250 zlotys from other capital holders, 3,750 zlotys from craftsmen, and 7,000 zlotys from students. These were astronomical sums compared to the wages in Poland. The wages of craftsmen during the Depression ranged from about 25 to 50 zlotys a month. During the period of prosperity earnings rose to 60-160 zlotys a month for a self-employed craftsman; 30-80 zlotys per month for a tailor in the city, and 20-40 zlotys a month for a tailor in the village.[351] The salary of an official in the Warsaw Zionist Office reached 300 zlotys a month.[352] Due to the growing impoverishment of Polish Jews, very few could afford the expense of *Aliyah*.

Given the huge gap between the number of people wanting to immigrate and the number of available immigration licenses, indirect immigration channels evolved: In addition to an increase in *Aliyah* disguised as tourism – an immigration route that required the economic means to finance the journey to Palestine, and the payment of guarantees – channels were developed to obtain licenses in illegal ways: bribes, counterfeits and so forth. All these required, in addition to determination and boldness, considerable sums of money. These demands and restrictions created, in effect, a selective *Aliyah*: only the affluent, the determined, and the courageous and resourceful of Polish Jews could immigrate to Palestine. Another criterion for selecting immigrants was age: the categories of *halutzim* and students were, of course, intended only for young people.

---

351 Landau, Tomaszewski (1981) p. 222,298; for details regarding the impoverishment of Polish Jews during the 1930s, see Mahler (1968) pp. 189-195.

352 The Aliyah Department to Sheffer, November 23, 1932, CZA S6/2515.

The *Aliyah* of relatives with recommendations was restricted up to the age of 25, and in some of the years between 1930 and 1939 – up to the age of 35. The *Aliyah* of craftsmen was also only an option for those up to the age of 35 or 45 at the most. The *Aliyah* of adults over the age of 35 or 45 was only possible within the "capital owners" category and relatives of the "requested" category.

Professional background was another criterion for immigration: Craftsmen, experts in various fields of industry, clergy and farmers could compete for a certificate in the categories made available to them within the quota of the Workers' *Aliyah*. Another essential criterion for immigration was family relationship to residents of Palestine. Only those who already had first-degree relatives in Palestine could immigrate as "recommended" or "required." Despite the limited data available, we will try to estimate the extent of the number of Polish Jews for whom immigration to Palestine was altogether a viable option:

Capital holders: We do not have data on the number of owners of major capital among Polish Jews in the 1930s, but we can estimate their numbers based on incomplete information: the £1,000 needed to immigrate as a "capital holder" was worth 25,000 zloty, a very high amount relative to wages in Poland at that time. The assumption that the number of Jewish capital holders was very small is enhanced in light of these figures: (1) Only half of the members of the large congregations in Warsaw and Lodz were assessed a community tax of 1,000 zlotys a year. Eighty percent of the members of the congregation were classified as impoverished and exempted from having to pay the community tax.[353] (2) Only about seven percent of independent Jewish businesses employed workers. (3)

---

353   Bronsztejn (1963) p. 70, 80; Mahler (1968) pp. 189-195.

Only 316 of the Jewish industrialists were "large industrialists" (factories with an average of 670 workers).[354] (4) Only about 11,000 Jews owned "medium-sized" enterprises (those with average 12 employees). (5) 86 percent of Jewish commerce was "petty commerce" – peddlers, market stalls, etc. Only 14 percent of merchants had larger businesses. (6) Of the more than 400,000 Jews engaged in retail trade, only 23,700 employed workers; (7) Only 5,800 Jews engaged in wholesale trade and less than 1,000 had employees; (8) Only 880 Jews owned real estate of 50 hectares or more. (9) Capital holders in Poland were mostly shareholders of large companies or held management positions in such companies; there were very few Jews among them.[355] According to all these figures and estimates, the number of Jewish capital owners in Poland was tiny. This assumption is also supported by the assessment of the *Aliyah* officials in Poland.[356] If we base ourselves on the maximal assumption that among Polish Jews half of the "medium-sized" industrialists and half of the merchants who employed workers possessed capital of at least £1,000, they numbered about 20,000 people at most. Since each holder of a license in the Capital Holders category could immigrate with their family, and an average family size was three, the maximum number of immigrants with £1,000 capital did not exceed 60,000, and more likely was far less. Of these, approximately 5,500 persons immigrated in the 1930s.

---

354   Mahler (1968) pp. 50, 90, 132-134, 184.

355   Tomaszewski (1993) p. 170; See also Tomaszewski's (1991) essay on the Jews of Lodz based on the 1931 Census.

356   In a report on the activities of the Warsaw Zionist Office for the years 1930-1931, the heads of the Warsaw to Office stated that there are very few with capital of £ 1,000, CZA S6/3556.

Halutzim: This category was only open to young men and women in their twenties, who made up about 10 percent of the population of Polish Jews. Therefore, the potential of number of immigrants did not exceed 300,000. However, they had to meet the conditions of training, seniority, and being judged as fit for *Aliyah*. For most of the period reviewed, competition for the small number of licenses allocated to them was extremely intense. *Halutzim* were required to finance the cost of their trip to Palestine, which was beyond the reach of many of them. Besides, their *Aliyah* entailed the separation from their families, and in many cases, the abandonment of their families in Poland who would be left without a livelihood. For many, this was impossible.

Students: Another category of young people who might consider immigration were those who could be admitted to educational institutions in Palestine, especially to higher education institutions: the Hebrew University and the Technion. In addition to financial opportunities, they had to have a high school diploma and have mastered Hebrew. The number of students who received a high school diploma among Polish Jews ranged from 2,000-2,500 a year.[357] The number of Hebrew-proficient high-school graduates in the 1930s can be estimated as no greater than 20,000 persons.

Relatives of Residents of Palestine: "Recommenders" and "Demanders." Among this group, as well, the number of immigrants was limited, and conditions were legislated that required a family relationship to the Palestine resident inviting them, who had to have sufficient economic means to guarantee the welfare of the immigrant, and the ability of the candidate to adjust to the employment needs in Palestine. In the early 1930s, there were about 40,000

---

357   School Statistics, 1935-1936, 1937-1938, GUS-SP, Table 20.

immigrants from Poland, and about 110,000 at the end. Assuming that every Polish native in Palestine had one relative in Poland who met the conditions for *Aliyah*, out of over three million Jews in Poland, the possibility of immigration in this category was no more than four percent of Polish Jews – about 120,000 persons.

A farewell photograph before immigrating to Palestine
"To the Aliyah of Our Friend Dov Mamlovsky,
See you soon, November 19, 1934"
Source: Beit Hatfutsot, Photo Archive 8965 Courtesy
of Rabbi Mamlowski-Sidransky

It turns out, therefore, that in the 1930s, the option of immigration was available to only a small proportion of Polish Jews – at most half a million people – out of over three million Polish Jews. These were primarily the very small group of capital owners; young high school graduates who could be admitted to educational institutions in Palestine whose families had the amounts needed to finance their studies; young people who could join the *HeHalutz* movement and compete with many other candidates for immigration in this field; affluent people who could afford the financing of immigration under the guise of tourism; and the few relatives of Palestine's residents and middle-class craftsmen and merchants who had a Zionist background and who had to compete against many others for a small number of immigration licenses. The majority of Polish Jewry did not have the opportunity to immigrate to Palestine. From that potential pool of about half a million immigrants, only about 100,000 successfully made *Aliyah*.

What other immigration options did Polish Jews face? The sad truth is that immigration options to countries other than Palestine were also minimal. The leading immigration countries in Europe were France and Belgium, and no more than a few hundred Jews managed to emigrate there every year. A major overseas immigration destination for Polish Jews was Argentina: between 1,000 and 2,000 Jews a year successfully emigrated there. The number of immigrants to the United States was several hundred and did not exceed 1,000 per year. At the beginning of the decade, Brazil accepted 1,000 to 1,400 Polish Jews a year, but the amount was later cut to 100-200 per year. The number of immigrants to other countries also did not exceed a few hundred per year. Various Jewish organizations in Poland made efforts to organize Jewish immigration to different countries, and Polish authorities also tried to help in this effort, but the fruits of their efforts were meager.

7

EPILOGUE

On a hot and sticky night of hamsin, with the windows open, all the souls flew back to Maków, to Krakow, to Jasa and to Chich, and the white houses at the seaside here were empty. During the day they pretended to be working, happy, and alive. At night, the city emptied, and everyone flew home.[358]

In the 1930s, after a thousand years of living in Poland, the Jews tried in every way to leave the country in which they and their ancestors were born, but only a small handful of the three million Polish Jews succeeded. The United States closed its doors, and Palestine became an almost exclusive destination for anyone trying to escape a country that no longer held out hope for the future of Jewish life. However, the gates of Palestine were also not open. The British government restricted immigration options, and the Jewish Agency distributed immigration licenses sparingly, with the building of the country and the development of the settlement at the center of its considerations. The consideration of saving Jews and

---

358   Heffner (1987) p. 46.

rescuing them under dangerous political and existential circumstances only applied to German Jews, whose suffering had become
apparent and blatant since Hitler came to power. The situation of
Polish Jews was considered less severe by the Jewish Agency and
even more so by the British government, even though the leaders
of the Yishuv in Palestine were well aware of their plight.

The aspiration to immigrate encompasses the masses of Jews
from all avenues and strata in Poland, and myriad eyes long toward
Aliyah as a life preserver from their poor lives and the destruction
that they are subject to . . .[359]

Who does not want to get a certificate? All the unemployed, all
that lack the means of a livelihood dream of emigration. At this
time, when all the gates are locked, there is no emigration but to
Palestine, and no immigration there except via certificates. They
hurry therefore, and send questionnaires to the Warsaw Zionist
Office and, more even more so, seek to register in one of the Zionist
parties.[360]

Against this background, a deep gap developed between the
urgent need for Polish Jews to come to Palestine and the dearth
of immigration licenses and their high cost. This distress caused
great unrest among aspirants for *Aliyah*. When it was decided that
organized craftsmen would take precedence in immigration, a wave
of organizations swept through the Jewish street adapting to the
requirements for a certificate; the possibility of *Aliyah* with a spouse
opened a wide door to fictitious marriages that the entire community cooperated in organizing. The frenzied spirit of entrepreneurship
also gave rise to corruption: fake professional credentials, trade in

---

359   Confidential Memorandum, Nov. 10, 1935, CZA S6/1499.

360   Sarid (1979) p. 419.

licenses, and various fraudulent acts. These all point to the intensity of will and creativity that were shattered on the brick wall of severe immigration restrictions and the lack of certificates.

Only a small minority of Polish Jews had any real possibility of immigrating to Israel. Contrary to the common belief that people did not come on *Aliyah* because they "did not want to" and "did not foresee" the catastrophe threatening them, Polish Jews were caught in a dead-end trap.

Research into immigration from Poland reveals a dire picture of the status of Polish Jews during this period. In addition to the well-known statistical and economic indicators that indicate severe economic distress, the struggle for every certificate – a fierce struggle that took place between organizations and individuals in Poland – indicates this dire distress. The plight of Polish Jews in the pre-World War II period was multi-faceted: In addition to the economic hardship, Polish Jewry suffered from severe anti-Semitism, which was exacerbated by alienation from the Polish authorities and elites. This resulted in discrimination against Polish Jews, causing them to be excluded by other citizens of the country. The combination of all these factors led to existential distress and loss of hope for any future in Poland. The fierce competition for the very few certificates, the willingness to take any legal or illegal path to receive them, to risk anything for them, and the willingness to abandon any remaining family if necessary – provided they could leave Poland – all indicate the desperate situation of the Jews during this period.

If we place on a graph the "archetypal immigrant" at one pole and the "archetypal refugee" at the other pole, the immigration from Poland in the 1930s is more similar to a refugee exit than to immigration, in which the destination and the date of emigration are freely chosen.[361] The immigrants from Poland aspired to leave at any cost, fought for their right to leave, and had almost no choice regarding their preferred destination. The decision to make *Aliyah* did not involve serious deliberations. In contrast, obtaining the immigration license required intense, complicated, and lengthy activity, and in most cases, ended in futility. Thus, at the root of the candidate's immigration activities, the decision was not whether to make *Aliyah* but rather whether to engage in the struggle for the possibility of *Aliyah*. In this regard, as well, immigrants from Poland were more like refugees than immigrants. This *Aliyah* differs from classical immigration in other ways. From the wealth of articles and reports on Palestine, published in the Jewish press in Poland in the 1930s and whose information was common knowledge on the Jewish street, it can be concluded that the immigrants were exposed to a great deal of information about what was happening in Palestine. Contrary to the situation of immigrants who, when moving to a new country, are brought to a "new and unknown world," Polish immigrants who came to Palestine did not come to the "unknown." From reading of newspapers, as from other sources of information, they had a deep knowledge of their target country. The immigrants knew the geography of the country, the climate, and the landscape of the country. They had information about the cities, the rural settlements, and the development of cities and colonies. They were exposed to information about the cultural events in the country, the economic development, and the mentality of the residents of the country. Although much of the information published in the press emphasized the positive and optimistic face of what was happening in Israel, readers could also come to know

---

361 Lavsky (2003) p. 164.

the darker sides of life there: the difficulties in earning a living, price hikes, negative attitude toward new immigrants and more. Moreover, while the official language of the settlement in Palestine was Hebrew, Yiddish was common for most Jewish residents, so that the language barrier, which was the main difficulty facing immigrants, hardly existed with regard to immigrants from Poland. Furthermore, the nature of the population that the immigrants had to integrate with was also known and close to them: the settlement was largely made up of Eastern Europeans, the greatest part of them Polish, so that the immigrants came into a well-known world, into some kind of "Poland in Palestine" or according to the wording of Jacob Shavit – "Warsaw in Tel Aviv."

A farewell photo of Shoshana Bohrer prior to her *Aliyah* to Israel, Lvov, 1935 (Except for Shoshana, all the family members in the picture perished in the Holocaust) Source: Beit Hatfutsot, Photo Archive 37208, Courtesy of Gershon Kvasnik-Aviel

The relationship between the Zionist leadership in Palestine and the Zionist delegation in Poland was rigidly hierarchical. The Center in Palestine dictated all the activities in Warsaw and micromanaged all its activities. The Jewish Agency in Jerusalem sent detailed instructions on every matter to the Warsaw Zionist Office: from detailed instructions on immigration permits to issues related to the day-to-day management of the office, the number of employees and their wages, members of the Office's committees and more. In this way, the Warsaw Zionist Office was "between the hammer and the anvil." On the one hand, they had to deal with the tens of thousands of immigration applicants, rejecting most of them. On the other hand, they were almost powerless: lists of immigrant candidates were sent to them from Palestine, lists of relatives, experts, and others. Potential immigrants for other categories were selected based on criteria dictated by the government and the *Aliyah* Department of the Jewish Agency, so that the Warsaw Zionist Office did not have any independent decision-making power. They, who interacted with the thousands who wanted to come on *Aliyah*, fought tirelessly to expand their powers. They felt that they were close to the realities on the ground, and thus their estimates were more accurate and just than those of the officials in Jerusalem. From the correspondence between the office in Jerusalem and the one in Warsaw, one can also feel condescension from the officials in the *Aliyah* department in Jerusalem toward the officials in Warsaw. The struggle of the Warsaw Zionist Office was unsuccessful, and in the hierarchy of the Zionist institutions, the place of the Warsaw Zionist Office remained at the bottom. The Office managers and officials were also dependent on the Jerusalem officials from a personal perspective, as they needed their approval for their personal *Aliyah* and that of their families.

The primary official criterion for selecting immigrants was their suitability and, in particular, their potential contribution to the country's economy and construction. Careful examination of the criteria indicates that immigration to the country was not possible at all for those Polish Jews who were without means. The few who met the criteria – relatives, craftsmen, students, clergy, experts, and farmers – were required to have capital, at least a basic amount, to meet the threshold conditions for immigration. Even the *halutzim* were required to raise their travel expenses on their own. One can, therefore, characterize Polish immigration in the 1930s as mainly middle-class people of some financial means; close relatives of residents of Palestine who were in a strong financial position; and craftsmen or masters of some profession that would allow them, at least seemingly, to earn a living in the country. Nevertheless, most immigrants also had to have connections, initiative and daring, and in many cases, have a willingness to act outside the legal framework in order to be included among the lucky ones who succeeded in immigrating. Polish immigrants of the 1930s came from the more established and more connected circles of Polish Jewry. Most regular folk were left behind.

Statistical analysis of immigration reports from Poland allows us to examine the characteristics of immigrants and compare them with immigration patterns at other times and in other circumstances. Most immigrants were 18 to 35 years old – young people of working age – similar to a classic immigration pattern. In contrast, the proportion of children up to the age of 16 among immigrants from Poland was only 18 percent, compared with 30 percent of the immigrants from the Russian Empire in the "Great Immigration" of the late 19th and early 20th centuries. This characteristic, in addition to the high proportion of single and married couples without children, indicates that immigration from Poland in the 1930s was less of a "family" nature than that of the Great Immigration.

The family and community character of the great wave of immigration was literarily portrayed in the Sholem Aleichem novel *Motl, Peysi the Cantor's Son*. Motl emigrated to America with his mother, brother, sister-in-law, friend Pinny and Pinny's wife; of the entire family only the father's grave remained in the Ukraine. At the same time, the parents of his sister-in-law, neighbors, and friends immigrated to America. They all met in New York and created a "Kasrilevke in New York." In contrast, most of the immigrants from Poland in the 1930s left behind their younger brothers, their older parents, and many other relatives who were unable to immigrate, and most of them perished in the Holocaust.

The emigration rate among all Polish Jews was tiny: Of the more than 3 million Polish Jews, only about 100,000 immigrated to Palestine in 1930-1939 (legal and illegal immigration). If we add the approximately 50,000 Jews who emigrated to other countries, the total of all emigrants during the entire decade was only about 5 percent of Polish Jewry. This is to be compared with the much higher proportion of German Jews who succeeded in leaving on the eve of World War II, and the very high proportion of emigrants from the Russian empire at the end of the 19th century and the beginning of the 20th century. The overwhelming majority of Polish Jewry remained behind. There was not one entire community that was brought to Eretz Israel, it was only a few lone families that were able to leave intact. This was another factor in the breakup and separation of family structures: while the new home was being built in Palestine, the core of the family and the old home remained in Poland. As opposed to the classic immigration pattern – which was mainly immigration across the ocean – this move was not accompanied by a feeling of a final separation, as the old home remained accessible within a few days of travel. Many immigrants returned to Poland to visit their parents and their families and to introduce them to their new spouses and children. For example, in her memoir, Shoshana Zelinger said: "We went to Poland to get married ... I went to my parents when I gave birth... "[362] In *Whose Little Boy Are You?* by Hanoch Bartov, the hero's mother makes plans for years to travel to Poland in order to show her son to her parents; he was "almost Bar Mitzvah" and did not know his family:

> ... I sigh, Mother says, for only one thing. I have no great demands, and I thank God for whatever we have. However, one thing I dream about, to see Mom again, our home ... just that. And the neighbor joins in her longing: "I, too, would want to ... glance even just for two weeks, even a week just to see the house and then come back."[363]

Many saw their *Aliyah* as an immigration of pioneers and hoped that this would result in their families joining them soon. One can only imagine the horrific disappointment of those immigrants when all their hopes and plans were destroyed with the onset of the war, and even more so - when the dimensions of the Holocaust became known. This is how Hankeh Lanzner described the parting as she left her parents' home on her way to Palestine in the early days of September 1939:

---

362   Gra (1988) p. 57.

363   Bartov (1986) pp. 218-219.

I informed my parents that I was going to Vilna, and from there, I would try to find a way to Eretz Yisrael. My parents begged me not to leave, and [that I should resolve that] what would happen to them should be my fate as well. How difficult were the days of separation from home! I had a feeling we would never see each other again, and no one would know which of us would be alive. In a thousand ways I was connected to my parents' home ... to mother ... to father ... to brothers and sisters. Today, as if my heart turned to stone - I said goodbye to them forever.[364]

And Rachel Schechter:

I sometimes think ... it would have been much nicer if we had all stayed with my parents and maybe gone with them. However, during the difficult days in the camps, perhaps they thought: At least this is our good fortune! Their children are alive and well; that as parents they did the right thing, and that Dad was right to send us to the free world ... I remember them escorting us to the train ... I see my little brother, who was last born, running after the train, I see him, I will see him until my last days, as he shouted: "I will come! Just a little longer, and I will come!"[365]

---

364   Book of Yagur (1964) p. 325.

365   Heffner (1987) pp. 188, 204.

And her husband, Zvi, reports:

> The train was full of immigrants, and we took a seat by
> the window ... Outside, below, the whole family stood ...
> And I look at them, and I know what I wanted, that the
> town's fence would be broken and I would have a way
> into the world, maybe it happened, and I didn't know
> that at this moment I am burning my past with them,
> and I do not know that I will not see them anymore.
> Moreover, in truth, I didn't see them as sick or healthy,
> neither sad nor happy, neither alive nor dead, they just
> wiped them away, and they were no longer.[366]

---

366 *Ibid*, p. 473.

Statistical Appendix

Table A1 - JEAS Activities in Poland 1935-1939

Table A2 - Jewish and non-Jewish immigrants from Poland according to immigration goals, 1931-1938

Table A3 - Percentage of Jews of all immigrants by immigration destinations, 19326-1938

Table A4 - Jewish immigrants out of the Jewish population by district, 1931-1938, rate per 1,000

Table A5 - Jewish Immigrants from Poland by District of Origin and Destination: Europe, Israel, and Other Countries, 1931-1938

Table A6 - Jewish Immigrants from Poland, 1931-1938, by Districts of Origin and Destination - Percentage

Table A7 - Number of Certificates according to Schedules 1931-1939

Table A8 - Number of Jewish Immigrants from Poland by Main Destination Countries, 1931-1938

Table A9- Number of Immigrants from Poland by Districts of Origin, 1931-1938

Table A10 - Distribution of Certificates to Immigrants "Type B" 1935-1936

Table A11 - Distribution of Certificates for "Tourism Elimination" 1935-1936

Table A12 - The number of immigrants from Poland, tourists from Poland and tourists who were allowed to settle in the country, according to various sources

Table A13 - Immigrants from Poland and all Immigrants to Palestine, 1930-1939

Table A14 - Immigrants from Poland by Immigration Categories, 1930-1939

Table A15 - Properties of Immigrants from Poland, 1933-1939

Table A16 - Number of Immigrant Halutzim and Members of the *HeHalutz* Zionist training program in Poland, 1929-1938

Table A17 - Immigrants from Poland, beginning in 1919, some of whom included in the Jewish community in Israel

Table A1 - JEAS Activity in Poland 1935-1939

Year	Oral appeals	Letters received	Jewish Emigrants from Poland, excluding Palestine
1935	38,900	86,900	5,945
1936	49,300	120,100	6,337
1937	54,000	157,100	6,002
1938	77,500	191,900	6,742

Source: Emigracja i Kolonizacja, February 4,1939, YIVO-RG 245.4.12.11

Table A2 - Jewish and non-Jewish emigrants from Poland by destination 1931-1938

Year	Emigrants from Poland			Emigrants to Europe			Emigrants to other continents		
	Total	Jews	Percent Jews	Total	Jews	Percent Jews	Total	Jews	Percent Jews
	(1)	(2)	(3)=(2)/(1)*100	(4)	(5)	(6)=(5)/(4)*100	(7)	(8)=(2)-(5)	(9)=(8)/(7)*100
1931	76,000	8,621	11.3	64,200	1,506	2.3	11,800	7,115	60.3
1932	21,400	8,625	40.3	11,800	1,350	11.4	9,600	7,275	75.8
1933	35,500	16,878	47.5	18,300	1,653	9	17,200	15,225	88.5
1934	42,600	16,986	44.6	21,800	989	4.5	20,800	17,997	86.5
1935	53,800	30,047	55.8	19,200	453	2.3	34,600	29,594	85.5
1936	54,600	16,932	31	29,800	403	1.3	24,800	16,529	66.6
1937	10,2500	8,829	8.6	78,600	436	0.6	23,900	8,393	35.1
1938	12,9100	9,153	7	107,800	385	0.4	21,300	8,768	41.2
Total	515,500	118,071	22.9	351,500	7,175	2	164,000	110,896	67.6

Table A3 - Percentage of Jews of all immigrants by immigration Destinations, 1926-1938

Destination	Jewish Percentage among Emigrants
Germany	1
Lithuania, Estonia, Denmark	0
France	5.2
Belgium	21.7
USA	54.5
Canada	13.8
Argentina	31.5
Brazil	40
Paraguay	0
Palestine	100
Other	22

Source: Janowska (1984) p. 42

Table A4 - Jewish emigrants out of the Jewish population by origin district, 1931-1938, rate per 1,000

Region	Number of Jews in 1931, thousands	1931	1932	1933	1934	1935	1936	1937	1938	Total 1931-1938
Total	3,114	2.8	2.8	5.4	6.1	9.7	5.4	2.8	2.9	37.9
Warszawa Region	571	3.4	3.2	5.7	7.2	9.9	5.3	2.9	3	40.6
City of Warszawa	352	3.9	3.8	6.5	8.4	11.2	5.9	3.1	3.3	46.1
Lo'dz	378	1.9	1.9	3.9	4.7	9	4.3	1.8	1.4	28.9
Kielce	317	1.8	1.8	2.4	4	5.4	7.6	5	1.9	29.9
Lublin	314	2.6	2.7	5.7	6.2	8.3	5.3	2.8	3	36.6
Total of Central Poland	1,582	2.5	2.6	4.9	6	8.9	5	2.4	2.3	34.8
Bialystok	197	5.4	5.3	9.4	10	16.5	9.8	6.7	6.2	69.3
Wilno	111	3.8	3.7	6	6.4	11.2	5.1	2.4	2.6	41.2
Nowogro'dek	83	3.8	3.8	8	6.8	12	6.4	3	4.2	48.0
Polesie	114	5.6	5.4	9.6	10.1	16.4	8.1	4.7	4.6	64.6
Wo'łyn	208	3.8	3.5	6.6	6.5	9.6	8	3.4	3.3	44.7
Total of Eastern Poland	713	4.5	4.4	7.9	8.1	13.1	7.9	4.3	4.3	54.5
Poznan'	7	1.4	1.6	3.4	5.6	4.2	9.7	4.1	13.7	43.8
Pomorze	3	3.6	4	5.3	7	10.7	10	4.3	34.3	79.2
S'lask	19	0.4	0.9	4	2.8	6.6	4.5	4	3.9	26.8
Total of Western Poland	29	1	1.4	3.9	3.8	6.3	6.2	4	9.2	35.7
Krako'w	174	0.9	0.9	3.8	3.6	6.4	3.1	1.4	2	22.1
Lwo'w	342	1.9	1.9	4.5	5.1	7.8	4.1	2.5	2.6	30.4
Stanislaw	140	1.3	1.9	4.1	4.2	10	3.8	2.1	2.9	30.3
Tarnopol	134	2.6	1.9	4	4.7	9.3	5.4	2.9	3.5	34.3
Total of South Poland	790	1.7	1.7	4.2	4.5	8.1	4	2.2	2.7	29.2

Source: GUS-ST 1930-1939

Table A5 - Jewish Emigrants from Poland by District of Origin in Poland and Destination: 1931-1938

District	Year	Total	To Europe	To Palestine	To Elsewhere
Total	1931	8,621	1,506	1,534	5,581
	1932	8,625	1,350	2,873	4,402
	1933	16,878	1,653	10,311	4,914
	1934	18,986	989	12,654	5,343
	1935	30,047	453	24,715	4,879
	1936	16,932	403	10,602	5,927
	1937	8,829	436	2,845	5,448
	1938	9,153	385	2,490	6,278
	1931-38	118,071	7,175	68,024	42,872
Central Poland	1931	4,026	1,111	567	2,348
	1932	4,151	986	1,127	2,038
	1933	7,816	1,167	4,259	2,390
	1934	9,530	760	6,061	2,709
	1935	14,073	287	11,289	2,497
	1936	7,925	239	4,914	2,772
	1937	3,849	243	1,194	2,412
	1938	3,698	207	959	2,532
	1931-38	55,068	5,000	30,370	19,698
Eastern Poland	1931	3,223	136	711	2,376
	1932	3,108	150	1,187	1,771
	1933	5,628	181	3,607	1,840
	1934	5,753	96	3,773	1,884
	1935	9,363	57	7,799	1,507
	1936	5,622	50	3,362	2,210
	1937	3,083	53	941	2,089
	1938	3,066	19	828	2,219
	1931-38	38,846	742	22,208	15,896

	1931	28	6	5	17
	1932	41	12	16	13
	1933	115	19	84	12
	1934	113	8	96	9
Western Poland	1935	186	9	165	12
	1936	183	4	143	36
	1937	118	6	60	52
	1938	272	16	99	157
	1931-38	1,056	80	668	308
	1931	1,344	253	251	840
	1932	1,325	202	543	580
	1933	3,319	286	2,361	672
	1934	3,590	125	2,724	721
Southern Poland	1935	6,425	100	5,462	863
	1936	3,202	110	2,183	909
	1937	1,779	134	650	995
	1938	2,117	143	604	1,370
	1931-38	23,101	1,353	14,778	6,970

Table A6 - Jewish Emigrants from Poland, 1931-1938, by Districts of Origin and Destination – By Percentage

	Total	To Europe	To Eretz Yisrael	Other Destinations
Total	100	6.1	57.6	36.3
Central	100	9.1	55.1	35.8
East	100	1.9	58.5	39.6
West	100	7.6	63.3	29.2
South	100	5.9	64	30.2

Table A7 - Number of Certificates according
to Schedules – 1930-1937

Schedule	Number of Certificates for Distribution by Jewish Agency		
	Total	Poland Allocation	Germany Allocation
Fall 1930 (Oct 1930-March 1931)		523 (1)	
Spring 1931 (April – September 1931)	345	157 (1)	
Fall 1931 (Oct 1931-March 1932)	221	195 (1)	
Spring 1932 (April – September 1932)	1,700	590	45
Fall 1932 (Oct 1932-March 1933)	4,215	1,473	118
Spring 1933 (April – September 1933)	4,950	1,310	1,300
Fall 1933 (Oct 1933-March 1934)	5,188	1,640	1,741
Spring 1934 (April – September 1934)	6,262	1,995	2,093
Fall 1934 (Oct 1934-March 1935)	7,200	3,072	1,361
Spring 1935 (April – September 1935)	7,600	2,975	1,350
Fall 1935 (Oct 1935-March 1936)	2,985	1,160	874
Spring 1936 (April – September 1936)	4,000	1,374	1,475
Fall 1936 (Oct 1936-March 1937)	1,300	536	295
Spring 1937 (April – September 1937)	620		400

Table A8 - Jewish Emigrants from Poland by Main
Destination Countries, 1931-1938

	1931	1932	1933	1934	1935
Total	8,632	6,408	16917	19,026	30,703
Total Europe	1,509	1,350	1656	990	407
France	646	529	899	602	85
Belgium	531	405	309	143	122
Other	332	416	448	245	247
Total Outside Europe	7,123	7,290	15261	18,036	30,249
USA	649	905	777	871	735
Canada	141	242	350	511	541
Mexico	56	87	215	88	163
Cuba	122	81	70	194	252
Argentina	476	1,335	1313	1,472	2,022
Brazil	753	931	1390	1,360	1,060
Uruguay	953	401	295	364	299
Palestine	1,535	2,879	10344	12,674	24,758

	1936	1937	1938	Total 1931-38
Total	16,942	8,856	9,328	118,954
Total Europe	407	445	389	72,00
France	112	209	98	3,190
Belgium	18	121	175	1,934
Other	167	115	116	2,086
Total other countries	16,535	8,411	8,849	111,754
USA	557	997	2,310	7,801
Canada	307	211	185	2,488
Mexico	233	86	45	973
Cuba	163	172	145	1,199
Argentina	2,750	2,433	2,175	13,976
Brazil	942	270	107	6,813
Uruguay	361	596	173	3,442
Palestine	10,605	2,854	2,514	68,163

Source: GUS-SP Years 1930-1939

(The small differences between the data in this table and the Data in Table N2 comes from differences in the source)

Table A9 - Emigrants from Poland to Palestine by Districts of Origin, 1931-1938

Year	1931	1932	1933	1934	1935	1936	1937	1938	1931-1938
Total	1,535	2,879	10,344	12,685	24,758	10,605	2,856	2,516	68,178
Warszawa City	145	386	1,305	1,996	3,226	1,311	356	263	8,998
Warszawa Area	69	156	622	790	1,445	612	186	96	3,976
Lodz'	142	199	956	1351	3,037	1,221	263	192	7,361
Kielce	94	200	654	974	1,791	966	214	185	5,078
Lublin	117	186	722	950	1,790	804	175	223	4,967
Bialystok	248	409	1,188	1,275	2,537	1,144	351	299	7,451
Wilno	75	125	394	466	1,021	384	183	116	2,688
Novogro'dek	79	124	465	391	834	347	80	95	2,415
Polesie	162	289	732	829	1,468	591	163	119	4,353
Volyn	143	240	828	812	1,939	896	244	199	5,301
Poznan'	2	3	15	30	22	59	12	35	178
Pomorze	0	2	11	19	29	29	5	39	134
Krakow	23	72	505	509	993	435	114	146	2,797
Lwow	115	221	1,041	1,286	2,196	949	288	259	6,355
Stanislaw	48	139	447	478	1,253	385	130	84	2,964
Tarnopol	65	111	368	451	1,020	414	118	115	2,662
Unknown	1	6	33	31	43	3	11	26	154

Source: GUS-SP years 1930-1939

Table N10 - Distribution of Certificates to Immigrants "Type B" 1935-1936

Party/Movement	Winter 1935-1936	Summer 1936
Agudat Yisrael	33	37
Poalei Zion	9	22
Zionists	6	20
Mizrachi	1	7
Poalei Zion Left (Activists)	7	6
Sadkov	14	--
Et Livnot	--	4
Hitahdut	--	2
Medinatiim	--	2
Others: Unaffiliated, Elders, etc.	132	379

Source: Reports of Warsaw Zionist Office, 1935-1936, CZA s6/6553

Table N11 - Distribution of Certificates for "Tourism Elimination" 1935-1936

Party/Movement	Winter 1935-1936	Summer 1936
Mizrachi	34	26
Medinatiim	7	15
Hitahdut	4	2
Activists	8	--
Et Livnot	2	7
Revisionists	1	4

Table A12 - immigrants from Poland, tourists from Poland and tourists allowed to settle in Palestine, according to various sources

Year	# of Olim based on Polish Statistical Sources (1)	# of Polish citizen Olim based on Jewish Agency (2)	# of Olim whose last residence was Poland based on Jewish Agency (3)	# of Tourists from Poland permitted to remain in Palestine (4)	# of Tourists from Poland in Palestine (5)	# of Olim who were registered (6)
1931	1,535	1,610	1,574	116	--	1,726
1932	2,879	2,987	2,943	312	2,037	3,299
1933	10,344	12,879	11,791	372	1,157	13,251
1934	12,674	16,829	15,014	894	2,593	17,723
1935	24,758	29,407	27,291	1,186	4,398	33,204
1936	10,605	12,929	11,436	327	2,876	14,210
1937	2,854	3,578	3,608	130		4,449
1938	2,514	3,346	2,973	296	--	4,986
Total 1931-39	68,163	83,565	76,630	3633		92,848

Source: (1) - GUS-SP, 1930-1939, (2) – G.G.B (1935 Table 6, (3)) – G.G.B (-1935) Table 7, (4) G.G.B (1935) Table 17, (5)) – G.G.B (1935-) Table 18, (6) Sicron (1957) Statistical Supplement, Table 10.

*Sicron's calculation for 1931-1934 was done by citizenship, and the source for the data is the Jewish Agency. The calculation for 1935-1938 was made by country of birth, and the source is the Mandate government. The Jewish Agency's figures on immigrants whose last place of residence were in Poland are higher than those provided by Polish statistics. The Agency based its data on reports issued by Zionist offices abroad regarding the number of immigration licenses issued. In contrast, the Polish government's statistics were based on Polish emigration forms filled at border points. The number of immigrant citizens from Poland likely includes those citizens who immigrated to Palestine from other countries.

Table A13 - Immigrants to Palestine from Poland and from other origins, 1930-1939

	Total Olim	Olim from Poland	Other Olim	Percentage of Olim from Poland
1930	4,134	2,328	1,806	56
1931	2,998	1,574	1,424	53
1932	5,480	2,943	2,537	54
1933	27,289	11,791	15,498	43
1934	36,619	15,014	21,605	41
1935	55,407	27,291	28,116	49
1936	26,976	11,436	15,540	42
1937	9,441	3,608	5,833	38
1938	11,222	2,973	8,249	26
1939	13,663	1,444	12,219	10

Source: GGB (1945) tab.7

Table N14 - Immigrants from Poland to Palestine by Immigration Categories, 1930-1939

	1930	1931	1932	1933	1934	1935	1936	1937	1938	1939 Jan-Apr	Total 1930-1939	Distribution by Percent Categories
A1	58 (1)	44 (1)	AN	897 (3)	1197 (3)	2348 (4)	564 (4)	153 (6)	138 (7)	111 (8)	5510	
A2	0	0	AN	7	0	0	0	0	0	0	7	
A3	9 (1)	6 (1)	AN	229 (3)	641 (3)	231 (4)	137 (4)	0	0	0	1253	
A4	2 (1)	3 (1)	AN	4 (3)	11 (3)	1 (4)	5 (4)	1 (6)	5 (7)	0	32	
A5	0	0	AN	7 (3)	16 (3)	12 (4)	7 (4)	0	0	0	42	
Total Capital Owners	69 (1)	63	281 (2)	1144	1865	2592	713	154	143	111	7125	10
B1	0	0	AN	0	0	0	3 (4)	0	0	0	3	
B2	0	0	AN	44 (3)	0	1502 (4)	537 (4)	9 (6)	0	0	2263	
B3	27 (1)	23 (1)	AN	130 (3)	990 (3)	1158 (4)	723 (4)	600 (6)	603 (7)	123 (8)	4377	
Total B	27	27	AN	174	1161	2660	1263	609	603	123	6643	9
Halutzim	886 (9)	488 (1)	1160 (9)	3473 (3)	2720 (3)	4584 (4)	1843 (4)	457 (6)	956 (7)	140 (8)	16707	
Recommended	810 (10)	416 (1)	AN	2199 (3)	1592 (3)	2829 (4)	737 (4)	72 (6)	205 (7)	17 (8)	8877	
Organized Laborers	0	0	AN	0	0 (3)	(4)	421 (5)	121 (6)	63 (7)	28 (8)	633	
Privates	16 (1)	164 (1)	AN	176 (3)	155 (3)	135 (4)	52 (4)	62 (6)	31 (7)	20 (8)	811	
Experts/Owners of Industry	0	0	AN	0	(3)	(4)	544 (5)	106 (6)	62 (7)	4 (8)	716	
Craftsmen, Middle class, Type B/others	0	0	AN	2172	2468 (3)	4188 (4)	799 (5)	120 (6)	111 (7)	33 (8)	9891	
Farmers C/H	0	0	AN	0	0	11 (4)	166 (4)	3 (6)	2 (7)	2 (8)	184	
Total Aliyah Workers	1712	1068	2067 (2)	8020	6935	11747	4562	941	1430	244	38726	52
Requested Persons	496 (1)	350 (1)	661 (2)	1164 (1)	3057 (3)	7771 (4)	4150 (4)	1111 (6)	402 (7)	372 (8)	19534	26
Tourists (13)	200 (1)	199 (1)	420 (2)	1101 (3)	162 (3)	223 (4)	74 (7)	91 (6)	135 (7)	172 (8)	2777	4
Total Olim	2504	1693	3429	11603	13180	24993	10762	2906	2713	1022	74805	100

Sources and Notes for Table A14

(1) The *Aliyah* movement from Poland to Eretz Israel through the Warsaw Zionist Office in 1930, 1931 (CZA S6/6553).

(2) The *Aliyah* movement from Poland to Eretz Israel through the Warsaw Zionist Office during its 16 years of existence 1920-1936 (Table A CZA S6/1394).

(3) The number of persons who immigrated to Palestine from Poland through the Warsaw Zionist Office during the period from Jan 1, 1933 to June 1, 1935 according to the categories (CZA S6/2435 p. 11).

(4) Report on *Aliyah* in 1935, Table 3, Warsaw Zionist Office (CZA S6/1394 p. 8).

(5) In the entire 1936 report, there is no record of professionals by organizations, industrial workers, etc. Total 1764 immigrant professionals in 1936.

In the available monthly reports for March-December 1936, this detail is recorded: Private - 52, Organizations - 421, Industry Workers - 544. According to this data, the number of middle-class immigrants is estimated to be 799.

(6) My Summary of Monthly Reports January-December 1937 (CZA S6/8453).

(7) Movement from Poland to Palestine through the Warsaw Zionist Office for 1938 (CZA S6/8453).

(8) My Summary of Monthly Reports for January-April 1939, (CZA S6/8453).

(9) Sarid (1979, p. 421).

(10) The rest of the total of *halutzim* and recommended relatives - 1696 immigrants (CZA S6/6553).

(11) The column does not add up because of a lack of 1932 data.

(12) Registration of craftsmen organized as a separate category began only from 1936.

(13) Tourists who were allowed to remain and settle. Government numbers for these tourists are generally higher because they relate to Polish subjects, while the numbers from the Warsaw Zionist Office relate to those whose place of residence was in Poland.

Table A 15 - Characterization of Immigrants from Poland, 1933-1939

	Request Relative	Recom Relative	Middle class & Type B	Organized laborers (3)	Capital owners > 250 £	Male Halutzim	Female Halutzim	Capital owners >1000 £	Students	Clerics	Tourists	Indust. Laborer	Private	Farmers	Total (4)
Tot. Olim 1930-39 (2)	16,393	8,877	10,312	212	1,253	16,707		5,610	4,377	2,263	2,777	716	811	184	73,392
Olim 1933-1939 monthly data	15,385	6,018	8,050	569	1,142	8,726	1,894	4,307	3,787	2,074	1,714	681	510	103	54,960
# of Singles	4,759	2,982	1,032	97	36	2,187	1,888	413	3,787	113	1,403	117	186	83	19,083
Family members	10,626	3,036	7,018	473	1,107	6,539	6	3,894	0	1,961	311	564	324	20	35,879
# of families	4,032	1,145	2,289	148	335	3,127	2	1,244	0	505	141	180	101	8	13,257
Avg family size	3	3	3	3	3	2	3	3	0	4	2	3	3	3	3
# licenses	8,791	4,127	3,321	245	371	5,314	1,890	1,657	3,787	615	1,544	297	287	91	32,337
Single license %	54	72	31	40	10	41	100	25	100	16	91	39	65	91	59
# Men	3,963	1,848	3,049	189	388	5,214	0	1,547	2,584	665	1,147	287	200	60	21,141
# Women	7,839	3,425	2,652	214	358	3,222	1,889	1,528	1,131	579	525	193	199	36	23,790
Children < 16 yr	3,592	744	2,349	166	396	290	5	1,229	104	829	42	201	111	8	10,066
Between 16-18	1,460	19	162	9	56	0	0	179	549	146	3	9	19	1	2,612
Between 18-35	1,723	4,892	3,936	323	356	8,231	1,887	1,203	3,125	308	582	325	271	83	27,240
Between 35-45	817	334	1,429	66	203	205	2	768	3	378	503	96	81	5	4,890
Older than 45	7,789	27	174	6	132	0	0	928	0	422	585	50	26	3	10,142
Farmers	67	155	321	8	0	411	51	94	6	0	2	1	6	22	1,144
Merchants	499	17	59	1	3	3	0	771	0	1	471	0	14	0	1,839
Students	67	23	13	0	0	39	3	8	3,551	0	7	0	6	0	3,717
Free Vocations	98	160	153	6	3	37	18	97	24	4	184	31	16	1	832
Religious Work	27	1	10	0	0	2	0	3	0	577	6	0	2	0	629
Industrialists	9	0	43	0	0	1	0	25	0	0	73	0	1	2	154
Craftsmen	857	2,613	2,196	216	372	2,588	500	256	29	0	134	249	109	5	10,124
Laborers and Halutzim	4	13	13	4	0	1,314	390	0	0	0	1	1	2	0	1,742
Artisans (5)	13,757	3,036	5,242	334	764	4,331	909	3,093	177	1,492	836	399	354	73	34,797

Sources and Notes for Table N15

(1) The table is based on monthly data which is partial and includes the following months: 1933 January-November; 1934 October-December; 1935 January-December; 1936 March-December; 1937 January-December; 1938 April-December; 1939 January-April.

(2) Source: Table N14 - Immigrants by categories.

(3) Some of the annual reports include craftsmen organizations in "Type B."

(4) The gap between total immigrants in accordance with this table (73,392) and total immigrants in Table 14 (74,664) is due to the fact that a number of categories were not included in this Table, such as Capital Owners of types A2 and A3, and a lack of detailed data for 1932.

(5) This category was introduced only in 1936.

Table N16 - Number of Immigrant Halutzim and Members of the HeHalutz Zionist training program in Poland, 1929-1938

Year	Immigrant Halutzim	Hachshara Members in Poland	HeHalutz members in Poland
1929	1,100	2,100	9,300 – 10,000
1930	900	1,000 – 2,800	18,000
1931	400	1,000 –1,400	10,000 – 18,000
1932	1,200	2,200	
1933	3,500	4,500 – 8,200	21,000 – 33,000
1934	1,700	7,500 – 9,000	29,000 – 32,000
1935	4,600	6,000 – 8,500	25,000 – 40,000
1936	1,800	6,000	
1937	460	4,500 – 6,000	
1938	1,000	3,000	

Source: Sarid (1979) pp. 415-418,467,473,552,553;
Autiker (1972) pp. 111-118.

Table N17 – Olim from Poland, 1919-1939, and their Proportion in the Jewish community

Years	# of Olim from Poland	Cumulative number End of Year	Emigrants to Poland	Net Olim from Poland	Jewish Population in Palestine	Percentage of Polish Olim among all Jews in Palestine
1919-1923	9,160					
1924	5,670	14,830				
1925	17,115	31,945	268	31,677		
1926	7,200	39,145	1,886	37,259		
1927	817	39,962	2,214	37,748		
1928	234	40,196	754	39,442		
1929	1,800	41,996	563	41,433		
1930	2,328	44,324	179	44,145		
1931	1,574	45,898	191	45,707		
1932	2,943	48,841	109	48,732	199,600	24.4
1933	11,791	60,632	66	60,566	245,700	24.6
1934	15,014	75,646	216	75,430	307,700	24.5
1935	27,291	102,937	298	102,639	375,400	27.3
1936	11,436	114,373	485	113,888	404,400	28.2
1937	3,608	117,981	379	117,602	416,200	28.2
1938	2,973	120,954	542	120,412	436,700	27.5
1939	1,444	122,398		122,398	474,600	25.8

Source: In years 1919-1923 – G.G.B. (1945) Table 4; Years 1924-1925 (1947) G.G.Z. pp. 104-5; Years 1926-1939 – G.G.B. (1945) Table 7; Emigrants – GUS (1990); Number of Jews in Palestine – G.G.B. (1945), Tables 2-3

These estimates were made not including natural population movements

Bibliography

Archives

Central Zionist Archives - CZA
Natanya's City Archive
Kibbutz Ramat Hakovesh's Archive
AAN - Archiwum Akt Nowych
GUS - Glowny Urzad Statystyczny
YIVO

Press, Periodicals

Baderech
Bustanay
Biuletyn Syndykatu Emigracyjnego
Wiadomosci dla Emigrantow
Biuletyn Urzedu Emigracyjnego BUE
Emigracja i Kolonizacja
Kwrtalnik Instytutu Naukowego Badania Emigracji
Miesziecznik Zydowski
Nasz Przeglad *N.P.*
Przeglad Emigrgacyjny
Przeglad Sociologiczny
Sprawy Narodosciowe
Wychodzca

Surveys, Censuses

G.G.B. – Gurewich. Gretz, Bachi. HaAliya,Hayishuw V'hatnuah H'tiviyt Shel H'uchlosiya
Alyia, 1934-35.

GGZ - Gurevich, D., Gertz, A., Zanker, A., Statistical Handbook of Palestine, 1947.

GUS-RS - Glowny Urzad Statystyczny, Rocznik Statystyczny, Warszawa, 1920-1939.

GUS-SP - Glowny Urzaad Statystyczny, Statystyka Pracy, 1920-1939.

GUS-MRS - Glowny Urzad Statystyczny, Maly Rocznik Statystyczny, 1920-1939.

Literature and Research Hebrew

Agnon, S. Y., Shira, 1971.

Alroey, G. Hamahapeha Hashketa, 2008.

Barlas, H. H'alyia ve Hamisrad H'eretz Israely B'Varsha in: Gruenbaum I, Enccyklopedia of the Jewish Diaspora. Warsaw, 1953.

Bartov, H. Shel Mi Ata Yeled? 1978.

Bartov, H. Yehudi Katan, 1980.

Bernstein, D. Nashim B'shulayim, 2008.

Cherniavsky, Irith. The Aliya Of Polish Jews in the 1930s: Thesis Submitted for the Degree "Doctor of Philosophy." The Hebrew University of Jerusalem, 2010.

Grah G., Even Yehuda. B'reshit Hayu Holot, 1988.

Dovrat, S. Zichronot Shel Ish Pashut, 1993.

Freilich, M. Hitbolelut Ve Polonizacyia B'kerev Yehudim B'polin Bein Milhamot Haolam, 1999.

Halamish, A. Hamilkud Hakaful Shel Yehudey Polin 1933-1929 in:

Proceedings of the Eleventh Congress of Jewish Studies, 1994.

—Aliyat, Baaley. Hon L'eretz Israel Bein Hamilhamot in: D. Hacohen, Ed. Kibbutz Galuyot. Mitos ve Metziuth, 1998.

—B'merotz Kaful Neged Hazman, 2006.

Heffner, A. Kolel Hakol, 1987.

Horowitz, D. and Lissak, M. M'ishuv L'medina, 1977.

Lavsky H. 2003, Leumiuth,Hagira Vehitiashvut in: Bareli A.,Karlinski N. ed. Yiunim B'tkumat Israel

Leichter, S. and Milkov, H. Sefer Oley Hasertifikatim, 1993.

Leshchinsky, J. Hapraot B'polin 1935-1937 in: Dapim Lecheker Hashoa Vehamered, 1952.

Mahler, R. Yehudey Polin Bein MIlchamot Haolam, 1968.

Melzer, E. Hadiplomatya Hapolanit U'baayat Hahagira Hayehudit in: GALED, 1973

—Lebaayot Hagizanut B'hevra Hapolanit: 1933-1939 in: GALED, 1995.

—Maavak Medini B'malkodet: 1935-1939, 1982.

Mendelsohn, E. Hatnuah Hatzionith B'polin. 1915-1926, 1982.

Naor, M. and Giladi D. Eretz Israel B'meah Haesrim, 1991.

Ofer D. Derech Bayam, Alyiah B 1939-1944, 1998.

Otiker, I. Tnuat Hehalutz B'Polin 1932-1935, 1972.

Oppenheim, I. Tnuat Hehalutz B'Polin 1929-1939, 1993.

Sarid, L. Hehalutz U'tnuot Hanoar B'Polin 1917-1939, 1979.

Sefer Yagur, 1964.

Shavit, Y. M'rov L'medina, 1978.

Shenfeld, R. Avot U'banim, Haalyia M'polin B'einey Hador Hasheni in: GALED, 1997.

Shmorak, H. Ivrit-Yidish-Polanit: Tarbut Yehudit Tlat Leshonit in: Shmorak H. and Versas, S., Ed.

  Bein Milhamot Haolam. Prakim M'haiey Hatarbut Shel Yehudey Polin, 1997.

Sicron, M. Ha'alyiah L'israel 1948-1953, 1957.

Warhaftig, Z. Palit V'Sarid B'imey Hashoa, 1994.

Literature and Research Polish

Bornstein, I. Uwagi o Charakterze i Przyczynach Zydowskiej Emigracji z. Polski. Warszawa, 1936.

Bronsztejn, Szyja. Ludnosc Zydowska w Polsce w Okresie Miedzywojennym Studium Statystyczne. Wroclaw-Warszawa-Krakow, 1963.

Cala, Alina Ed. Ostatnie Pokolenie. Warszawa, 2003.

Eder, W. "Ruch Wychodzczy Ludnosci Polskiej do Belgii w Okresie Miedzywojennym." Przeglad Polonyjny. Z. 4, pp. 79- 95, 1981.

Fuks, Marian. Prasa Zydowska w Warszawie 1823-1939. Warszawa, 1979.

Garncarska-Kadary, Bina. Zydowska ludnosc pracujaca w Polsce 1918-1939. Warszawa, 2001.

GUS - Glowny, Urzad Statystyczny, Historia Polski w Liczbach. Warszawa, 1990.

Hersch, Liebman. Syjonizm i Tragedja Palestynska. Krakow, 1930.

Janowska, Halina. "Emigracja z Polski w Latach 1918-1939." 1981.

Kicinger, Anna. Polityka Emigracyjna II Rzeczpospoliej, Central European Forum for Migration Research. Warsaw, 2005.

Landau, Z. and Tomaszewski, J. Zarys Historii Gospodarczej Polski 1918-1939. Warszawa, 1981.

—Landau, Z. and Tomaszewski, J. Gospodarka Polski Miedzywojennej Tom III, 1930-1935. Warszawa, 1982a.

—Landau, Z. and Tomaszewski, J. Gospodarka Polski Miedzywojennej Tom IV, 1936-1939. Warszawa, 1982b.

Linder Menachem. "Emigracja Zydow z Polski w Okresie Kryzysu 1929-1933." Ellenberg Zygmunt Redaktor, Miesiecznik Zydowski. Warszawa, 1935.

Mendelson, Ezra. "Jewish Historiography on Polish Jewry in the Interwar Period." Polin, Vol. 8, pp. 3-14, 1994.

Metzer, J. The Divided Economy of Mandatory Palestine. Cambridge, 2002.

Mitchell, B. R. International Historical Statistics Europe 1750-1988. New York, 1992.

Pilch, Andrzej. Redaktor Emigracja z Ziem Polskich w Czasach Nowozytnych i Najnowszych. Warszawa, pp. 326- 450, 1984.

Shandler, J. Awakening Lives. London, 2002.

Shapiro, Robert Moses. "The Polish Kehillah Elections of 1936: A Revolution Re-examined." Polin, Vol. 8, pp. 206-226, 1994.

Steinlauf, Michael. "The Polish-Jewish Daily Press." Polin, Vol. 2, pp. 219-239, 1987.

Tomaszewski, J. "Jews in Lodz in 1931 According to Statistics." Polin, Vol.6, pp. 173-201, 1991.

Pollner, Majer. Emigracja i Przewarstwienie Zydow Polskich. Warszawa, 1939.

Preker, M. Zagadninie Przyosobienia Emigrantow do Palestyny. Warszawa, 1936.

Reczynska, A. "Dane Statystyczne Dotyczace Emigracji Z Polski do Kanady w Latach, 1918-1939." Przeglad Polonyjny, z.4 pp. 103-115, 1981.

Reczynska, A. Emigracja z Polski do Kanady w Okresie Miedzywojennym. Warszawa, 1986.

Reif, N. "Rozwoj i warunki emigracji Zydowskiej z Polski." Sprawy Narodosciowe, X p. 223, Warszawa, 1937.

Rosner, Leopold. Szkice Palestynskie. Krakow, 1936.

Rudnicki, Szymon. Oboz Narodowo Radykalny. Warszawa, 1985.

Tartakower, A. "Pauperizacja Zydow Polskich." Ellenberg Zygmunt Redaktor, Miesiecznik Zydowski. Warszawa, Marzec-Kwiecien, 1935.

Tartakower, A. Emigracja Zydowska z Polski. Warszawa, 1937.

Tomaszewki, J. "Niepodlegla Rzeczpospolita." Najnowsze Dzieje Zydow w Polsce. Warszawa, 1993.

Tomaszewski, J. "Memorial z 1938 w Sprawie Polityki Panstwa Polskiego wobec Zydow. W Archiwum Akt Nowych w Warszawie, waktach Departamentu Konsularnego Ministerstwa Spraw Zagranicznych." Naczelna Dyrekcja Archiwow Panstwowych, Archiwum Akt Nowych, Teki Archiwalne, seria nowa t.1 23, 1996.

Zarychta, Apolonjusz. Emigracja Polska 1918-1931. Warszawa, 1933.

Zieminski, Jan. Problem Emigracji Zydowskiej. Warszawa, 1937.

Zyndul, Jolanta. Zajscia antyzydowskie w Polsce w latach 1935-1937. 1994.

Literature and Research English

Bachi, Roberto. Population distribution and internal migration in Israel. Jerusalem, 1965.

Bachi, Roberto. The Population of Israel. Jerusalem, 1976.

Hatton, T. J. and Williamson, J. G. The Age of Mass Migration. New York, 1998.

Lee, E. V. "A Theory of Migration." Demography, Vol 3 no.1, pp. 47-57, 1966.

Markus, Joseph. Social and Political History of the Jews in Poland, 1919-1939. Berlin, New York, Amsterdam, 1983.

Mendelson, Ezra. The Jews of East-Central Europe between the World Wars. Bloomington, 1987.

Mendelson, Ezra. "Jewish Historiography on Polish Jewry in the Interwar Period." Polin, Vol. 8, pp. 3-14, 1994.

Metzer, J. The Divided Economy of Mandatory Palestine. Cambridge, 2002.

Mitchell, B. R. International Historical Statistics Europe 1750-1988. New York, 1992.

Shandler, J. Awakening Lives. London, 2002.

Shapiro, Robert Moses. "The Polish Kehillah Elections of 1936: A Revolution Re-examined." Polin, Vol. 8, pp. 206-226, 1994.

Steinlauf, Michael. "The Polish-Jewish Daily Press." Polin, Vol. 2, pp. 219-239, 1987.

Tomaszewski, J. "Jews in Lodz in 1931 According to Statistics." Polin, Vol.6, pp. 173-201, 1991.

Printed in Great Britain
by Amazon